Never Smile at Strangers

JENNIFER JAYNES

Never
Smile at
Strangers

f THOMAS & MERCER

Published by Thomas & Mercer, Seattle

www.apub.com

Amazon, the Amazon logo, and Thomas & Mercer are trademarks of Amazon.com, Inc., or its affiliates.

ISBN-13: 9781477821916
ISBN-10: 1477821910

Cover design by Cyanotype Book Architects

Library of Congress Control Number: 2014949871

Printed in the United States of America

For Brian.

Thank you for believing in me.

PROLOGUE

THE BOY OPENED his eyes and turned to the window. It was late, and the screen door to the back of the house had just slammed shut.

Thunder rumbled, and raindrops struck the glass in loud, maddening beats. Wide-eyed, he clutched the wool army blanket that reeked of urine and watched the downpour through his tiny bedroom window.

A burst of lightning streaked across the sky, illuminating the branches from the giant oak outside and the Spanish moss that clung to them. The flash disappeared, and the world grew pitch black.

An oak branch scraped the filthy glass, and the screen door banged shut a second time.

A restless energy filled him.

Something wasn't right.

His room, not much larger than a closet, smelled of mildewed wood. The nasty odor grew thicker during a storm, more menacing. Gulping musty air, he reluctantly crawled out of bed and tiptoed down the hallway.

He stood outside his mother's bedroom door, listening for her usual drunken snores. All he heard was the ticking of her wind-up alarm clock.

Something was smeared against the doorjamb.

Blood.

His heart skipped a beat. There was blood on the floor, too.

Moving into the tiny kitchen, the scarred linoleum cool and bloody beneath his bare feet, he stood at the window and watched the storm. The weeping willows leaned, overpowered by the screaming wind. He looked out at the moonless night and tried to remember if he'd flipped the pirogue, the small boat they kept out back.

Earlier that afternoon, his little sister, Allie, had followed him to the pond. Her eyes had been teeny, mischievous. She wasn't supposed to wander past the small yard. He'd been too worried about convincing her to follow him back to the house to even consider the boat. But he worried now. If Mother saw it filled with rainwater, there'd be trouble.

They usually didn't lock the house, but he now flipped the latch on the screen door. He grimaced, imagining his mother in the morning, her thin mouth set in a stiff line, furious about the slamming door that had kept her up at all hours of the night, whether it did so or not.

He couldn't risk it.

Lightning struck, illuminating the rusted Buick that for all of his nine years had sat atop concrete blocks next to the old, splintering shed. The night became dark. In the blackness, he thought he saw something move. A moment later, he saw it again.

He flipped on the porch light, bathing the yard in a dull, yellow haze. He had to blink twice before he believed what he saw.

Trembling, he backed away from the window.

His mother, naked and standing in the yard, stared up at him through a tangle of rain-soaked hair, her eyes wild. As he bolted from the window, he could hear her calling to him.

Ten years later

"IT'S GOING TO be another muggy day in Grand Trespass with a high of 91 degrees and a relative humidity of 94 percent. Expect it to be partly cloudy with wind gusts from the west-south-west. Not entirely unpleasant, but none too comfortable, either. Now, here's Billy with the traffic."

CHAPTER 1

HALEY LANDRY FOLLOWED her best friend, Tiffany Perron, into Provost's, a small bar that lay at the fringe of Grand Trespass, Louisiana.

The town was little more than a post office, a filling station, man-made ponds used to harvest crawfish and catfish, a diner, a tackle shop, a church, and an old general store with a faded, oversize RC Cola billboard.

Grand Trespass was so inconsequential, its name was rarely uttered outside a ten-mile radius of its rusted "Welcome" sign. That fact made certain locals feel insignificant as well.

Nineteen-year-old Haley was one of them. Her only dream for as long as she could remember was to escape Grand Trespass.

To find out who she was.

Who she *could* be.

That was something she envisioned being able to do only by going away to college—but college was increasingly becoming less of a reality. For the first time in her life, she had responsibilities. Huge ones . . . ones she wasn't sure she could handle.

They found a table near the bathrooms and ordered. Tiffany plucked a cigarette from a pack and held out the box. "Want one?"

Haley shook her head.

"You okay?" Tiffany asked. "You look a little pale."

"I'm fine."

Going out just to have fun tonight seemed wrong. Her father was killed in a gruesome accident seven months earlier, and she'd barely been out of the house since. But she didn't want to ruin Tiffany's evening.

She straightened in her seat and tried her best to look more okay than she felt. She knew the illusion was thin.

Tiffany blew a stream of smoke over her shoulder, then her eyes narrowed. "You know, you have to start getting out. It's been months since—"

"I know," Haley interrupted. Cigarette smoke, sweat, a mixture of cheap colognes, and the smell of fried food made her queasy. She wanted to go home.

After the waitress returned and set their cheese sticks and sodas on the table, Tiffany leaned forward, her eyes serious. "Look, I've got something to tell you."

"What?" she asked, glad to change the subject.

"Okay, now don't freak. It's about a guy. And it's not Charles." She lowered her cigarette. "I know it's not right, especially after Tom and all." Her eyes grew wider, more emphatic, the way they always did when she was trying to sell Haley something.

"You know how much I love Charles. I mean, I love *things* about Charles. Certain wonderful things . . . but then there are things I don't love. Like, how he's so disgustingly infatuated with me."

"I thought that was one of the things you loved?"

Tiffany sighed and pushed her long, strawberry-blond hair from her face.

"I did. It felt cool at first, but I'm so over that now. He always wants to be with me. I don't do well on a leash."

"He's your boyfriend. He should want to be with you. Besides, it's hardly like he has you on a leash."

Tiffany tilted her head and twisted her gold necklace around her thumb, a nervous habit since Haley's mother had given them matching twenty-four karat ones with monogrammed heart-shaped pendants for their high-school graduation.

"I don't know. Maybe I'm not cut out for a boyfriend," Tiffany said. "I mean, I like too *many* boys." She untwisted the necklace and let it fall back against her neck. She smirked. "Maybe my mama's right. I'm hopelessly boy crazy, and Jesus is gonna make me pay for my lust in the afterlife."

Haley had no reason not to like Charles Johnson. He was bright, warm, polite . . . decent. Although she'd been as surprised as anyone that Tiffany had decided to date a black guy, Haley had no problem with it. She thought he was good for Tiffany.

But Tiffany wasn't so good for him, especially after her affair with Tom Anderson, a professor at the community college—an ordeal for which Charles had just forgiven her. And now they were having *this* conversation.

"I think Charles wants to marry me. Say I marry him. Then what am I supposed to do? Stay here? Grow old in Grand Trespass with a *black* man? It's bad enough to think I might be stuck here at all. But being with Charles in the first place was more about screwing with my mama's head than truly loving *him*."

Haley groaned. She hated how her friend treated guys. Everything always had to be about her, with little to no consideration of them.

"Don't get me wrong, Charles is a doll. An absolute doll. Well, usually. But since the thing with Tom, he's become almost, I don't know, obsessed." She sighed. "Well, anyway, there's this guy. I'm not going to tell you his name because . . . well, you're just going to have to, um, trust me on why."

Trust, Haley thought. She loved Tiffany, but trusting her was a lot to ask. The guy probably had a girlfriend or a wife. Or worse, children.

Just then, Haley saw Charles work his way through the crowd. His eyes quickly settled on the two girls, and he walked toward them.

"Anyway, this other guy and me," Tiffany continued, "we've been kind of flirting, and I think that he likes me. I mean, of course, he likes—"

"Shhh," Haley interrupted, her voice low. She lifted her chin in Charles's direction. "He's here."

"Who?" Tiffany asked, turning to see.

Charles stopped at their table. An overhead light in the hazy room cast a shadow across his dark face. "Thought you two were hanging at Haley's tonight."

He took a seat and crossed his arms across his chest, fixing his eyes on Tiffany. "Stopped by her house and was told you came here instead."

"We changed our minds," Tiffany said, irritated. "Haley needed to talk and wanted to get out of the house. Her mother's still in a bad way."

Charles looked at Haley. His expression softened. "Your mother still having a tough time?"

She nodded. Her mother had been grieving since the accident. The woman who once brimmed with life, an eternal optimist, now was silent and much too thin. She lay in bed night and day, detached from the world.

The part that *wasn't* true was the original plan to stay at her house. She wasn't sure what lies Tiffany had told him and didn't want to get involved. Her friend lied too much, and Haley wasn't in the business of keeping track.

"If there's anything I can do to help out, let me know, okay?" Charles said.

"Thanks." Haley studied the crowd and saw an old friend of her father's, standing in the distance. "Excuse me," she said, relieved to have an excuse—any excuse—to get up. "I see someone I should go and say hi to."

A moment later she was across the room, and the man, whose name she'd forgotten, was beaming down at her. "Look at you. Growin' like a weed, *mon cher!*" His smiling lips gave way to tobacco-stained teeth. His face was ruddy and sagged with years of alcohol and too much Louisiana sun. "Your father sure did make one pretty youngster," he gushed.

I'm not pretty, she thought. *Tiffany is the pretty one.*

The man was one of her daddy's childhood friends from Weston. Haley's father had become a math professor at Cavelier La Salle Community College, which kids from Chester, Truro, Weston, and Grand Trespass usually attended before they dropped out and started their own families.

Haley glanced past him at her friends. Charles was leaning across the table. Tiffany's face was drawn. She twirled the necklace over her thumb and shook her head.

"How's that mother of yours holding up?" the man asked.

Not so well. Actually, not well at all. "She's, uh . . . fine. Nice seeing you," Haley said. "Sorry, I need to run."

She went to the bathroom and splashed cool water on her face, then locked herself in a stall. She leaned against the rusted avocado-colored door. She knew she shouldn't have gone out, but Tiffany had begged her. Now she was fighting with Charles. Who knew how long they'd be?

She took a few deep breaths and focused on the wall in front of her because if she closed her eyes, she knew her mind would take her places she was too afraid to go.

CHAPTER 2

HE WAS A liar. Lying was what kept him safe, alive, and relatively sane when he was little and his mother would crawl into his bed . . . and when he became older and she continued.

He lied about everything and to everyone: his wearisome, red-faced manager at the Winn-Dixie; the employer at his second part-time job; the filthy sister he'd been forced to care for; anyone he encountered outside the house; anyone he'd ever met. Sometimes, when he was lucky, he even managed to lie to himself.

He was sure that people liked him because of the person he pretended to be. If they knew who he really was, they'd hurt him. The thought unsettled him almost as much as the terror trapped inside his head.

Some people thought they were close to him. They weren't. He made sure of it.

It was dark now in the woods. Still. A sharp contrast to the slew of horrid, dangerous thoughts exploding like fireworks, overcrowding his skull.

He felt far from at peace and always had, but something about this summer made everything worse. His mind was a pressure cooker that desperately needed release.

Screaming at the pond wasn't enough anymore.

They'd begun to scream back.

Brushing away a low-slung limb, he trudged forward. A pair of yellow eyes studied him from within the tall grass. His chest tightened.

It was the sickly stray cat that he'd named Ian. It followed him everywhere these days: to the pond, through the woods. Its heinous eyes even peered through his tiny bedroom window at the worst of moments. He wanted nothing to do with the revolting animal. "Leave me alone, Ian!" he yelled, but the cat didn't budge.

"I said, fuck off!" He lunged at it.

It shrieked and shot into the darkness.

He headed back to the small house he shared with his sister. He knew he wouldn't be able to stay there for long. He avoided it as much as possible. It'd been hers, his mother's. Inside of it, he was still a frightened, angry little boy.

Outside, he could usually fake who he was and become almost normal. But not in the house, a place that would remain a cruel part of his life until his sister graduated from high school.

Or until he was forced to destroy her.

Once he neared the house, he couldn't bear to enter. The light in his sister's room was off, which meant she was out. But she wasn't the only one he had to worry about. Some nights, his dead mother's presence just felt too strong.

He decided to take a drive.

CHAPTER 3

FIFTEEN, MAYBE TWENTY minutes passed before Haley left the bathroom. She glanced around the bar. Tiffany and Charles hadn't returned. The cheese sticks and sodas were on the table, untouched. She left a five-dollar bill and headed to the back door.

She pushed it open and stepped out into the warm, sticky night. The putrid odor of Trespass Bayou hung in the air. "Tiff?" she shouted into the parking lot. "Charles?"

She waited.

No one answered.

Heat lightning rippled in the night sky as she walked deeper into the gravel lot.

Tiffany's black Ford Mustang was still parked there, but so many trucks resembled Charles's. She couldn't tell which was his and if it was still there. Wandering up and down the rows, she peered into each large truck, thinking maybe she'd see them arguing inside one of the cabs.

They were all empty.

Glancing out at the line of woods on the east side of the lot, she thought she saw something move. "Tiffany?" she called.

The night was still, silent.

She shouted louder. "Tiffany! Charles!"

Again, nothing. Just an owl, screeching in the distance.

CHAPTER 4

SUNDAY MORNING, THE aroma of sautéed andouille sausage, garlic, and onions clung to the air as Haley chopped scallions in the kitchen, careful to make them fine like Nana used to do.

She was afraid. Afraid for her mother, who looked more like death every day. Afraid for her sister, Becky, who'd never openly mourned her father. Afraid for her life, which had unraveled nearly a year ago.

She wished Nana was still around to tell her what to do. When her maternal grandmother was alive, she had been the centerpiece of the family. Daddy was the voice of reason, but Nana was the voice that spoke of reasons, deeds, and notions no one wanted to think about, much less believe.

Haley's mother always said to pay her no mind, that Nana was growing senile. But Nana had been alert and full of life, more so than most of the kids Haley's age. If Nana were alive now, she'd know exactly how to whip her family back into shape.

Haley's boyfriend, Mac, sat at the kitchen counter, his nose buried in a fishing magazine. He was a vision of health: tall, tanned, athletic, confident, and always relaxed. Nothing seemed to ever bother him. She'd become the opposite of him over the long months: pale, puffy, stressed, and uncertain. Haley wasn't even sure why he still wanted to be around her.

Still, she knew she didn't have the luxury of drowning in a depression. Her mother had claimed that path before anyone else had the chance. Someone had to care for her, Becky, and the house. There was no one else.

"You have a good fishing trip?"

"Yeah," Mac said, not looking up. "Relaxing."

"Get back last night?"

"Yesterday afternoon. Put in a couple of hours for Lloyd. Would've called but couldn't get a damn signal at the site. By the time I got home, it was pretty late."

Mac worked for Lloyd's Towing in Weston. He put in odd on-call hours any chance he could. Since he was fifteen, he also worked other part-time jobs on occasion, including cutting lawns.

Haley wiped beads of sweat from her temples with the heel of her hand. The wall-mounted air-conditioning unit in the living room barely cooled both rooms, and lately the unit in Becky's bedroom had been on the brink. She needed to call a repairman, but the bill would run them a couple hundred dollars.

She dropped a handful of chopped scallions into the skillet, then gently stirred them into a crackling mixture of flour and oil. On the refrigerator door, along with old report cards, her high-school graduation photo, and an old "To Do" list was a note from her father, saying he went to buy Sheetrock. It was a note he'd posted just hours before he died, held by one of the magnets he used to pass out at parish fairs.

"Education Is Forever," it read.

How about when you're dead? she wondered.

She couldn't bring herself to take down the note. Apparently, Becky and her mother couldn't, either.

Mac set down his magazine, then pulled off his LSU ball cap and began working the bill between his thick, strong hands. His forehead and cheeks were sunburned, and just above the collar of his T-shirt were three jagged, red lines on his neck.

"What happened?" Haley asked.

"Ah, nothin'." Mac pulled his cap back on, then lightly fingered the scratches. "A branch got me while I was fishing is all. Wasn't payin' attention." The corners of his eyes crinkled as he flashed her a tired smile.

"They look pretty bad. You put anything on them?"

"It's nothing, Hale. Believe me, looks worse than it is."

Haley decided to take him at his word. Men didn't like women who nagged. Besides, she had enough to worry about.

Mac walked around the counter and kissed her cheek. "I'm goin' to go lie on the couch and have me a little nap. After that, I'll take you for a snow cone. How's that sound?"

Haley was folding towels when the phone rang half an hour later. It was Julia Perron, Tiffany's mother. Haley told her Tiffany wasn't there.

"Weren't you with her last night?" Mrs. Perron snapped.

"Yes, Mrs. Perron, I was. We went to Provost's."

"And she's not there?" she asked skeptically, as though Haley would now say yes.

"No, ma'am."

There was a brief silence on the other end of the line. "Haley, this wouldn't have anything to do with the little argument she and I had yesterday morning, would it?"

Mac stirred from where he lay on the couch.

Haley lowered her voice, not wanting to wake him. "I . . . I don't know."

"Could you tell me who I should call then? She wouldn't be with that *Charles* boy, would she?"

Months earlier, Mrs. Perron had forbidden Tiffany from dating Charles, one of only a handful of blacks in Grand Trespass and the surrounding towns. Families like the Perrons—white, working class, and sometimes narrow in their views of what and who were acceptable—didn't look kindly on minorities. When Mrs. Perron found out that Tiffany was secretly dating Charles, she demanded that Tiffany not see him anymore. She hadn't told Mr. Perron for the sake of his bad heart, but she'd threatened to disown Tiffany if she continued seeing Charles behind her back.

"No, ma'am, I wouldn't think so," Haley said, cradling the phone between her shoulder and ear as she folded a blanket.

After hanging up with Tiffany's mother, Haley tried Tiffany's cell phone but got her voice mail. She left a message and walked to the kitchen. Mac had already awakened and was placing a new bottle on the Culligan cooler.

"Sounds like Tiffany's going to be in hot water the rest of the summer." She sighed. "That's if she's not disowned."

"She stay out last night?" Mac mumbled.

"Yeah, guess so. And her mother's pissed."

Mac grabbed a dish towel and wiped his hands. "She with Charles?"

"I guess. I can't think of anyone else she'd be with."

But she could. Tiffany could be with the guy she'd begun to tell her about.

CHAPTER 5

MAC EASED THE truck to the side of Main Street and killed the ignition. The Ford shook for a few seconds, then became quiet. Wondering if Tiffany had made it home yet, Haley pushed open the passenger-side door and climbed out.

Her bare feet burned against the sun-beaten asphalt. She took slow, deliberate steps. While she concentrated on the blistering heat, she couldn't think of anything else: her father, her mother, her insomnia, her future . . . The asphalt was agonizing but also therapeutic in a way. A Southern antidepressant.

Dead, dried-up worms stuck to the blacktop. She slowly made her way across the road, trying to avoid stepping on their mangled bodies.

"The tar's gotta be blazin'. Shit, I can feel the heat clear up to my ankles," Mac said, waiting on the other side. "Why you walkin' so slow?"

"It's not that hot," she said and tried not to wince. "Really."

The snow-cone stand was a run-down trailer that had been parked on the side of Main Street for as long as she could remember. Haley noticed a girl her age, Erica Duvall, standing on the side of the road several yards away. She was staring into the woods, a backpack hanging low on her back.

"What do you reckon she's doin'?" Mac asked, squinting against the sunlight. He handed a blue snow cone to Haley.

"Don't know."

"She hangs out in the woods an awful lot," he said, taking another cone from the kid at the counter. "You'd figure a girl our age would've grown out of that type of play. Moved on and become a young lady."

"She doesn't have any friends," Haley said, watching Erica disappear into the woods. Haley found Erica beautiful and mysterious.

"You two get along okay at Luke's?"

To help her family with the bills, Haley had taken a job a few weeks earlier as a waitress at Luke's Diner, where Erica and Tiffany also worked. She bit into the ice, barely tasting the sweet syrup on the tip of her tongue. "Yeah, she's quiet, but nice enough."

Haley had found herself mesmerized with the quiet, petite girl who was also a waitress there. She was much different from the others, always reading, always writing, always in a different world.

Tiffany had a much different impression of Erica. She found Erica weird and a bit freaky and, like she did with so many other people, looked down on her.

Erica's family had moved to Grand Trespass from San Francisco when she was in the first grade. Haley remembered when she first saw Erica at school. She was small and skinny, with the same long, brunette hair framing her tiny face. Both her clothes and her eyes had looked way too big for her.

Sadly, Erica had the same number of friends walking into the classroom that day as she'd had the day she graduated from high school. None.

Four o'clock that afternoon, Haley carefully skimmed the scum that had settled at the top of the gumbo pot. Setting the wooden spoon back on the stove, she went to her mother's bedroom and eased open the door. The only part of her body that Haley could make out in the bedcovers was the crown of her head. She hadn't come out all day. It was as though she was attempting to sleep away the reality of her husband's death.

Haley closed the door and walked to the recliner. Mac's six-foot-one frame was sprawled out on the large couch against the wall. His empty snow-cone cup was on the floor by his side, next to a crumpled can of Coors Light.

"You think you should call Dr. Broussard?" he asked. "This has been going on for far too long. It's not healthy for her to stay holed up like that."

"He was just here a couple of weeks ago. She wanted some pills to help her sleep. Now she stays in there and sleeps more than she did before." Haley sighed. "I don't know what to do."

The phone rang. Haley sprang up and hurried into the kitchen. "That's gotta be Tiffany."

When she answered, she immediately heard terror in the voice on the other end of the line. "Please tell me Tiffany's there," Mrs. Perron croaked.

Haley glanced at her watch, and her heart began to race. *Where could Tiffany be?*

CHAPTER 6

FIVE MINUTES AFTER the phone call, Mrs. Perron climbed into Mac's truck and thrust an ample hip into Haley's side. Haley squeezed closer to Mac, and Mrs. Perron slammed the door closed.

"*Le bon Dieu!*" she cried, mascara smeared into the deep recesses beneath her worried eyes. "It's not like my Tiffany to run off like this!"

Mac threw the truck into gear and headed to Trespass Gardens, where Charles lived. Haley looked out at the dusty road as the big cypress trees whizzed by, their branches seeming to reach for the truck. She folded her arms over her body and held herself tight.

In the distance, a cottonmouth slithered across the blacktop. Mac skillfully eased the truck across the yellow dotted lines, sparing its life. As Haley glanced behind her, watching the reptile hurry into the unkempt grass at the edge of the woods, she thought again of what Tiffany had begun to tell her. She wondered if she knew the mysterious guy who had caught Tiffany's eye.

If he could have had anything to do with her not returning home.

But just as quickly as the thought had come, she dismissed it. *Tiffany is with Charles. She's okay.*

A few minutes later, they pulled off the two-lane blacktop road and bounced their way into Trespass Gardens, a park on the opposite end of Trespass Bayou that housed trailers and small houses.

Gravel crunched beneath the truck as they crawled past one old trailer after another. Several shack-like houses appeared. Haley took in the porches that sagged beneath tattered couches and disfigured toys. Trash barrels of all sizes and colors lined up for collection.

Soiled-faced children played freeze tag in front of the homes, running through sprinklers and beneath clotheslines that groaned with drying wash.

"There," Haley said, pointing to a small white house in the distance. "That's Charles's house."

Mac pulled off the path. As soon as he yanked the emergency brake, Mrs. Perron was out the truck door and hurrying up to the porch. At the top of the steps, she yanked open the screen door and rapped loudly.

Mac's engine popped and hissed as the two sat watching the older woman. "How many times have you been out here?" Mac asked.

"Just once."

Mac fumbled for his cigarettes. "This ain't a good place for young girls to be hangin' around."

Haley had known Mac would comment about Trespass Gardens. He was always worrying about her. Had been for the whole year they'd been together.

He produced a cigarette. "Just want you to be safe is all."

She looked into her boyfriend's eyes. He had stood by her side at her father's funeral and afterward, taking care of the things her father had before he passed: the yard, the gutters, the siding, her tears.

"You worry about me too much."

"Well, if I don't, who will?"

Sticking the cigarette between his lips, he reached for the door. Before opening it, he glanced up at Mrs. Perron and shook his head. "The girl's not right in the head. Making her mama worry like this is just plain wrong. A nice, wholesome girl like you would be better off with more upstanding friends. But you know where I stand on that subject," he said. Then he jumped out of the truck.

Mac had never liked Tiffany because he thought she was too promiscuous and self-centered. He was as polite to Tiffany as he was to everyone else, but it was more than obvious that he didn't care for the girl and never would.

Haley climbed out of the truck to find him pulling down the tailgate. He sat and lit his cigarette. Several yards away, a bunch of kids were squealing, hopping over sprinklers and sliding across a faded Slip'N Slide.

Mrs. Perron was still knocking on the front door. "Anybody home?" she shouted, becoming more agitated. "Anybody? Tiffany? You in there?"

Haley wandered around the house into the backyard. A thick plume of smoke curled into the air, rising from a distant neighbor's barbecue. Its tangy, mesquite scent filled her nostrils.

She stopped at a tall anthill, slid off a flip-flop, and pushed her foot into its soft center. In a matter of seconds, ants swarmed out and up her ankle. She watched as they slowly spread up her shin, past her knee. She savored the sting of their tiny bites. But once they reached mid-thigh, she pulled her throbbing leg to safety and brushed the insects off.

She glanced at the house, startled. Someone was peering out from behind a window shade, watching her. Quickly, the shade fell back against the window.

She hurried back to the front yard. Mrs. Perron was still speaking to the front door.

"Tiffany, if you're in there, you'd better come out right now," she threatened, her voice trembling. "If you don't, I'll make sure your father knows everything. I mean *everything*. Bad heart or not!"

Mac flicked his cigarette ash into the grass as Haley approached. "No one home?"

"I saw someone in the window out back. But whoever it is, isn't answering," she said.

"Was it Tiffany?"

"I don't know. I couldn't see."

"We can come on back here after we take her home," he said, picking an ant off of Haley's arm. "If she's in there, she'll probably open up if her mother ain't around."

CHAPTER 7

HALEY'S HOME WAS no different than most of the ranch-style homes the middle-class families had built in Grand Trespass in the seventies and eighties. At the front door, one would walk into a small room that connected to a nice-size kitchen, then a relatively spacious living room.

The bedrooms and one bathroom were located off the living room. Standing at the front door, one could see clear through the house to the back door and vice versa, the architecture not lending itself to much privacy.

The women in Grand Trespass liked the floor plan because they were able to cook and still keep an eye on their children playing in the living room. Haley liked it because she could easily keep an eye on both Becky and her mother when they weren't in their bedrooms.

"Who's the kid?" Mac asked, letting the screen door snap shut behind them.

Cigarette smoke hung in the air. Haley had seen a bicycle leaning against the house when they'd pulled up but figured it belonged to Sadie, her sister's friend. Sadie's mother was always buying Sadie things, trying to make up for the time she ran the child over in the driveway, leaving her with a lame right arm.

"I don't know." She walked past the kitchen and into the living room. Becky and a dark-haired teenage girl were watching television.

"Hey," Haley said.

Fifteen-year-old Becky turned to her with a practiced look of boredom, an irritating expression she seemed to have mastered overnight. "Hey," she answered, pulling her thin, mousy hair into a ponytail. She pointed to the girl. "Haley, this is my new friend, Seacrest. Seacrest, this is my sister, Haley, and her boyfriend, Mac."

The girl blew out a steady stream of smoke and fixed her gray eyes on Haley's. "Hey," she muttered.

Haley winced, watching the smoke spiral into the air.

"The Landrys don't smoke in the house," Mac said, his voice matter-of-fact but polite, one of the many mannerisms Haley admired in him.

The girl smirked. "Well, then, I'll go on outside." She stood and pulled at the hem of her short denim shorts. Then she sauntered out the back, letting the screen door slam shut behind her.

"Why'd you tell her she could smoke in the house?" Haley asked, exasperated.

"She didn't ask," Becky replied. Her feet, stained brown on the bottoms from walking around barefoot, dangled from the arm of the big recliner. She twisted in the chair, lowering them to the floor.

"Well, who is she?" It wasn't every day that Becky brought a new friend to the house. In fact, she couldn't think of the last time she had. Sadie was Becky's only friend.

Becky shrugged and smeared some lip balm on her cracked lips. "I don't know. Just some girl."

Mac took a seat on the couch. "What do you mean you don't know?"

"I just met her. She was riding her bike out front, and we just started talking. She's pretty, huh?"

"Does she go to your school?" Haley asked.

She shook her head. "She lives in Weston."

"I don't like that she smokes," Haley mumbled, trying Tiffany's cell phone again. She'd grown anxious. She and Mac had just driven to Trespass Gardens for a second time—this time without Mrs. Perron—but again, no one had answered the door. She didn't have Charles's cell-phone number, and directory assistance said that his home number was unlisted.

"What's wrong with smoking? Tiffany smokes," Becky said. She lifted her chin in Mac's direction. "So does Mac."

"They are *adults*," Haley pointed out, checking the answering machine for messages. There were none. "Did Tiffany call?"

Becky shook her head.

Haley sighed. *Where the hell is she?*

"And Mom. Has she come out of her room at all?"

"No."

CHAPTER 8

HE ROLLED A polished half-dollar-size stone around his palm. He'd found it on the bank of the pond and hoped it would remind him of the power he'd had with those who now rested at its bottom. Although it was only morning, the air was already humid. It made his hand uncomfortably moist.

He dropped the stone in his pocket and rubbed his palm against his pant leg. Once it was dry, he studied the faint scars inside both hands, an unpleasant reminder of the morning his mother held both palms against a hot burner on the stove. He was nine, and she'd been in one of her moods. The seared skin had smelled awful. Her laughter still rang in his ears.

He heard a scream, and his head shot up. Trembling, he looked out at the pond to the place where he'd sunk the girl's body. It was black, its surface unblemished.

He walked closer to the water's edge. Something in the tall grass plopped into the water. Stepping sideways, he tripped on a thick branch. He steadied himself, but the wetness from the pond's edge already had seeped into his muddy rubber boots.

He heard it again.

The cry of a human in agony.

The sound was deafening. He shook harder.

Still staring at the pond, he covered his ears and stumbled backward. "It's okay to be afraid," he whispered. "It's okay. I'm afraid, too."

He thought back to her face as he'd wrapped her in the lawn bag. The pale lips and the pastiness of her skin. The dead had a rigid stare, unforgiving. He was relieved that he'd duct-taped her eyes shut so he wouldn't have to feel their blaring judgment.

He'd breathed freely after killing her, feeling an elation and blissful calm no other act that he knew of could bring. He would have kept her longer if it hadn't been for his sister. If she found out, it would be all over for him.

He finished wrapping the girl and, an hour before daybreak, he was done. Carrying the body in his arms, he'd felt a startling rush of power. He'd even begun smiling.

He took her to the far end of the pond, the place where he docked the small boat. As the girl's body sank, another scream rang out and echoed against the still sky.

He shuddered with joy.

CHAPTER 9

ERICA DUVALL WAS a loner. She always had been. Her mother had been a loner as well, not understood, not wanting or needing to be. Her mother had hated the people of Grand Trespass and had wanted nothing more than to get away.

Now she was gone.

After she finished the mystery novel she'd been writing, she left. Ten years earlier, with only a backpack, the clothes on her back, and a dream, she'd crept out of the house and fled Grand Trespass. But she made a mistake. She'd left Erica, the person who'd loved her most. To this day, Erica didn't understand why she hadn't taken her along or why she hadn't at least said good-bye.

Erica had always been different from the other kids. She always felt awkward and uncomfortable in anyone's presence, but that rarely bothered her anymore. She didn't need anyone in her life except for her mother.

Now across the living-room floor were magazine clippings, a thesaurus, balled-up scraps of paper, and scribbled-on receipts. Erica sat on the leather couch, staring into a notebook. For the last three days, she hadn't been able to string more than two sentences together. She was stuck between chapters five and six, and she wasn't even sure the first five chapters were good enough. The short stories hadn't been this difficult. In fact, they had come easily. Her teachers always had marveled at them.

The trouble was, she had to write a novel—not just any novel, but a great one, one her mother would be proud of. If she were proud, she couldn't help but love her again.

She wondered if her mother had ever fought the demon of writer's block. Every time Erica had watched her write, the words seemed to come so naturally. She had her routines. In the mornings, she'd pace for a half hour or so in her pajamas with her favorite mug between her hands, a University of San Francisco mug she carried everywhere. She called it her muse.

She drank coffee from that mug and tried to get the rhythm she needed for her writing by swaying to a Janis Joplin album. Sometimes she listened to Fleetwood Mac or Meatloaf, depending on her mood or the material on which she was working. She never listened to the Cajun music Erica's father liked, full of its whining accordions and muddy soul, the music that often blared when he was passed out drunk on the couch or the kitchen floor.

Her mother had despised that music and everything it represented. She was a native of San Francisco, not a Southerner from a Podunk town that barely existed on a map. She'd often told Erica that her greatest mistake had been following her father to Grand Trespass. She said she'd been blinded by love, a mistake she seemed to work night and day to fix.

After finishing her writing for the day, her mother would dress, and they'd make a snack together, usually pan-fried beignets. Then they'd sprawl on either end of the couch, eat, and watch old movies together.

But those days were over—at least for now.

Erica had been nine and her mother twenty-six the year she left. That was ten years ago, around the time her father began coming home late from work. For the long months leading up to her departure, writing was all her mother could think about. She tackled it as though she was making up for wasted time.

Erica sighed and tossed her notebook aside.

She flipped off the lamp and closed her eyes.

———

An hour later, the front door swung open. Disoriented, Erica opened her eyes. The overhead light flooded the room, and she sat up. She blinked, waiting for her eyes to adjust.

It was her father, and he was talking to someone.

A musky odor filled her nose, and she sneezed. She watched her father scan the room.

"Oh, hi, hon."

He carried a paper bag in his left hand and held the hand of a busty, blond woman—the source of the atrocious smell—with his right.

Erica sized up the woman's long red fingernails, a color her mother would never stoop to wearing. It sent men the wrong message—or maybe with her father, the right one.

Erica scrambled to pick up her things from the floor. Her thoughts were private, not for her father to see, much less some blond bimbo.

"Erica, this is Pamela."

Pamela took a step toward Erica and extended her hand. She noticed the woman wasn't much older than she was.

"Hi. It's so nice to finally meet yooooou!" she squealed.

Finally? A mixture of anger and confusion washed over Erica. She shoved everything into her backpack and stood, not accepting the woman's hand.

Her father cleared his throat. "Erica's a writer," he said, smiling. It was a fake smile, the type he used when he was selling used cars at the lot or when there were strange women in the house, though she'd never seen one quite this young. "She's working on a novel."

"You are?" Pamela asked, apparently unaffected, her voice still annoyingly cheerful.

Erica groaned and marched across the living room, toward her room.

————

Nineteen tea candles lit Erica's bedroom. She'd dumped the twentieth candle into her bedside garbage can, part of a ceremonial act she'd seen her mother perform several times. Nineteen flames now twisted on their wicks, swaying against the air conditioner that had just kicked on in the small room.

She leaned against her headboard, listening to one of her mother's Janis Joplin CDs. A cheap bottle of white wine she'd swiped from the diner rested between her legs. She took a sip, watching the flames' shadows dance across the walls and the splintering bookshelves.

Her mother had believed the candles gave her creative energy. Erica sipped as she waited to feel some of her own, but she was distracted. Images of the new hussy's young face and long red nails preoccupied her. She shook the images from her mind and took a longer sip, then another.

Someone knocked on her door.

"What?" She yelled.

Her father opened the door. "Honey . . ." he started, coming in and sitting on her bed.

She moved to the chair by her window.

"Honey, we need to talk."

"About?" she asked, trying to sound as indignant as possible. Her mother had been indignant with him, especially after his late nights at the car lot.

"It's about your manners. Your attitude."

She studied the floor. She hated people's eyes; they made her anxious. She didn't like what she saw in them: judgment, indifference, hate, ignorance. She couldn't even bear to look into her own father's eyes most times. He was as ignorant as all of them.

Her words were an angry hiss. "Excuse me?"

He glanced at her nightstand and saw the wine bottle.

"You were very rude to Pamela tonight. I don't—"

"She's still here, isn't she?" Erica interrupted. He'd said nothing about the alcohol, but instead of relief, she felt more infuriated. It was already ten o'clock. There was no reason for that strange woman to be in the house.

"Well, yeah. Pamela's still here. And she'll be here a while. She's . . . staying over." He pointed to the candles on the windowsill. "You need to be careful with those. Make sure to blow them out before you go to—"

"Sleeping over? Where? Where will she *sleep*?"

"Erica, how many times do we need to—"

Her head was spinning from the alcohol. "In your bed?"

"I'm a grown man, honey. If Pamela—"

"You're still married!" Erica shouted. Tears swelled behind her eyes, and she turned so that he couldn't see her face. She was disappointed that she'd raised her voice. He'd mistake it for her caring, which she didn't.

The muscles in her stomach knotted when she thought of her father sleeping with another woman, but she wasn't sure why. She knew her mother would never return to him or Grand Trespass, so it shouldn't even matter.

The voice behind her softened. "Your mother hasn't contacted us in ten years. I looked for her and I couldn't find her, honey. I'm not sure what happened . . . or why she hasn't tried to get in touch with you, kiddo. I know she loves you."

Erica didn't want to believe him. She wanted to believe that her mother had contacted her father, that she had tried to get in touch with Erica but her father had in some way come between them. Her mother was perfect, something her father definitely wasn't.

"Erica, I don't understand why you have to make things so difficult. I try. I really do."

He tries?

She hadn't seen him try. Did he think that the last several years of courting loose women and working late most evenings at the dealership was trying? How about giving her a rickety decade-old Ford F-150 that broke down twice a month, or caring nothing about her life? Was that trying?

Her father stood. "I'm sorry you feel this way. I really am. But I have a life, too. And I have to live it, honey."

He walked to her bedroom door, then turned. "You'll like Pamela. She's a great lady. She's different than the others. You'll see."

With that, he closed the door.

Now that she was alone, the tears skidded down her cheeks. She wanted to scream at the door and say things that would hurt him. She wanted to hurl the wine bottle. She hated him. He was the reason her mother left her.

CHAPTER 10

LUKE'S DINER WAS never empty. Someone was always sitting at a table or lingering at the counter between the hours of six o'clock in the morning and eleven o'clock at night. Sometimes it was the attendant from the gas station across the street who hung out there to avoid her husband. Other times, it was some lonely widower, blue-collar worker, or weary person or family passing through town.

Lazy-eyed Chris Guidry owned Luke's. Black-and-white photographs of his family and Grand Trespass adorned the walls. Among them was a nearly life-size photo of his late daughter, Luke Anne, who had died two years earlier in a drowning accident on Trespass Bayou.

Haley found something eerie about the little girl's gaze. Every time she saw the photograph, she was forced to turn her eyes away. Maybe it was the fact that the girl had died so young. She just looked too wise in the photo, too knowing.

Chris didn't seem old enough to have a child, especially a dead one. Usually when folks had kids, they had a haggard look about them as though they were simply aging faster or had grown up in a way that was impossible for those who were childless. Chris didn't.

Haley had stopped at Tiffany's house before her shift that morning to find the usually well put-together Mrs. Perron naked of her daily face spackle and in her robe, clutching their poodle so tight that he yelped. Seeing Mrs. Perron, incoherent and with dark circles beneath her swollen eyes, she had a flashback of her own mother in the hospital the night of her father's accident.

Haley took two food orders and passed the order slips through the window to the kitchen trailer out back. Standing in front of the coffee urns, she massaged her temples. There was an excruciating pain behind her eyes, the pressure she always suffered when she'd had too little sleep or was under too much stress. She'd managed to get only an hour of sleep the night before. The Nyquil she kept at the side of her bed for insomnia no longer did the job.

She stroked the heart-shaped pendant that hung around her neck, the replica of Tiffany's, and whispered, "Where are you, Tiffany?"

"You say something?" asked Austin Thibodeaux, the diner's cook, setting the food order on the counter.

Haley jolted. "Oh, sorry. Didn't realize you were there. Was just talking to myself, I guess."

He flashed her a grin. "I wouldn't let that get too out of hand. We'll have to start worrying about you."

He studied her, and the sparkle in his blue eyes faded. "Hey, you okay?"

"Yeah. I'm fine."

But she was far from fine. Two nights had come and gone since anyone had seen or heard from Tiffany. Several men were now at city hall with the Perrons. At nine o'clock, a search party would begin scouting the woods.

"You sure you're okay?" Austin asked. "You don't look so good."

"I'm sure."

He grabbed a newspaper from the counter, fished out the crossword puzzle and folded it in half. Before returning to the kitchen trailer out back, he rested his hand on the trailer door. "If you need anything, just holler. You know where I'll be."

She nodded.

The cowbells dangling from the front door of the diner rang, and the diner's owner, Chris, entered. Haley shielded her eyes from a ray of sunlight that found its way in through one of the diner's dusty windows and went to pour him a cup of coffee. As she set the pot back down on its burner, she felt Chris's hand on her shoulder. Chris had always been touchy-feely, but as much as she didn't like it, she knew he meant no harm.

"Just heard about Tiffany," he said. "Any new word?"

She shook her head and handed him the coffee.

"Sweet Jesus," he murmured. "You know, when you mix with folks you shouldn't mix with, you're just asking for trouble."

"She isn't with Charles. Sheriff said he spoke with him last night."

Chris mumbled something under his breath and reached beneath the counter for the shift schedule. "If you want, you can go on home. Kim can cover the floor before Erica's shift. She should be in any minute."

"No, it's okay. Better to keep busy," she said, wiping the counter.

He stood with the schedule and studied it briefly. Then his good eye met hers while the lazy one seemed to study the two customers behind her. "I'm sure she's just run off with some boy. No need troubling yourself any more than you already are with your daddy and all."

Tiffany hadn't run off. Haley was sure of it. But she was too tired to argue, so she said nothing.

Chris's hand was on her shoulder again. He gave it a little rub, and Haley tried not to shrink away. "Change your mind about taking off early today, let me know. I'll be out back."

CHAPTER 11

BY TWO O'CLOCK, the lunch crowd at Luke's had moved out. Chris and Austin were scrubbing the grills in the trailer out back, preparing for the dinner crowd, and Erica was working the floor. As Erica walked through the front door of Luke's for her shift, Haley was leaving, too rattled to finish out the day.

Erica hauled a rack of clean silverware from the kitchen and set up at the counter to roll it, all the while mulling over the possibility that something really could have happened to Tiffany Perron. She'd heard men shouting the girl's name in the woods that morning and wondered what was going on. The word was she went out on Saturday night and no one had seen her since.

Most of the townsfolk who frequented Luke's that morning didn't seem quick to get excited about her disappearance. The ones who knew the girl seemed to suspect she was just off somewhere with a boy. It was the people who didn't know her who seemed to be doing the majority of the worrying.

Grand Trespass, albeit small, wasn't innocent of its share of crime. Erica's mother, having done exhaustive research on the town for her mystery novel, used to tell her about the ugly goings-on that most tried to hush. An estranged spouse planting a bomb in a mailbox. Domestic disputes resulting in six bullet wounds to the head. Drunk-driving fatalities, home invasions, prostitution, check fraud, ritualistic acts involving the town's domestic animals.

Grand Trespass wasn't a close-knit town by any means. Rightfully, people tended to be mistrusting. They kept to themselves, shielding their private business from town criers—and the smart ones locked their doors. Her mother had speculated that boredom, rampant alcoholism, and general malaise were the chief culprits of the town's woes.

The plump, fiftyish attendant from the gas station across the street sat at the counter talking with Kim Theriot, Chris's manager. Erica listened to the two as she rolled the silverware.

"What do you suppose happened to the Perron girl?" the attendant asked, lighting a cigarette. When she exhaled, Erica could see that the butt bore a disgusting red ring from the woman's lipstick.

Kim wore a New Orleans Saints T-shirt and was squeezed into a pair of blue jeans. She sat slumped next to the cash register, focusing on a crossword puzzle. "No tellin'," she muttered. "Tiffany has ants in her pants. Always has. Probably up and left the state, knowin' her. That's all she ever talks about anyway. Goin' off. Leavin'. Becoming some big movie star." She chuckled. "As if."

Erica hated Kim more than she did Tiffany—and that was saying a lot. Kim was two years older and had been one of the nastiest bullies Erica had to deal with growing up. In grammar school and high school, Kim had picked on her relentlessly, spreading rumors and labeling her a devil worshiper. Once, in the gym bathroom, she even threw a live cockroach in Erica's hair.

Erica acted as though she didn't give the older girl a second thought. She'd never admit to Kim or anybody that she could be hurt. "Show them your weaknesses, and you'll be forced to own them. That's all they'll be able to see in you," her mother had told her. She'd been right, but still, it hadn't protected her from the constant pain.

Chris wandered in from the trailer and went quietly to the front door. He stared at the sugarcane field across the street.

"A bunch of folks from Chester and Truro just began a new shift in that search of theirs," the attendant said. "A man from Lafayette and some hounds of his are out there with them."

"Sounds like the sheriff is takin' this pretty serious," Chris muttered.

"He's just protecting his ass is all, because she's Julia Perron's daughter." Kim grunted, setting the puzzle aside. She unwrapped a piece of gum. "Knows he won't have a peaceful dinner 'til she has some answers. But you mark my word. There's goin' to be a lot of pissed-off people when they find out she's just out gallivanting. That girl's lived a charmed life. She always will with those looks of hers." She shook her head. "It's a shame. All those poor folks spendin' their blessed Monday not getting paid a red cent because they're tryin' to find her. They already have trouble enough puttin' food on the table."

Moments later, the cowbells clattered, and Rachel Anderson, the creative-writing teacher from the community college, walked in. Rachel, wearing a floor-skimming lavender skirt, her long, blond hair pulled into a neat French braid, scanned the diner. Settling her sunglasses on the top of her head, she went to the counter and politely addressed the group.

"Good afternoon."

Erica noticed Kim and the attendant glance at each other.

Everyone in Luke's knew about Tiffany's affair with Rachel's professor husband, Tom, and they knew that Rachel only came in to intimidate her. Before learning about the affair, she'd never stepped foot inside Luke's.

Erica admired the woman for being so confrontational. She had balls. There was no mistaking that the woman was strong . . . and Erica liked strong.

"Just a cup of coffee, please," Rachel said, smoothing out her skirt and sitting.

Instantly soothed by the woman's presence, Erica reached for the pot of coffee.

"They're out searching the woods by the Johnson's old place now," the attendant said. "I hear the brush is so bad out there, it could take hours to cover just a few hundred feet."

"Searching the woods? Did I miss something?" Rachel asked, tearing open a packet of sugar. Erica studied Rachel's long, thin fingers, her polished nails, clear and beautifully shaped. She admired the elegant way her hands moved as she tore open the small square package. Rachel was perfect, just like her mother.

"Tiffany," Kim announced. "She's gone missing. You didn't hear?"

Rachel's eyes darted from Kim to the attendant. "What do you mean *missing*?"

"No one's seen her in two days. She left her Mustang in the parking lot over at Provost's Saturday night. Never made it home."

Rachel dropped the sugar packet, and granules spilled onto the counter. She stirred her coffee with a shaky hand. "They have any idea where she could be?"

"Sheriff talked to her boyfriend," Kim said. "He says he doesn't know where she is. No one knows much else."

The diner went silent.

The attendant pulled her tube of lipstick from her pocketbook and smeared it against her thin lips. Erica noticed that every now and again, she would study Rachel. She wasn't sure if it was out of envy, curiosity, or suspicion. People in Grand Trespass generally were suspicious of folks who stood out, and most women particularly didn't seem to care for Rachel. Erica believed this was only because they were jealous. Like Erica's mother, Rachel didn't talk like the other ladies. "Sugah," "sugah darlin'," and "*cher*" this and that. "*Cher bebe*" and "*Mon cher!*" She didn't dress in muumuus and walking shorts and leave the house in old sweats. No, Rachel had pride, grace, style, and an education—assets that ruffled the feathers of many of the women in Grand Trespass.

Erica had admired her since taking her first writing course at the community college. Now she was taking a writing course for each of the summer terms. She was one of the few people Erica had ever grown to like.

And she liked her a lot.

She was the closest thing to her mother she had ever known.

"Haley Landry was the last to see her. They went to Provost's together," the attendant said. "Sheriff's been making his rounds, talkin' to folks. The Perrons organized a search party. Folks have been searching the woods all day."

"Any signs of foul play?" Rachel asked.

"Not that we know of," Kim said. "That's why I think all of this is bullshit. If she was someone else, no one would get questioned for at least another day or two. *I'm* convinced she's just run off. Either a stunt for attention, or she's found some new boy."

The attendant shook her head, lipstick stuck to a yellowed top tooth. "I don't know. Haley and Tiffany are best friends. She'd know if Tiffany just ran off. But the poor gal looked like death when she left. And after the horrible, horrible way her daddy died, bless her little heart. I hate to say it," she said, crossing herself, "but I don't have a good feelin' about the Perron girl. Not a good feelin' a'tall."

CHAPTER 12

AROUND TWO-THIRTY, SHERIFF Bill Hebert walked into Luke's clutching his campaign hat between his thick hands. "Afternoon," he said, nodding to the group. Slightly bowlegged, the fiftyish man sauntered to the counter, set down his hat, and took a seat next to the attendant. Purple circles the shade of Easter-egg dye framed his crinkled lower lids.

"How's the search going?" Chris asked.

The sheriff cleared his throat. "I suspect it's goin' just fine."

"I'll head out there around four if there's no news before then. Join the late shift," Chris volunteered. "If there still is one."

Sheriff Hebert nodded. He reached into his shirt pocket, took out a pack of unfiltered Camels, and then returned them. His laugh was gravelly. "Tryin' to quit, but I don't believe in goin' cold turkey."

Erica set a cup of coffee in front of him and picked up Rachel's still-full cup. She'd left minutes ago, her face pale.

"You care for a sandwich? Some soup? Gotta mean shrimp bisque back there," Chris said.

Hebert shook his head. He surveyed the room. His blue eyes were as cool as lake water but more stern than any eyes Erica had ever seen. He was a quiet man, preferring to talk very little, but when he did, he easily took command. "There's goin' to be a young detective fella comin' by to speak to a few of y'all about the Perron girl sometime tomorrow. Will you be around, Chris?"

"Absolutely."

"Haley Landry on the schedule?" he asked, his thick, stained fingers returning to the cigarette pack. Before they got there, he lowered his arm.

"Yep, mornin' shift," Chris said.

"I'll tell the detective she'll be here in the mornin' then. Name's Eddie Guitreaux. Seems like a decent young man from what I've seen. Bright, somewhat hungry. Ex-football hero. Used to be a real big shot in Baton Rouge. He'll be comin' around to ask folks some questions. I trust everyone will be as helpful as possible."

He took a long slug of his coffee. "It's also been brought to my attention that there's been a Peepin' Tom in town for the last couple of months. Not sure if it's related. And it's never smart to jump to conclusions. Besides, there are no signs of foul play here. Hard facts, that's what the detective will be lookin' for. I expect that's what he'll git."

Kim's eyes lit up. "Peeping Tom?"

There was nothing Kim liked better than a juicy piece of gossip. Her mouth served as the town's FOX News.

The sheriff set down his coffee cup. "Yes, ma'am, someone peekin' into folks' windows. He's been doin' it in Chester for as long as I can remember. In Weston, too. We can't seem to find the bugger, and it seems as though he's becomin' more active. Folks been gittin' prank calls, too. They think it's the same fella." He paused. "But I reckon I shouldn't say any more about that right now. I just ask that y'all keep your eyes peeled. Call the station if you see anythin' out of the ordinary. In the meantime, I'm sure Guitreaux will be keepin' everyone fine company."

CHAPTER 13

ERICA RIPPED A page out of her notebook and crumbled it. She tossed it to the floor and scowled at the next blank page. Tears stained her cheeks.

The scenes still weren't working, and when she tried to write them anyway, they sounded contrived. She would have to start all over. Write something completely different.

She eyed the oversize plastic Heineken bottle that served as a bank for her New York City fund, the money that would take her to the East Coast so that she could find her mother. It was four feet tall and more than half-filled with dollar bills and coins. Her goal was to have it completely filled by the end of the summer. Now realizing that she might have the money but no novel, her heart sped up.

She kicked the gray top sheet to the foot of her bed in a futile effort to release some of the nasty anxiety, then reached for her wineglass only to find it empty. "Un-freakin-believable," she said with a groan.

Slipping out of bed, she pulled on a pair of sweatpants, then shuffled down the hallway toward the kitchen. The air conditioner was set low, and the house was chilly.

"Hello," a soft voice said behind her.

Erica stiffened.

"Oh, sorry, darlin'. Did I frighten you?"

Pamela sat on Erica's mother's leather couch, a romance novel in her hands. A sheer pink nightie barely covered her body.

Erica folded her arms across her chest. "Did my father give you a key?"

Pamela laid down the book and cocked her head. Erica could see that the lacy material barely contained the woman's breasts. "If he had, *cher*," she replied slowly, "would that be a problem?"

Feeling her nostrils flare, Erica stormed from the room and into the kitchen. She threw open the refrigerator door to find two tomatoes, a cucumber she'd taken from a garden on the way home the night before, a case of Diet Coke, a jar of olives, and three cans of Miller Lite.

She pulled out two beers and was balancing the beers, a box of tea candles, and some matches when Pamela walked into the kitchen.

"If you don't want me here when your daddy's not home, I won't come over," she said softly. "Is that what you want?"

The woman looked even younger than before with her hair pulled back and no makeup. She was actually much prettier without it—well, as pretty as a cheap-looking bimbo could possibly be.

"Do whatever you want. It's his house."

"But it's your house, too, darlin'."

Erica moved past her.

The woman's voice followed. "You know, I haven't decided. Either you're into witchcraft, or you're thinking about it. You into witchcraft, *cher*?"

Erica whirled around, nearly losing a can to the hardwood floor. "What?"

"Just somethin' I noticed."

Erica thought of the deck of tarot cards on her dresser and the valerian root, a relaxant that she used when she was messing around with simple spells that her mother used to cast. "You've been in my room?"

"I wasn't prowlin' or anything. I was lookin' to borrow some cold cream is all, and noticed some things. Your incense. The book of invocations."

"Don't *ever* go into my room again! You hear me?"

Pamela's face fell. "I just wanted to talk to you about maybe castin' me a little spell. Don't worry, I won't go tellin' your daddy or nothin'. It's a girl thing anyway. Business that should be left between us women."

Erica shot her a dirty look. *Us women?* She and this woman were nothing alike. "Tell him what you want. But you'd better stay out of my room," she said, "or I'll make sure my father puts a leash on you."

CHAPTER 14

HE SHIFTED HIS gaze from the television to the wall. The phone was ringing. It hardly rang, but when it did, it was always a sales call.

"Hello?"

"Hi, sir. My name is Andrea, and I'm calling from Total Decks," a squeaky, hopeful voice began. "How are you today?"

He didn't answer.

"Great, I hope," she continued cheerfully. "May I ask if you currently own a deck?"

"No."

"No, you don't? Fantastic. Then we would like to send someone out to your home to give you a free estimate. When would be a good time?"

"Not interested," he replied, glancing at his watch. Nine p.m. It seemed too late to be getting a sales call. Weren't small children in bed by now?

"You sure, sir? It's complimentary. That means it's free."

"Yes," he said, not concealing his annoyance.

The screen door opened, and his sister, Allie, appeared. She glanced at him and shook her head disapprovingly. Her long hair was down again, and she smelled strongly of liquor and lotion. She stumbled past him, then slammed her bedroom door.

"Are you sure?" the voice on the phone continued. "We can just come out and give you that estimate. I promise it's free. And Grady's Custom Decks are rated the . . ."

Music erupted from inside Allie's room. He could feel the vibration in his hands, his skull. He hung up the phone and sat back down. Grabbing his beer, he picked up the remote. Alarming images of female flesh flashed across the screen as he flipped through the channels.

When Allie was home, he couldn't relax. Since their mother had passed, she had become even more frightening.

Ian, the mangy cat, mewed outside.

Allie's door flew open. She tottered to the kitchen and flipped on the fluorescent light, bathing the room blue-white.

"Staying in again?" she asked.

His eyes went back to the television. A *Seinfeld* rerun filled the screen. His eyes moved blindly over the characters. He'd never gotten into television. It was impossible for him to concentrate on one thing for even half an hour while he was inside the house. There was too much going on inside his head.

Plus, it disturbed him.

Aside from the black-and-white sitcoms and dramas that were taped in the fifties through the early seventies, the rest of the programming was nothing but filth.

Out the corner of his eye, he watched her at the refrigerator. She opened it and looked inside, her hands on her hips. "Don't you have two jobs? You know, if I had two jobs, I'd buy groceries every once in a while."

"What do you need?"

"Uh, let's see," she answered. "Two, or even one of the four food groups? Something besides a can of tobacco and cheap beer?

You're supposed to be the adult, you know. You should really start acting like one."

She slammed the refrigerator door and twisted the cap off a beer bottle.

He hadn't asked for this job, and he knew he wasn't any good at it. "Five," he said.

"What?" she asked, tugging at her gauzy top.

"Five. There are five food groups."

"Whatever."

"I leave you money."

"I *spend* the money. And not on food. On other stuff. Like condoms and blow."

He stole a quick glance at her and saw that she was smirking. He loathed her attitude and her outfit. All the girls her age dressed like tramps. Didn't they realize how unsafe that was? What it did to certain men?

Men like him.

His eyes settled on the beer. "You're too young for that."

She snorted. "Too young? What, now you think you're my father? Oh, please, you're not even an adult. You never will be."

He turned back to the television screen. It had grown fuzzy. He cracked his neck and looked at the coffee table, where a cereal bowl sat, half-filled with congealed milk.

A cockroach scuttled across the floor behind the television, then slipped through a crack in the wall. He shuddered. He'd always been afraid of roaches, even as a kid when Allie would chase them and laugh as she crushed them between her small palms.

But she was older now, on to more dangerous things.

She tossed the bottle into the trash can with the rest of the empty bottles and Styrofoam take-out containers and picked up her purse. "Don't you wish you had a life?" Her eyes took in the room.

He watched them flit from the stained carpeting to the large, gold-framed St. Bart's print that hung lopsided on the wall.

He watched her, knowing this wasn't where Allie wanted to be. But he didn't want to be here, either. As soon as she turned eighteen, he'd be gone. He'd drive to Nevada and finally get a place of his own. He'd move far, far away from this place and the constant reminders of his late mother, of the torment. He'd be a different person. He'd begin a normal life.

If that was even possible.

Allie walked across the room, her chin upturned. "And one day, I'll walk out this door, and I'll be gone forever," she said, her words slurred. "You'll be lonely, won't you?"

He thought about Tiffany. The fear in her eyes as she realized she was about to die. She'd wanted to leave, too. She never had, not in the way she imagined she would. He remembered her muffled screams, how rigid her body had grown.

"Are you drunk?" he asked.

Her steely eyes bore into him, and he tried not to let his nervousness show. She could *never* know how uncomfortable he was around her, the power she had over him. She'd use it to her advantage. Women always did.

"No, I'm not drunk. Anyway, why should you care? You barely exist."

He knew she was trying to get a rise out of him. His eyes returned to the television.

He was aware he'd grown more attractive over the years, losing all the horrible baby fat. The changes had ended the name-calling and the laughter from the kids at school. But to his sister, he remained just as hideous and insignificant as always.

She smirked. "And for your info, I *know* you had a girl in here the other night. I saw her purse, and there's a lipstick stain on the couch," she said, pointing, her eyes small. "Unless it was just you . . . and you've started cross-dressing and wearing shitty shades of lipstick. Oh, not that I'd be surprised." She snorted at her own joke.

He didn't react.

Her face turned serious again. "So, who was she?"

He picked up his beer.

"Was she pretty?"

He glanced at her face and realized his sister was jealous. Their family was demented.

"Did she have big tits?"

"Yes, and they were very nice," he mumbled.

Her eyes grew even smaller. "You screw her?"

"I did." He began to shake.

The room went still. A long moment later, her laughter cut the silence. "Whatever. I don't believe it." She smoothed her skirt and marched to the front of the house. "God, am I glad I'm not you!" she hooted. She let the screen door snap shut behind her and was gone.

He studied the place where she'd been standing. She'd be gone until tomorrow. He always felt safer when she was gone.

He pulled on his rubber boots and walked to the back door.

CHAPTER 15

RACHEL ANDERSON OPENED the door to her son's room and sighed. Clothes and magazines littered the floor, and despite the house rules, a ketchup-smeared plate and two crumpled Coke cans were on top of his dresser.

She was having a terrible year. A few months earlier, she'd discovered that her husband, Tom, had been having an affair with one of his teenage students: Tiffany Perron. She would have sworn just a year ago Tom would never stray. Tom was someone she always thought of as a fine man, a faithful man. To say her perception of him had been flawed would be a colossal understatement.

"Tommy!" she shouted for her son.

Since she'd heard the news about Tiffany, her stomach wouldn't untwist. She stopped by the diner to show the girl that she was watching her.

It had become a tradition.

She had visited ever since she found out about Tom's affair, hoping to keep her family together, to warn the younger girl to stay away from her husband. What had seemed like a clever plan before suddenly sounded horribly asinine. The girl now was missing. She'd probably just run off, but nonetheless, she was missing. Somehow that made what Rachel had been doing seem highly juvenile.

Pathetic, even.

"Tommy!" she yelled again. "I thought you told me you cleaned your room!"

She began to collect the dirty clothes. Then, thinking better of it, she dropped what she'd picked up and shuffled into the living room. Was this what her life had become? The jaded wife of a philandering husband? An insecure thirty-six-year-old woman going out of her way to challenge teenage girls? A woman forced to *compete* with teenage girls?

Rachel thought of the unfinished manuscript she kept buried in her closet. She once had big dreams; then she became pregnant with Kelsey. She married Tom, ten years her senior, and in her progesterone bliss, she thought there'd be nothing but positive things to come: a healthy marriage, a beautiful child, a successful career as a novelist. But money became tight, and she had been forced to take up teaching. Not long after, little Tommy came along. Then Tom started taking his trips.

Several of them.

In the last year, the trips nearly doubled in frequency.

In the living room, eleven-year-old Tommy lay on his stomach in front of the television with a bowl of Apple Jacks. Rachel picked up the remote by his side and pressed the power button. The screen went black.

Tommy twisted, the spoon still in his hand, his big eyes confused.

"You told me your room was clean, Tommy."

"It is," he answered, his words slow and even, like his father's often were.

She planted her hands on her hips. "Tommy?"

"God, Mom!"

"God, Mom, what?"

"Just . . . can't you relax for once? You act like the sky is falling, and guess what? It's not."

Rachel winced. Those were the words he'd heard his father say many times, words she despised. She had a reason not to be relaxed. It wasn't as if she was the innately tense person they made her out to be. She had reasons. Good ones, dammit! "Don't ever tell me to relax, Tommy."

He sat up and scowled. "But you're always getting on my case! I'm so sick of it. Is Kelsey's room clean? Did you get on *her* case?"

Rachel regarded her son. He was becoming more like her husband every day. His wavy blond hair. His stubborn, defiant tone. The way he tilted his head when he watched television.

The anger on his face.

She took in the long, lean legs that were now sprouting more peach fuzz, the feet that had seemed to grow large overnight.

"Tommy, we're talking about *your* room," she said, trying to keep her tone in check.

It had become difficult around the house in the last year. She was always on edge, and she knew her children felt it. She wondered if they knew about the affair. The town was small, and she was sure that others knew.

But who?

And how many?

Was Tom still cheating despite his insistence that he wasn't? Had he cheated before, or had this really been the first time? Rachel forced the wave of questions into the back of her mind. "This conversation is about *your* room, Tommy," Rachel repeated. "You told me it was clean."

"You see? You're always on my case and not hers!" He snorted. "You know, she's not as perfect as you think."

Rachel raised an eyebrow. Her sixteen-year-old daughter, Kelsey, had changed a lot lately. She'd become rebellious, and Rachel was beginning to worry if she was okay. "She's not?" She looked out the living-room window and watched the handsome young man who cut their grass ride the length of their backyard on the big John Deere lawn mower they'd inherited from Tom's now-dead father.

She picked up a cushion from the floor and situated it on the couch, wondering what the best tactic would be to coax Tommy into giving her some information.

After a few seconds, she turned back to her angry son and said something she knew that a good mother wouldn't say. "I think she's pretty darn close to perfect, Tommy. Kelsey's a good girl. You could stand being more like her."

Tommy's eyes smoldered. "Yeah, she's a good girl, all right. If you call sneaking out your window in the middle of the night *good*, then, sure, Kelsey's a *great* girl. If only I could be like her."

Rachel's breath caught in her throat. *Kelsey was sneaking out? To do what? And with whom?*

She dropped to the couch. "How do you know this, Tommy?" she asked, nervously fingering her bracelet.

"I've seen her. She did it last night, too. She always does it." Tommy shook his head. "And you think she's so dang perfect."

An hour later, the phone rang. It was Myrna, one of Rachel's colleagues at the college.

"I just wanted to let you know," Myrna said. "Oh, dear. How do I say this?"

Rachel tossed a stack of student essays on the kitchen table. "Say what? Just say it, Myrna."

"There's been . . . talk," Myrna said. She said the word *talk* so softly, Rachel could barely hear it. Having known Myrna for years, however, she knew that had indeed been the word she'd used. Rachel could imagine the woman right now, probably sitting in her bedroom, bubbling with anticipation, dying to tell her the juicy, hurtful news.

Rachel swallowed. "Talk?" *What about? Tom? About Tom and Tiffany?*

"I'm not sure how to say this."

Rachel headed to the liquor cabinet. "Just *say* it, Myrna," she said, desperate to maintain her composure.

"It was about Tom's . . . his affair."

Rachel tried not to acknowledge the tears in her eyes as she filled a shot glass with whiskey. She downed it and winced. So Myrna knew about the affair. And if Myrna knew, then—

"And now that the Perron girl has disappeared, people are . . . Well, you know how they are. They think that maybe Tom . . ."

Rachel's heart sank. She wrapped her free arm tightly around her middle and tried to hold herself together. She managed to keep her voice even. "What are you saying? You think this is something more than just a young girl rebelling and running away from this small town? You think something went awry and that Tom had something to do with it? Because if that's what you're saying, I have to tell you that you couldn't be further from the truth."

There were footsteps behind her, then a young voice. "Mom, I'm going to Stephanie's."

Rachel turned to see Kelsey, dressed in a black T-shirt and the black Texas A&M sweats Tom had bought her during a recent conference at the university.

Rachel suddenly wanted to speak to Kelsey. Since it now seemed the rest of Grand Trespass had learned of the affair, she wanted to find out exactly what her children knew. "Hold on, Myrna," Rachel said into the phone, her voice just a croak. She covered the mouthpiece with a shaky hand. "No. I don't want you to leave the house. Not now."

Kelsey's jaw dropped. "But Mom!"

"I said *no*, Kelsey."

"Dammit, Mom!" the girl shouted, although the two stood only a few feet apart.

"Don't curse in this house, young lady," Rachel whispered, concentrating on not dropping the phone. She felt sick from the news, the whiskey, the sudden shouting.

Rachel could hear Myrna's voice, teeny in the phone. "Oh, dear. Do you want to call me back?"

"But why? Why *can't* I go to Stephanie's?" Kelsey asked.

"Because you and I need to talk," Rachel whispered. "When I get off the phone—"

"Oooh! I can't wait to turn eighteen!" Kelsey shouted louder. "I hate your stupid rules. You don't understand me. You don't understand *anything!*" She whirled and stormed off.

Rachel swallowed hard, listening to the angry footsteps in the hallway, then a door banging shut.

"Myrna? You still there?" she asked.

"I'm sorry to have to bring up such a sore subject," the woman replied.

Sure you are.

"No. No, I appreciate the call," Rachel said. "I'll see you tomorrow?"

There was a brief silence, then, "Sure. I'll see you tomorrow, Rachel. Chin up."

Chin up? What the hell was that supposed to mean? And how long had people known about the affair? Longer than she had? Without hesitating to think, she hurled the phone against the wall.

The house was silent as she poured her next drink.

And the next.

She'd probably been the laughingstock of the college all this time. They were still gossiping about her during the summer term, and now this? Thinking Tom could be involved in what was just a silly girl's rebellious tantrum? Surely, that was all this was—at least, the ladies at the diner seemed to think so.

She had the urge to do something awful to Tom, to really hurt him. Maybe put a knife to his throat while he slept, while he dreamed of young, beautiful girls.

What had changed? Wasn't she still attractive? Why did she suddenly not make him happy? The thoughts infuriated her. She could have married many men, but Tom had been the one she loved most. He'd seemed to be so taken with her.

So loyal.

Now they couldn't talk. He was distant, hard, cold—but not to the kids, just her. Is this what happened to men when they entered their mid-forties?

Then there was the conversation about trading in the Pathfinder for a sports car, some ridiculous, red thing. Had he always been like this? Had she just been oblivious?

She downed another shot of whiskey.

CHAPTER 16

TUESDAY MORNING, HALEY led Detective Guitreaux to Chris's small, dusty office in the kitchen trailer behind the diner. She took a seat in the chair that faced the desk and studied the young detective who stood across from her.

He was about Mac's height, six-foot-one, but much beefier. Olive-skinned, he had small, uninspiring, wide-set eyes and a cleft chin. His suit looked expensive, but it was badly in need of pressing.

"I hear you and Tiffany were best friends?" he said softly, his eyes probing hers.

"Not were. *Are.*"

Tiffany had now been missing for three nights. Haley had no clue where she could be. If she'd gone somewhere voluntarily, she would have told her.

She needed answers.

She needed sleep.

Although she'd tried her best to talk with Charles to find out what exactly happened on Saturday, she hadn't been successful.

"You were with her on Saturday night at a bar—" He paused and flipped open a notebook encased in a black leather cover. "Provost's. You were at Provost's with her the night she disappeared?"

Disappeared. The word sounded horrible.

Haley studied the detective's long, square face. His Cajun French accent was thick and soft, but his eyes seemed hard. He had a thin nose that flared out slightly at the tip as though he were smiling. But he wasn't.

"Yes, sir. We were together Saturday night at Provost's."

His eyes seemed to soften. "Call me Eddie, *cher*," he said. "I call my father *sir*. And the two of us are like motor oil and kitchen matches. Now, can you do me the honor of telling me what transpired that night? The full story, please."

She fidgeted in her chair, then took a deep breath. "Tiffany picked me up at my house, and we left for Provost's a little before nine o'clock. We were only there a few minutes, maybe fifteen, before Charles, Tiffany's boyfriend, got there. I didn't see her for long after that."

"Why is that?"

"I went to the bathroom." She felt lightheaded as she again recalled the night's events.

The detective tapped a large ring against Chris's desk. Austin had told her that it was a college championship ring. Supposedly the detective had played football for LSU for a couple of years before an injury cut his career short.

"Then what happened?"

She remembered waiting in the bathroom stall, upset that she'd gone out. At the time, she had no idea that her friend would vanish. If she had, she never would have left her alone.

"I waited in there awhile."

"Waited?"

"Yeah. Tiffany and Charles were . . . arguing. They needed privacy."

"Was it out of the ordinary? The fighting?"

"No."

He watched her for a moment before he opened his notebook again and examined something. "How long were you in this bathroom?"

"Maybe fifteen minutes. I wasn't wearing a watch."

He jotted a long note into his book, then looked up again. "And then?"

"I walked out to the parking lot, but I couldn't find her."

"So, what did you do?"

"I walked home."

"Did you find it odd that she'd leave you at the bar alone?"

Haley shrugged. "No, not odd. I just thought they left together. That maybe they made up and forgot about me."

He tapped his ring against the desk again. "I wouldn't be very happy if a friend did that to me. I'd find it strange."

"Well, you don't know Tiffany. Sometimes she's inconsiderate. It wasn't really unusual for her."

"Did you hear from her after you left?"

"No, but I got a call the next morning from her mom. She asked where Tiffany was. She was worried."

"Has Tiffany run off before?"

Haley shook her head.

"Spent the night away from her house without her mother knowing? Or talked about leaving town?"

Haley straightened in the chair. "She sneaks out of the house sometimes, but she's always careful. She worries too much about her mother catching her. And no, she never talked about leaving town. Not like this. It just isn't something she'd do."

"Most nineteen-year-olds aren't expected to be so accountable to their mothers," Guitreaux observed.

"You don't know her mother. She's very overbearing. She still treats Tiffany like a child."

"Is that right? Any idea why Tiffany would put up with that? From what I've gathered, she's pretty strong-willed."

"Money. Her parents control a big trust until she turns twenty-one. She does her best to stay in her mother's good graces, but it's difficult for her. She feels like her mother breathes down her neck, and she hates her for it."

Guitreaux nodded. "I see." He tapped his pen against his upper lip for a few moments, looking thoughtful. "Let's talk about Tiffany's relationship with Charles. For starters, what were they arguing about?"

"I think she was seeing someone else, or at least thinking about it. Charles might have known."

"You talk to Charles since Saturday night?"

Haley shook her head.

"Not at all?"

"No."

"The two of you, you and Charles. Would you say that you're close?"

"Not terribly, but yes, we're friends through Tiffany. Why?"

"Well, it just would seem that you two would want to talk after someone you both cared about disappeared."

"I haven't been able to find him. I've tried."

The detective's eyes seemed to sparkle. "I see." He studied his notes for a long beat. "Do you know the gentleman that she might have been seeing?"

"No, sir, I don't."

"No?"

"No."

"No clue who it could be?"

"No."

"You and Tiffany. Were you getting along okay that night?"

"Yeah? Why?"

"No disagreements? Arguments of any kind?"

Haley frowned. "No, none. Why do you ask?"

He looked into his notebook again. "Part of my job." His eyes met hers. "So the last time you saw Tiffany, it was around nine-thirty, nine-forty-five p.m., and she was having an argument with her boyfriend, Charles. That was the last you saw or heard from her."

"Yes."

"Okay, good. I think I have enough for now. Unless, of course, there's anything else you can tell me that would help us find your friend?"

"I've told you everything," she said, feeling deflated. But as she said the words, she flashed back to something Tiffany had told her that night, something that hadn't bothered her when it was said but disturbed her now. "This probably doesn't mean anything, but . . . one of the last things Tiffany told me on Saturday was that Charles had been acting . . . obsessed. It was the first time she ever told me anything like that about him."

CHAPTER 17

AFTER LEAVING DETECTIVE Guitreaux, Haley fumbled in the parking lot outside the diner for her car keys. Though there were only five keys on the ring, she had a difficult time finding the right one.

Her hands shook, and her lungs revolted against the hot, humid air. She coughed, and an excruciating pain shot through her head. Recounting that night had drained her, stripping her of the little energy she had left. Although she didn't think Charles had it in him to do something horrible to Tiffany, why else would he avoid her?

She heard someone call her name. Squinting in the harsh sunlight, she saw Austin jog toward her. "You're in no shape to drive. C'mon, let me take you home."

"No, I'm okay," she insisted, dropping the keys, then bending to pick them up. She grabbed at them, also scooping up several pieces of gravel. She straightened and wiped the gravel off her hands. "I am. Really, I'm fine."

But when she tried to look up and show him she was okay, the tears surged forward.

"It's going to be okay," he assured her. "Let's get you home. Chris said he can get your car to you sometime this evening."

She trembled as they drove down Main Street. Too many horrible things were happening, and she wasn't sure how much more stress she could take. Chris suggested she take a few more days off. It was a relief because focusing on something as small as placing an order was becoming difficult. Her head was too muddled.

She'd spent the previous day holed up in her room, downing double shots of Nyquil and trying to sleep. But sleep didn't come until late at night, after she'd spent hours staring at a crack on her bedroom ceiling. When it did come, it was in the form of a vivid nightmare: Her riding her bicycle to the grocery store, only to realize that she didn't know the way back home. As she rode, nothing had looked familiar. It was as if she were in another town. She pedaled around and around, terrified.

"Is the AC too cold?" Austin asked, pressing his palm against one of the vents.

"No, I'm fine." She sniffed. "You'll want to turn left at the church." She glanced at Austin. She'd had a little crush on him for months, making small talk with him on several occasions but not as much as she'd like since he and Chris spent most of their time out back.

She knew her crush was innocent, just something to take her mind off her troubles. She knew she'd never act upon it.

Women like her—plain, predictable, and responsible—went for boys like Mac and stayed with them. Besides, Mac was good to her. Austin had a serious girlfriend, Beth, a freshman at Texas A&M. Rumor had it, he was going to ask her to marry him, just as Haley was likely to someday marry Mac.

"How's Beth?"

The edges of Austin's mouth turned up. "She's good. Real good. And Mac, how's he?"

"Doing well. I didn't realize you knew him."

"Oh, I don't. Just seen him around the diner," he said. "And, of course, Mrs. Motormouth talks about him from time to time."

Haley smiled at the nickname he'd given Kim.

"So, how often do you get to see Beth?"

"We shoot for every other weekend and, of course, college breaks. It's not a short drive by any stretch of the imagination."

"Yeah, I know," Haley said, wondering if she could have a long-distance relationship with Mac. She quickly decided she could. Even though they lived only ten miles apart, it wasn't like they saw each other every day anyway.

He usually stopped by three times a week, sometimes more, sometimes less. When he did, he seemed much more interested in making sure that she and her family were okay than wanting to make out or do anything romantic. But she had no complaints. The relationship, as it stood, was perfect for her. Since her father died, she had lost most of her interest in conversation. She usually worried that she was a bore when she was with him anyway.

She was no longer the witty girl she'd been when they first met. But Mac, not much of a conversationalist himself, didn't seem to mind. They did things that didn't require much talking. Sometimes he just fiddled around alone, repairing something in the house, cutting the lawn, painting the trim.

Haley rested her head against the passenger seat. She closed her eyes and inhaled. Austin's truck had some of the same comforting grease smells that Mac's had, minus the stale, smoky odor, and it was less dusty.

Austin stopped in front of her house and yanked the emergency brake. In the time it took for her to pick her purse up from the floorboard, he was at the passenger door, opening it for her. He helped her out like Mac always did.

But when his hand touched hers, a jolt of electricity shot through her body.

"You get some rest," he said, walking her to her front door. "Chris said he'll bring your car by this evening."

"Thanks," she said, shielding her eyes from the sunlight. "I guess I *did* need the ride." She wiped at her eyes. All of a sudden, she realized that she felt a little better.

"See you at the diner when you're ready to come back. Chris is concerned about you."

Two pecans fell onto the porch. Haley bent to pick them up. "By the way, did Chris ask you to take me?"

He nodded.

"Oh," she said, realizing she had wished it had been his idea. "Please thank him for me."

"I'll do that. Take care of yourself." He walked back down the dirt driveway.

Haley stood on the porch and rolled the pecans around in her palm as she watched him walk away and climb back into his truck.

Sighing, she opened her front door.

CHAPTER 18

ERICA LOVED THE way Rachel wrote on the chalkboard. Her writing was straight, sharp, always in capital letters, very legible. She double-underlined the important words, the ones she wanted to emphasize.

The chalk often made her sneeze. When she did, "Bless you" bounced off the walls of the small auditorium. Everyone loved her.

But not as much as Erica did.

Erica enjoyed Rachel's fluid, confident movements as she walked back and forth, teaching the importance of dialogue, the way her eyebrows became perfect v's when she asked her class a question. The genuine smile that spread across her face when a student answered correctly.

More than once, Erica heard the boys discuss Rachel.

"What a knockout."

"She's hot, for an older chick."

"Hell, I'd do her."

Erica bet her mother was just as beautiful these days, if not more, if that were possible. She longed to see her again, to know for certain what she looked like.

Today, Erica could barely sit still. She'd had a breakthrough with her writing that morning, a *brilliant* new idea.

An epiphany.

Rachel glanced at her watch. "Let's recap before moving on," she said, peering up at the class, her slender hands clasped together. "Dialogue is so much more than words. In fact, it is one of the most important tools you will use in moving your stories forward. You will also use dialogue to help develop your . . ."

Erica usually sat in front, but she was late that morning and now sat in the back row. Earlier, she'd gone to the little cemetery off Harper's Road to brainstorm. It was another one of her mother's writing traditions, another of her muses.

Sometimes her mother would sit there for hours with just the dead and her thoughts, concocting macabre situations and worlds.

So Erica tried it, too.

Erica felt a unique calm at the cemetery. The people who lay below her weren't threatening, unlike the ones she interacted with on a daily basis.

But as she'd cut through the woods on her way home that morning, she was startled to realize that someone else was with her.

Someone alive.

Leaves had rustled, then she'd glimpsed someone about thirty feet away. She'd called out, and the person ran away.

Why would someone run?

A knock on the classroom door. Rachel excused herself, then after a few hushed whispers outside the classroom, she poked her head back in. "I'd like you to begin doing the exercises at the end of chapter ten," she said. "At ten fifty, you're all free to go."

"Think it's the police?" a tall girl sitting in front of and slightly to the right of Erica asked a freckled girl.

"The police? Why would it be the police?"

"Because that girl was sleeping with her husband."

73

Erica quit thumbing her way to chapter ten. Her fingers slipped out of the text. She didn't like where the conversation was heading.

"What girl?" the freckled girl asked, scrunching up her forehead.

"Where have you been? The *missing* girl. Tiffany something."

Erica watched the girl's jaw drop. "Mrs. Anderson's husband was sleeping with her?"

"Sure was."

The freckled girl looked skeptical. "How do you know that?"

"Everybody knows. Mrs. Anderson found out about it and freaked. Some people think maybe she's the reason the girl's missing."

"No shit?"

"No shit."

Erica bit into her lower lip, willing herself not to say anything. These girls were stupid. What did they know anyway? She kicked the back of the tall girl's seat.

The tall girl turned.

"Accident," Erica muttered, staring at her text.

She felt the girl gaze at her for a quick moment before turning back around.

The freckled girl whispered, "She doesn't look like a killer."

"*Hello?* Did Dahmer? Bundy?"

"Dahmer did."

The tall girl ignored her. "Well, Mrs. Anderson isn't as perfect as she looks. She obviously had a motive. And get this: She's been visiting the diner in Grand Trespass where this Tiffany worked. Like clockwork. Like some sort of stalker."

Erica kicked the back of her chair again.

The tall girl turned.

"Oops," Erica said, her voice hard, her eyes boring into the girl's.

The girl studied her for a few seconds, the expression on her face a mixture of anger and confusion. Then, understanding the unspoken message, she turned around and said nothing for the rest of the period.

CHAPTER 19

WEDNESDAY EVENING, HALEY sat at her father's grave. "We're having such a hard time, Daddy," she told him. "Everyone's so miserable without you. I just want so badly for things to go back to the way they were."

As each new day passed, her memory of those old days seemed to fade. There were times when she couldn't even remember what her father had looked like. Sometimes she forgot how his laugh had sounded.

Forgetting terrified her.

She reached out for a dandelion blossom and began picking it apart, tears stinging her eyes. "And Tiffany still hasn't come home. No one seems to have any idea what happened to her. I wish you were here to help us."

She knew that even if her father were still alive, he wouldn't be able to do much. It wasn't as though he were a detective or a bounty hunter. He had been a bookworm, a college professor, a slight, gentle man. That didn't stop her from aching to see his face again, feeling his thin arms around her shoulders trying to comfort her.

She hugged her knees and looked out at the trash on the side of the dirt road that led to the cemetery: beer cans, abandoned fishing tackle, a Wendy's wrapper. The barbed wire that was meant to shelter the cemetery was loose in places and leaning, hardly a protector of anything.

None of the headstones were as nice as her daddy's or Nana's. Some of the dead only had markers such as license plates with their names and dates of birth and death. Other markers were mere stones, some odd-shaped, some jagged. She noticed a lawn chair had fallen across one that read *Mother* in sharp, pointy letters.

She thought of her own mother. "Mama's still in bad shape. She won't even get out of bed," Haley whispered. "I don't think she wants to live without you."

She tried to push back an awful thought, one that had come to her over and over in the months since the accident: wishing her mother, not her father, had died that night. Aside from Tiffany, her father and Nana had been her best friends. In most ways, she had been much closer to them.

While Becky had been attached to her mother's hip, it had been Daddy to whom Haley was attached the most. They were able to talk about anything, and they often did. She also knew that if it had been Mama who'd died, her father wouldn't have abandoned them as Mama had. He would have been stronger, even if just for his girls.

Several feet away, a branch snapped.

Haley let go of her knees. Feeling her body stiffen, she peered out at the woods with the dandelion between two fingers.

"Someone there?"

Another branch snapped.

Her breath caught in her throat. She squatted and planted her feet firmly on the ground, prepared to run.

After a terrifying moment, she heard a familiar female voice. "Sorry. It's just me."

She saw a hand, then a head full of hair emerge from the brush. In the murky light, it took her a second to realize that it was Erica Duvall.

"Hey," Erica said, nervously brushing off her T-shirt. "I'm sorry. I didn't know anyone was out here."

She turned to go.

"No. Don't go," Haley called. "You can stay." She shuffled back to her father's grave and sat.

Erica stood still for a few seconds, as though trying to decide what to do. Finally, she walked toward Haley and set down her backpack. "Any news about Tiffany?"

Haley's chest ached. "No. None."

Erica fumbled with her backpack and pulled out a bottle of wine. She twisted the top off and took a swig. "The wind is shifting," she muttered, holding out the bottle for Haley but not meeting her eyes. "It's going to storm."

Haley studied the bottle before reluctantly accepting it. She had drunk alcohol only once in her life, but she wondered if it might, for one short moment, help her forget. She took a sip of the bittersweet liquid, then grimaced and handed it back.

"You visit him every day?" Erica asked, glancing over to where Haley's father lay.

Haley hugged herself against the chill in the air. The cemetery always seemed cooler than the rest of the town. "Most days."

"I've seen you here before," Erica said. "I figured you needed to be alone, so I left."

Haley watched her drink more wine and wondered how often her conversations with her father had been overheard. "Why do you come out here?"

"There's a different energy here," Erica said, handing the bottle back to her.

Haley took a longer swig of the wine and winced at its sharpness. She marveled that after all these years she actually was sitting across from Erica Duvall, having a real conversation. Out of all the people she'd ever known, she couldn't think of anyone who fascinated her more. The girl had a dark sense of mystery about her that no one else she knew possessed. Although barely five feet tall and rail-thin, she also possessed a certain toughness—not the feigned toughness a lot of teenage girls tried to pull off, but the real thing.

The wind shifted, and Haley wrinkled her nose. An overbearing, musky odor blanketed the air. "I smell a skunk."

"Yeah, there's a dead one on Harper's Road," Erica said, pointing to the dirt road to their right, easing her feet out of her flip-flops and rubbing them across the grass. "Lying with his legs in the air. His beady black eyes staring up at the Lord. Not that there really is one, of course."

Haley could tell by the way the girl slurred her words that she was drunk. She studied Erica's bare feet. "Aren't you afraid to go barefoot around here?"

"No, not really. My feet are tough. Besides, it's better to feel the world around you. People let themselves become too desensitized."

Darkness blanketed the graveyard in a matter of minutes, bathing the cemetery in eerie shadows. Erica lit a cigarette, and the two passed it back and forth. The orange ember was the only light in the graveyard besides the dull, bluish glow of faraway stars.

They remained sitting, passing the wine and cigarette to each other. Soon, Haley's head was spinning with alcohol and nicotine.

"This is the longest we've gone without talking since we were like three," Haley said.

"You and Tiffany?"

Haley nodded. "If she was okay, she would have called me. But she's not okay. She's either hurt or . . ."

The ember of Erica's cigarette grew bright against the night as she inhaled. She said nothing, but her silence spoke volumes.

"You know, it's probably not the right time to say this," Erica said, "but I never liked Tiffany. Not to say I hope anything bad happened to her. I just don't want to lie to you. Just thought you should know how I feel about her."

Haley shrugged. "Not everyone likes her. Or me, for that matter."

"Are you kidding? Everyone likes you."

Haley thought about it and silently agreed. After all, she'd never had an enemy.

A branch snapped a few yards away. Haley jumped. "Did you hear that?" she whispered, not taking her eyes off the woods.

"Shhh. Stay still."

Another branch snapped, then leaves crunched as something or someone made its way closer to the tree line. An owl screeched from somewhere up high, then a dull, circular light appeared. It bumped between the tree line and the cemetery.

A flashlight.

As quickly as it appeared, it was gone, and darkness returned.

"Quiet," Erica whispered.

Haley nodded and held her breath.

For several long seconds, the two sat quietly. Haley's ears strained against the night, but she couldn't hear a thing out of the ordinary, just a chorus of bullfrogs and the night breeze stirring the leaves above them.

Then she felt Erica's small hand on her wrist, and the girl jerked her up. Before she realized it, she and Erica were running toward Harper's Road. Fat raindrops began to fall from the sky as they ran.

Erica had been right.

A storm was coming.

CHAPTER 20

AT THE ANDERSON house, Tom glared at his wife, his face flushed. "I'm not validating that question," he snapped.

"Validating?" Rachel asked from the edge of the bed. "I'm not one of your students, Tom. Were you or were you not truthful about ending your affair with her when you said you did?"

She took a good look at her husband and tried to see him from an objective point of view. His hair had receded, the strands now gray. A hangdog expression had taken over his once-strong jaw, and as he angrily waved his hands, she noticed several sunspots.

"I've answered that question a million times! I'm not answering it again. I told you the truth, so either you believe me, or you don't. It's your decision."

Did he seriously think it was as easy as that? That their world was still so black and white? Even after his betrayal, his lies? No, their world was now shades of the dreariest gray. As hard as she tried, she couldn't tell what was true and what wasn't.

"I don't know what to believe," she said honestly.

His arms fell to his sides. "I've apologized. Over and over, I've catered to your doubts and tried to make you feel better, Rachel. I can't do anything more."

Her laugh was sarcastic. "For your wife, you can't do anything more? What's that say about our relationship? Just where are we, huh? Where are we, Tom?" She realized she didn't want to hear the answer.

He turned his back to her and opened his closet door.

Her heart pounding, she repeated her question. "You said you can't do anything more. What exactly does that mean?"

"Just what I said."

Rachel glanced at the purple comforter they'd picked out at JCPenney the weekend before and the valances they'd hung together. The expensive impressionistic canvas they'd chosen on the Internet minutes before they'd made love for the first time in months. Somehow she had thought the new décor would help them start over, that it would offer them a clean slate. She'd had plans for the kitchen, too, and the carpet in the den.

Thunder rumbled outside. She peered out the bedroom window. It had begun to storm. "So where does that leave us? You not being able to do anything more? You being unable to fathom why I'd have a problem with believing the words coming out of your mouth after running around with that little *whore* for three months?"

"Rachel!" Tom spat.

"Rachel, what?" she screamed. "What do you mean?" She fingered the bracelet on her wrist with such intensity, it could have snapped in half.

"I'm sick and tired of this game. That's what."

"Game?"

"Yes, game! I'm sure it makes you feel better, but it's driving me nuts. Fucking insane."

Had she ever heard him say that word before? She didn't think so. "Do you know where that girl is?" she heard herself ask, not being able to conceal the question any longer.

He whirled around. "For God's sake, how should I know? Just what are you accusing me of?"

She formed her words slowly. "There was no accusation."

His mouth contorted into a grimace, then an odd grin. "But there was. You asked me if I knew where Tiffany was. You were insinuating that I—"

"Don't say that name in this house!" she shouted. It was a rule, just like no dishes in the kids' rooms or the living room. She'd be the firmest with this one.

A door slammed in the hallway. One of the kids.

The air was still for several seconds before Tom spoke again. "To answer your question, dear wife, no. No, I don't know where the missing girl is."

She watched her husband pull out an overnight bag for a conference in San Francisco. "People at the college are talking."

Tom paused briefly, a shirt in his hand. "Let them talk."

"And let them think that one of us did something to that girl?"

He threw the shirt into the bag. "If that's what they want to talk about, then sure."

She hated the tone in his voice, how he made her feel so out of line so very often. "Am I such a bitch to ask you these questions? Am I such a bitch to ask if you know the whereabouts of the missing girl you were—" She fell silent, staring at the purple comforter beneath her. It now looked all wrong, childish, like something one of her students would pick, not the style of someone her age. The valances looked just as adolescent. Suddenly, she had the urge to rip them down.

Tom tossed an empty hanger on the carpet and reached for a pale-blue polo shirt.

She retrieved the hanger from the floor. "Am I?" she pleaded. "Am I wrong to ask you? Is everything I say or ask these days so wrong?"

He threw a tie into his bag.

She reached for her wineglass and downed what was left, rage swelling inside her chest.

"It's nice to see you're drinking again," he muttered. "That always makes things easy for us."

"Easy?" Rachel laughed. "And you do? You make things easy for our marriage? For the kids?" Her eyes burned, but she was reluctant to let herself shed any tears. She'd shed so many over him, too many. "Will you at least be back from San Francisco in time for family night?"

After making up, she and Tom had agreed that a new tradition would be healthy for the family, so they had declared Saturdays to be family night.

"I don't know."

Rachel sighed and watched her husband finish packing. She felt miserable, neglected, and powerless. She hated her life and what she'd become. "Tommy told me that Kelsey's sneaking out of her room at night," she said, a last-ditch effort that some common ground might help unite them.

Tom closed his bag. "So talk to her, Rachel. But don't do it while you're drinking. She doesn't need to deal with that."

The anger inside was too much to handle. She inhaled sharply, feeling as though she would suffocate if she didn't. "Screw you," she said, rising on wobbly legs. She walked to their bedroom door and turned. "Screw you and the affair. You know, you might as well be a stranger to me."

She gazed at him, into the eyes of the person she'd once trusted with her life, then stumbled out of the room.

CHAPTER 21

THE STENCH OF wet manure hung in the air as the two girls reached Haley's porch. Erica bent, trying to work out a cramp in her hamstring.

"Who do you think that could have been?" Haley asked, breathing hard.

The moments that had just passed were only a blur for Erica. She had drunk too much. Had someone been in the woods again?

Erica shrugged. "Could have been anything. Maybe an animal."

"With a flashlight?"

"You saw a flashlight?" she asked, thinking again of the person who had fled when she'd called out earlier in the week.

"Yeah, I think so."

"You sure? Could have been the moon. It's pretty low tonight." Haley giggled.

Erica stiffened. *Did I say something wrong?* "What's so funny?"

Thunder rumbled overhead as Haley broke out in longer, harder laughter. "I don't—" Haley started, then fought to pull air into her lungs. "I've never drank this much. I . . . think I'm drunk."

Erica slowly relaxed, relieved that Haley wasn't laughing at her. She peered down at her filthy feet. They were on fire from all of the running, but her body was filled with so much adrenaline, she couldn't feel any pain. She had been buzzed long before she reached the cemetery. If she hadn't been, she knew she wouldn't have stayed.

"I don't *get* drunk. I'm responsible," Haley insisted. She laughed again. "But this feels *incredible*." She pushed her damp bangs from her eyes and grinned. Her face was so close, Erica could smell the wine on her breath. Her eyes danced beneath the porch light, more full of life than she'd seen them in a long while. She seemed to have, at least for the moment, forgotten her troubles.

Haley pushed the front door open. Erica could see two teenage girls and a little boy inside. All three were staring at them. She turned to go, but Haley grabbed her hand.

"Hay-wee!" the little boy screamed, cutting the silence. He rushed up to Haley, almost bowling her over as he latched on to her. He was a clownish-looking child with several awkward cowlicks and a pair of thick-lensed glasses that magnified his eyes. Seeing him, Erica wondered if he would suffer the same fate she had when she entered school, the torturous teasing from not belonging.

Haley laughed at the little boy.

"Why are you so happy? Did they find Tiffany or something?" the teenager with the brown hair asked, looking hopeful, a two-liter of Coke in her hand.

Haley stopped laughing.

Erica reluctantly took a seat at the oak table, next to the other girl. Setting her backpack beside her, she decided she would only stay a few minutes, then she'd go back to the cemetery, get her flip-flops and poke around the woods a little bit before going home to work on her book.

"Wawre's Teefany?" the little boy asked, his words distorted for a child she guessed to be about five or six years old. The boy cupped his hands over his small mouth and began running in crooked circles.

"Erica, this is my sister, Becky," Haley said. "Her friend, Seacrest," she said of the dark-haired girl, "and this little one here is Sasha." She pointed to the splotchy-skinned boy who had just fallen on the floor from a dizzy spell. "Becky babysits him."

"Hi," Becky said, a friendly smile on her face.

Seacrest just glanced at her as if she were bored.

"Where'd you get the McDonald's?" Haley asked her sister.

Becky quietly concentrated on pouring Coke into three glasses. She was almost as odd-looking as the little boy. Her features were mismatched. She had stringy, brown hair, close-set eyes, and a nose that was too wide for her face. She looked nothing like her pretty sister.

"Becky?" Haley repeated when her sister didn't answer her.

"We got a ride into Chester," Becky finally said nonchalantly, handing one of the glasses to Sasha, who was now sitting upright on the floor.

"Who with?" Haley asked.

Becky handed a burger to Sasha. "I don't know. Just some guy."

"Just some guy?"

Seacrest snickered.

"Okay, we hitched a ride," Becky said, flustered.

"You *what*?" Haley exclaimed.

"What's heetched, Hay-wee?" Sasha asked from the floor, bread and meat in his mouth.

Erica shifted uncomfortably. She pulled at her damp T-shirt, and chilly air rose between the cotton and her skin. She studied Seacrest, who stood out from the wholesome Landrys not just in appearance but in energy. She was dressed in tight-fitting shorts and a halter top and had a malevolent, unkind air about her. Seacrest must have felt her stare because she turned and threw Erica a pinched once-over before grabbing a glass of Coke out of Becky's hand.

The exchange made Erica's cheeks burn. It was déjà vu of the dreadful years of school.

Being sized up.

Being judged.

The fact that a girl so much younger could affect her that way left her feeling mostly ashamed of herself, weak, and pathetic. She reminded herself of a quotation that her mother used to whisper to herself after fights with her father: *No one can make you feel inferior without your consent.* With that as fuel, she straightened in her seat.

"It's no big deal," Becky pleaded.

"Hitchhiking is no big deal?" Haley snapped.

Erica noticed Haley's eyes looked strange, unfocused. She was definitely wasted.

Haley wavered a little, then steadied herself against the table. "Don't you know Tiffany's missing?"

"Wawre's Teefany?" Sasha asked again, this time looking concerned.

"Seacrest does it all the time," Becky insisted. She pointed at the girl. "And look, no one's cut her into tiny little pieces."

A bunch of excited words spilled out of Haley's mouth, but none were discernable.

Becky gaped at her. "Oh, my God, you're drunk! *That's* why you're acting so weird!"

"What?" Haley asked, fighting for composure.

Erica didn't want to witness any more. If she wanted family discord, she could get it at her own house. Seeing an opportunity to slip out, she grabbed her backpack and headed to the front door. En route, she heard Becky's voice rise, the daggers still pointed at her sister.

"You're so drunk you can barely talk! And you're lecturing *me*? What a freakin' hypocrite."

CHAPTER 22

HE AWOKE IN a panic, his skin damp with sweat. It was two o'clock on Thursday morning. Five days since his kill, and the law still hadn't shown. Like those times years earlier, they hadn't a clue.

He thought of the nightmare that had come to him as he slept, of the night ten years earlier when he awoke to find his mother out in the yard.

His jaw tensed, and he lay back against his pillow.

He was just nine years old then, running from the kitchen window to slip back into bed. Curling up beneath the scratchy blanket, he'd squeezed his eyes shut. He'd been dreaming, he told himself. It had been a nightmare, nothing more. His mother was drunk in bed where she belonged—not out in the rain—and he was here in his bed, warm . . . and reasonably safe until daybreak.

A branch outside tapped at his window as though it were a frail finger, vying for his attention. *Tap, tap. TAP! Tap, tap.* He sunk lower into the bed and grabbed his knees.

The bedroom door swung open, slamming into the wall. "You try to lock me out, *cher*?" his mother snapped, her tone dangerous. "Next time it might help if you lock the front door, too!" She ripped the blanket from his bed and peered down at him, her breath fiery with whiskey. "Get up!"

Cool water dripped from her naked body, onto his pale face and neck. Bony fingers seized his wrist and yanked him out of bed. "I said get up and help me!"

Outside, the rain fell in sheets, soaking his bare skin and underwear. He'd peered down at a half-naked man who lay on the ground, his face covered in blood.

The man's eyes were closed, his jaw opened at an odd angle. He wore only a white undershirt. His own young eyes had moved quickly, taking in the hairy, bloated belly, the stumpy legs. Then his gaze returned to the man's face.

His mother pressed her fingers against the man's neck. "Grab his wrist," she demanded.

He bent and hesitantly touched the man's wrist. "Is . . . is he dead?"

"I said grab his wrist, boy!"

For the next few minutes, they pulled the man the hundred or so yards past the house to the pond. As they pulled, he felt something warm explode inside of him. It formed first at his middle, then surged through his veins: a mixture of panic, fear, and an odd exhilaration—a feeling that, strangely, wasn't entirely bad.

The sky cracked open above them, and the man coughed. He dropped the man's wrist and stepped back. "He's alive!" he screamed.

"What are you doin'? Pick up that goddamned wrist and pull!"

The man went still again, and the two pulled him to the pond's edge. The rain had let up, and the moon began to shine through the clouds. Two water moccasins sliced across the murky water and slithered to where the old pirogue rested, belly down.

He avoided his mother's eyes and focused on the snakes. He wondered if they could smell the danger that hung in the air, the stranger's impending death. Death was a place he had dreamed about, wondering often if it was a better place than the one he'd known during his young life.

"You wait here," she demanded. "I'll be right back." And with that, his mother had disappeared into the night.

"Dariah?" the man had whispered, his voice hoarse. His eyes opened halfway. "What are you—" he began, then fell silent, his shallow gurgling almost drowned out by the loud croaks of distant bullfrogs.

A moment later, his mother had returned out of breath, carrying a shovel. She threw it to the ground, then grabbed his small shoulders and dug her long, red nails deep into his skin.

"Dariah?" the man had whispered again. "What's—?"

She released him and gazed at the man for a long moment. Suddenly, she went calm. When she spoke next, she formed her words slowly. "I'm going to the house." She handed him the shovel. "When I get back, I don't want him breathing none, you hear?"

An odd light had clicked on inside his head. It glowed brightly, then dimmed. The rain felt like popsicles on his bare back as the man started the repulsive gurgling again.

"I don't want you to think that you can go into town and start tellin' stories. You can't, because you'll be as guilty as me. You hear what I'm tellin' you? We're in this together." A grin crept across her face. "If you don't remember anything else, you remember that."

"But—"

"But nothing!" she snarled, rainwater dripping from her chin. "I'm your mama, and you do what I say!" She pointed at the shovel. "You just do what I told you, and after I gather the things we need, I'll be back."

She charged toward the house, and he watched until he couldn't make out her form any longer against the night. Then he turned to the man, who was still gurgling, his eyes small and frightened.

"Son, you . . . gotta help me," the man managed. "You've got to hide me from Dariah. Somethin's . . . somethin's snapped in that fool woman's head."

He cocked his head and studied the man. He remembered his heart had pounded so hard, he thought he'd topple. He didn't want to do it. He didn't even know if he could. But if he didn't, she'd make things far worse for him, and he knew he couldn't bear anything worse.

The man was having trouble breathing.

"Please, boy," the man pleaded. "Please. I can't feel my legs . . . and we don't have much time. That woman'll hunt us both down. She'll kill the both of us. You gotta . . . you gotta hide me."

But he'd already come to his conclusion. It was either the stranger or him, and it would have to be the stranger. Taking short, uneven breaths, he raised the shovel high above his head.

"God . . . please forgive me," he begged.

Then his and the man's screams pierced the night as he did what his mother had told him to do.

CHAPTER 23

HALEY BLINKED IN the darkness and turned her head so she could see the time: three o'clock. It was already Thursday morning. Odds were that Tiffany was still missing.

She wiped beads of sweat from her forehead and untangled her feet from the top sheet. A sliver of light streamed in from Becky's room, and she could hear Becky's new friend, Seacrest, laughing.

She rose and peered through the moth-eaten tarp that covered the spaces in the unfinished wall that separated her room from Becky's. Since Haley and Becky were getting older and sharing a room was growing uncomfortable, their father had decided to build a wall in the middle of the large room to give them each privacy. But he died before getting the chance to finish it.

Now, Seacrest lay on her stomach across the foot of Becky's bed in only a pair of red panties and a small T-shirt. Her dark hair partially hid her face as she flipped through a magazine.

Becky sat against her headboard, also with a magazine. She tapped a finger against her mouth, concentrating on something she was reading.

"No shit," Seacrest muttered, shaking her head. She giggled. "I don't care how bad you have to pee, you *always* turn on the bathroom light before sitting on the toilet."

"Huh?" Becky said absently.

"This chick was at her friend's house and ran into the bathroom without turning on the light. She went to sit on the toilet and ended up sitting on this dude's lap," Seacrest said, shaking her head again. She rose to her knees and pulled back her long hair. "And she had a crush on this guy. She peed on him. Right on his lap. How stupid is that?"

Becky giggled.

Seacrest stretched and exposed her abdomen. Her full lips parted in a yawn, and her emerald nose ring glistened. Haley realized with a touch of envy that even when the girl didn't try to look stunning, she was.

Seacrest turned to Becky. "You said your sister is friends with that girl, right? The one who disappeared?"

Becky laid her magazine on her chest. "Tiffany. Yeah, they're best friends."

"Think she's dead?"

"No way."

"Then what do you think happened to her?"

"I don't know," Becky said slowly. "But things like that . . . they don't happen around here."

"I bet she's dead."

Becky's brow furrowed. "Don't let Haley hear you say that. She'd have puppies."

"Bet that boyfriend of hers killed her," Seacrest said. "Happens all the time. Sometimes they don't find people until years later when they start finding pieces of them in different towns. Fingers, feet, arms. Sometimes their heads. They found a head in that dude Dahmer's apartment. He was a necrophiliac."

Haley crawled back in bed, burying her head in her pillow. She didn't want to hear any more. She wished Becky hadn't met Seacrest. She was what Mama would call *canaille*, mischievous and wayward. Bad news from the other side of the tracks, or at least the other side of town.

Foul-mouthed and a questionable dresser, she was a bad influence for Becky, who like the rest of them, still didn't know quite who she was.

And to talk about Tiffany like that. What right did she have to say she was—

A floorboard creaked in the living room. Haley propped herself back up and saw that both of the girls were still in Becky's bedroom, silent and reading.

She swung her legs over the side of the bed and stood, pulling on a pair of shorts. She felt grit beneath her feet: fine sawdust from her father's work on the wall. Sometimes she even felt it in her sheets. Feeling it always made her think that her father was close by.

Opening her bedroom door, Haley saw her mother at the kitchen sink. Wrigley, the eleven-year-old greyhound who rarely left her mother's side, gazed drowsily at her from her place on the floor.

"Mama? Can I get you something?" Haley asked, walking to her.

Her mother shook her head. "No, Possum, I'm just getting a little drink for Wrigley." *Possum*. Her mother hadn't called her that since before the accident.

She placed a hand on her mother's bony shoulder. "Are you sure? I made gumbo. I can heat some up real quick?"

The older woman's hair was disheveled and greasy. Outside of Haley's nightmares, this was the first time Haley had seen her awake in nearly five days.

"I'm not hungry, darling," the woman said, shutting off the water. "Wrigley just needed to go out."

Haley caught a whiff of the sour, unclean odor that clung to her mother. She also noticed two pills in her hand.

"Are you okay?"

"I'm fine, honey. Just fine." She placed the pills on her tongue and washed them down with a cup of water. "These are just the sleeping pills Dr. Broussard prescribed for me. They help me . . . get by."

She walked past Haley with a bowl of water and headed across the living room, back to her room. Her body moved under her tacky yellow robe, not with the feminine sweeps it had before the accident but as though she were transporting the whole world beneath it.

Arthritis-ridden Wrigley grunted as she rose to follow her.

"Tiffany's missing," Haley said.

The older woman loosened her grip on the bedroom doorknob. "Missing?" Her face twisted with confusion. "How awful. I should call Julia," she said, referring to Tiffany's mother. "When did this happen?"

"No one's seen her since Saturday."

"Today's Monday?"

"Thursday."

"Oh." The bowl of water trembled in her hand. "Is she with a boy?"

Haley shook her head. "No. She would have told me."

"Yes, I guess so, darling. But I'm sure she'll turn up. I'll say a prayer."

"Sheriff Hebert came by, but you were sleeping. He said he didn't want to disturb you. There's a detective going around with him, too. He said he'll want to talk to everyone in town, so I'm sure he'll be by again."

Her mother nodded. "How's your sister?"

"Fine."

"Good. That's good." she said and flashed a weak smile. Haley noticed her teeth had yellowed in the last several months. "And you, Haley?"

"I'm doing good, too."

"How's school?"

Concerned that it would only worry her, Haley hadn't told her mother that she didn't sign up for summer classes. Her original plan had been to take them to catch up for her lost first semester. "Good," she said.

"You having any trouble getting back and forth to Lafayette?"

Haley shook her head.

"Good, good. I need to get me a little rest now. Goodnight, darling." She and Wrigley went into the room. The door closed behind them.

Haley stood next to the door for a long moment. "*C'est l'heure du lit*," she whispered, remembering Nana's soft words at bedtime. "Goodnight, Mama."

———

Haley opened her eyes for the second time that night. She sat up and peered at the clock radio. It was almost four in the morning.

What had woken her this time?

She heard it again. Someone was screaming. She bolted out of bed and ran into Becky's room. The overhead light was on, and Becky was crouched in the corner behind her bed, dried pimple cream caked across her nose and chin.

"Someone's outside the window," a voice behind her whispered. Haley turned and saw Seacrest kneeling against the side of the dresser. Her face also was dotted with pimple cream, and she was pointing to the window.

"Becky, go to my room," Haley whispered.

Becky didn't move.

Someone tapped softly at the glass. Haley's heart raced faster. A hushed voice called out from the other side. Then a face was at the window, but she couldn't make out whose.

Holding her breath, Haley took a step forward. "Tiffany? Is that you?"

The voice called out again: "No, it's Charles."

CHAPTER 24

HALEY FLIPPED ON the porch light and stepped out the front door. Charles sat on the porch swing. He wore a wrinkled white T-shirt and a pair of loose-fitting jeans and clutched one of the fliers Mrs. Perron had made. The woman had posted them everywhere: on tree trunks, traffic signs, storefronts, in public bathrooms, the sides of mailboxes, and automobiles. It was impossible to be in town without seeing at least a dozen copies of Tiffany's likeness.

"Where have you been?" Haley asked.

Charles seemed to ponder his words before saying them. When he finally broke the silence, his voice was low and hoarse. "You know I didn't hurt Tiffany, don't you?"

Less than a week ago, she would have said no to Charles's question. She wouldn't have thought in a million years that he'd hurt Tiffany.

"You didn't answer me. Where have you been?" she asked.

"Home . . . mostly."

"I've been out there, Charles. Many times. Either no one answers, or your mother says you're not home. You've been avoiding me."

"My mom thought it would be best that I lay low until Tiffany turned up." He concentrated on the flier, carefully folding it in half. "I know how this looks, Haley. I'm not stupid. I thought she'd turn up, but she hasn't."

"What happened Saturday? Where is she?"

"I don't know. And I know when I say that I don't know where she is, it sounds . . ." He lowered his head. "Look, we've been arguing. For the last two weeks, nothing but arguments. And on Saturday night, she just . . . disappeared."

"Disappeared?"

"Shit! You see what I mean?" He turned, and the chains on the swing protested under the strain. "I knew once I told you that I didn't know anything, you'd think I hurt her. That's exactly what the sheriff thinks. And that sorry-ass hick detective who keeps comin' around my house."

He paced up and down the porch, the flier waving in his hands. "Tiffany was seeing someone again, Haley. She denied it, but I knew she was. She was acting different. Just like she did with the Anderson dude."

He stopped pacing and sat on the top step. His foot tapped loudly against the wood, but Haley tried to ignore it. She knew the girls weren't sleeping. And her mother . . . like *she'd* wake up.

Charles shook his head in frustration before he spoke again. "We argued in the parking lot at Provost's, and she just took off. That's the last I saw of her."

"Took off? Where did she go?"

"Into the woods."

"Why would she go in the woods? She hates the woods, Charles. They scare her."

He shrugged. "She always takes off when we argue. I guess the woods were convenient."

"Well, did you follow her?"

"Not at first. You see, I'm always chasing after her. She'd come to expect the attention. I didn't want to play that game anymore, so I waited. But when she didn't come out for a while, I went in to get her."

Haley remembered thinking she'd seen something move in the woods that night. Could it have been Tiffany or Charles, or—

An armadillo trotted across the yard, then sensing their presence, froze. Haley watched it as she listened.

"I called out to her. Then I just figured she was sitting somewhere, pouting and not answering me. So after about ten minutes or so, I got in my truck and left. Tiff only does things when she's ready, Haley. You can't tell her a damn thing. You know that. And you sure as shit can't tell her *not* to do anything she wants to do.

"If only I'd stayed and waited for her a little longer, maybe none of this would be happening. Trust me, I won't be able to live with myself if something . . . you know . . . bad . . . happened to her."

Haley tried to process his words.

"Do you think she could have run off with someone?" he asked.

She shook her head, watching the armadillo scurry off.

"Do you know who she was seeing?"

"No."

"But you knew she was seeing *someone*?"

"I honestly don't know if she was or wasn't."

"I don't want to pressure you," Charles said. "It's just tough because I know how tight you two are. I know she tells you things."

He said *are,* not *were.* It was a good sign.

"Charles, Tiffany told me that you've been acting strange lately. Obsessed."

"Obsessed." He snorted. "Yeah, sounds like something she'd say. C'mon, Haley, you know how dramatic she can be. If she barely scraped her head on a kitchen cabinet, she's likely to say that it sliced her scalp wide open. If one guy happened to flirt with her while she was at the supermarket, she'd make it three."

Charles was right.

He ran his fingers through his hair and studied the porch. "I don't know what to do. They keep asking me questions. The same questions over and over again to see if I'll slip up and change my answers. It's like a really bad episode of *Law & Order* or some shit. I'm freakin' the shit out."

Haley moved to the swing and sat.

"The sheriff and that asshole detective who know *dick* about solving a missing person's case think I'm behind this, and they're making me out to be some kind of freak. And it sure as hell doesn't help that I'm a black man in a town of backwoods, racist asses. They've searched my mom's house twice. My truck. I don't know how many hours I've spent at the station for questioning. I think they're downright pissed because they can't pin anything on me." He wrung his hands together. "My God, I didn't *do* anything to her. I never would. She's created a world of hurt for me, but I still love that girl like crazy."

CHAPTER 25

ON SATURDAY, HALEY returned to work. She was taking a customer's order when Tyler Jeffries walked into Luke's, holding the hand of a girl who looked to be Becky's age.

Her chest tightened, and the notepad in her hand plopped onto the black-and-white-checkered tiles. She was overcome with the sensation she was going to faint.

"Lookie what the cat dragged in!" Kim gushed, hurrying around the counter to give her cousin a hug. "Where have you been, Mr. Tyler? I haven't seen you for *ages!*"

As Haley knelt to pick up the notepad, she imagined—not for the first time—what Tyler must have looked like that night out on Coontz Road when he'd killed her father.

He must have been sweaty, his eyes wide as he realized what he'd hit.

Sweat snaked along the back of Haley's neck. She didn't think she could bring herself to walk across the diner to the front door, not with him there. But what were her choices? Staring at Tyler, she realized he looked so fresh-faced and happy. Too happy. He didn't deserve to look so—

She was still looking at him when he glanced over and saw her. His face clouded over, and he quickly looked away.

The cowbells clattered, and Mac walked in. He nodded hello to everyone. Tyler peered hesitantly at Mac.

"Miss, did you hear me? Are you okay?" her customer asked.

Haley saw Kim glance at her, the realization finally creeping into her ruddy face. She pointed to where Haley stood, and Mac headed toward her, concern flooding his big, brown eyes.

"You okay?" Mac whispered. "No, of course you ain't. Go sit in my truck." He handed her the keys. "I'll tell Kim you're taking the rest of the day off."

———

The vinyl seats in Mac's truck burned the backs of her legs and arms, but Haley barely noticed.

"I realize it could have happened to anybody," Haley said, her hair blowing in her eyes. She rolled the window up a little. "After all, Daddy was walking on the side of the road, and it was dark and raining, and there was the sharp turn . . . but he was my father. And Tyler killed him. I can't just act like nothing happened."

Mac rested a hand on Haley's knee. "I know, babe. I know."

Haley watched the trees whiz by, trying not to think about that night.

"Think you can stay over?" she asked.

Mac slowed the truck and turned onto her road. "I don't know. I've got to work pretty late. That's why I was stoppin' by the diner to say hello."

"You've been working late so much lately," Haley said. She instantly felt a little guilty for complaining. After all, it wasn't unlike Mac to need his space. He had always needed it, a lot of it. She was the one who was changing, not him.

But she was desperate for the company, so she decided to play the neediness card. If there was anything Mac desired, it was being needed. She needed more help through this. In the days since Tiffany had disappeared, they'd barely even talked about it.

"Please? I need you."

Mac's face slowly eased into a smile. "You do need me, don't you?" he said, patting her knee. He parked the truck in front of her house. "How about I come on over around ten? We'll drive by the diner to get your car, and then we can come back here. Sound like a plan?"

Haley nodded, relieved.

"What do you think happened to Tiffany?" she asked, the words tumbling out before she'd even decided to say them.

"Aw, don't worry yourself about her none. I'm sure that wherever she is, she's just fine. You have enough to worry about as it is, Hale. Her mother's just paranoid. Got everyone in an uproar right now, but it'll all die down once Tiffany calls home."

"How can you say that? There's no way she's just fine. If she'd gone somewhere willingly, she would have called me. You know that."

Mac sighed. "Look, I really have to get goin'. Let's talk about this later, okay?"

It was then that she reached to pick up her purse from the floorboard and spotted something glossy peeking from beneath the seat. She picked it up. It was a copy of *Hustler* magazine. Her adrenaline spiked from the shock of seeing it in Mac's truck.

She studied the titillating cover for a long while, her heart racing. Although she wasn't sure where she stood on the issue of pornography, Mac had brought it up on a few occasions while they'd been together, insisting that it turned him off.

Why would he say that if he hadn't meant it?

The fact that he had the magazine also frightened her. The only thing familiar, constant, and dependable in her life these days was Mac. It was too out of character.

She tossed the magazine on his lap. "How many times have you told me that you don't like pornography? That you like women to be wholesome?"

The magazine teetered from where it had landed on his lap and fell to the floorboard.

Mac, his cheeks flushed, refused to meet her eyes. Instead, he looked ahead, at the house.

"Was it a lie?"

He didn't answer.

Her heart pounding angrily in her chest, she jumped out of the truck. "You can forget about coming over tonight. I'd rather be alone than with someone who lies to me."

She slammed the door and marched to her front door, wondering what else in her life would go wrong.

Becky smelled like raspberries, scented lotion she probably bought during her and Seacrest's hitchhiking escapade. But Haley was hesitant to lecture her. She didn't want Becky to start spending even more time away from the house, like she had with Sadie for the first few months after their father had passed. If she did that, then Haley wouldn't have a clue what her sister was doing. Her being out with Seacrest concerned her much more than when the girls were at their home.

Becky now lay next to Haley in her twin-size bed. A floor fan oscillated in front of them, blowing tepid air in their faces. Sasha lay sleeping on top of a *Teletubbies* sleeping bag on the floor, his tiny jaw relaxed, his mouth opened in a perfect half-moon.

Haley felt sorry for the little boy. He spent much more time at their house than his own. His mother was a stripper who seemed to prefer being with her customers. Although Becky was irresponsible at times, between her and Haley, he got much better care at their house than with his mother in their trailer in Trespass Gardens.

Rubbing her temples, Haley tried to push the argument she'd just had with Mac to the back of her head. She wasn't ready to deal with it.

"I saw Tyler Jeffries today," Haley said.

Becky's jaw dropped. "You did? Where?"

"The diner."

Becky screwed up her face. "That—" she started, then stopped, seeming to be at a loss for the appropriate word. "Asshole murderer," she said finally. The corners of her mouth drooped, but she looked to be more deeply in thought than upset.

The two lay quietly, listening to the steady click of the fan.

"Will Mama ever get better?" Becky asked, her face pressed into a pillow, the brown freckles sprinkled across the ridge of her nose contrasting against her fair skin.

"She'll be okay," Haley answered, relieved and more than a little surprised that her sister had mentioned their mother at last. It was one of the first times since the accident.

"When? When will she get better?"

Haley propped herself up with her elbow. "I'm not sure."

"It's been forever and a day," Becky complained. "And she acts like she doesn't know us anymore. How can she do that to us?"

She was angry, probably as angry as Haley was.

"She's not thinking clearly, Beck. She's really, really depressed."

Becky sighed, then lay on her stomach and crossed her ankles. A brown tendril hung against her milky forehead. "Can we do anything? Anything Dr. Broussard can't do?"

"You can go in and talk to her sometimes, you know," Haley said.

Becky shook her head, staring off into space. "I don't like seeing her like that. I don't like going into that smelly room and seeing her look so sick in the head." Becky glanced at her. "Would she do something stupid? Like hurt herself?"

"Oh God, no," Haley said quickly, then shivered. She didn't want to think of the possibility, not now. Her mind desperately needed some peace and quiet.

"How's Sadie?" she asked. "I haven't seen her around lately."

"Don't know. We're not friends anymore."

"What?"

"I like Seacrest better, and she hates Sadie."

"But y'all have been friends forever, Beck."

Becky shrugged. "Isn't she pretty? Seacrest, I mean."

Haley thought about the question. She was beyond pretty. Stunning, in fact. But it just seemed so unfair to whom God gave the beauty. "She's pretty, I guess. But only on the outside."

Becky curled her brown tendrils around a chubby finger and looked thoughtful. "Do you think I'm pretty?"

Haley knew that neither she nor her sister would ever grace the cover of a magazine, but that didn't mean that they weren't attractive. "Of course," she answered. "You're beautiful, inside and out."

"But I'm nothing compared to Seacrest. Even her name's crazy cool." She pursed her lips and grew quiet for a moment. "There's this boy, Richard. I like him, but I think he's going to like her more than me. I mean, why wouldn't he? I would, too." She sighed. "Anyone would."

Haley wanted to kiss her sister and hold her close. She knew Becky was just like her, lonely, mixed up, and as confused and scared as she'd ever been.

"I think Seacrest's nothing compared to *you*. Richard would be crazy to ever pick her over you. You're smarter and classier. Plus, I think her name's kinda stupid."

Becky looked doubtful. "You're not saying that just because you're my sister?"

"Nope, cross my heart."

Becky's eyes grew softer. "Do you still miss Dad?"

"Yeah, I'll always miss Dad."

"Yeah, me too," Becky whispered. "And Tiff?"

"Yeah, I miss her, too," Haley said.

"Think she's dead? If she wasn't, don't you think she would've called us?"

Haley swallowed, and tears filled her eyes. She reached for the pendant around her neck and rubbed it between her fingers. "Yeah, I do, Beck . . . I think she is."

CHAPTER 26

THE ANDERSON FAMILY sat in the living room: Kelsey in a chair, Rachel on the love seat, Tom on the couch, and little Tommy stretched out on the floor, a DVD in his hands.

"But I've seen that one already," Kelsey complained. "Let's watch the other one."

"It's not my problem you've seen everything!" Tommy shot back.

"Quit shouting," Rachel said, trying not to snap. She was tense. Tiffany still hadn't shown up, and it had everyone at the college talking about her and Tom . . . about their marriage. Something they had no business discussing.

She filed her nails although she had filed them too short just a day earlier. The faint music of wind chimes sounded out back, the metal rods tinkling against one another in the stifling darkness. She glanced out the window behind the television, but it was so dark outside she couldn't see a thing.

Tom had insisted that they not cover the big window that extended from the floor to the twenty-foot ceiling, that there was no need because it backed into the privacy of the woods. But being in the living room at night with the window uncovered made her feel uneasy, especially now with the girl missing and a potential murderer on the loose.

"She's not going to get her way again, is she?" Tommy asked, twisting around to look at his mother.

"We'll watch the one nobody has seen," his father said. "Put it in, Tommy."

With a huff, Tommy snatched a blue DVD case from the coffee table.

"Ha-ha," Kelsey gloated under her breath.

"Kelsey, stop!" Rachel scolded, her tone harsher than she'd intended. "Your father made a decision. Now live with it."

Kelsey glared at her. "Who's shouting now?"

"Kelsey, don't talk to your mother that way," Tom said.

"Oh, please," Kelsey replied.

Rachel bit her tongue. It was family night. She'd let this one go and choose her battles wisely. Besides, it felt nice to have Tom return early from San Francisco. Maybe that meant something?

They watched the previews in silence. Before the feature was a commercial of models selling makeup. One of them reminded her of Tiffany. She had reddish hair and bright, young eyes. Rachel thought about her own eyes and how tired-looking they'd become. When had that happened?

The model had a thin, lithe body like Tiffany's, and her skin boasted a youthful glow. Another model was a little older and wearing a bikini. Was it body makeup, or did these women not have an ounce of cellulite? At the end of the commercial, the models smiled into the camera, their teeth like piranhas. They looked so desirable, even to her.

She remembered when she was desired. In those early days, Tom had considered her quite the prize. Stopping by her dormitory in the mornings with steaming coffee and glazed donuts, then walking her to class, Tom was eager to be by her side. He'd leave the sweetest love notes in her box at the post office and listen to her talk about her dreams for hours on end, always seeming curious for more.

He'd loved her so deeply and honestly, he'd given her no reason to doubt that he'd always be there for her. But that was a long time ago. A lot had changed.

Kelsey suddenly stood. "I have homework to do."

"On a Saturday night?" Rachel asked, tossing the nail file on the end table.

"Sure you do," Tommy said.

"I do!" Kelsey snarled.

"Kelsey, sit down," Rachel said. "We're doing something as a family right now. If you have homework, you can do it tomorrow."

"Why'd you argue about the damn movie if you were going to pull this?" Tommy hissed.

"Shut the hell up!" Kelsey barked. "I hate Saturdays! Family night is the stupidest thing I've ever heard of! Daddy, I just want to go and do my homework. I don't want to sit here for two hours worrying over it."

Tom cradled his forehead with his hand as though he had a terrible headache. When he spoke, he sounded resigned. "Go ahead. Go do your homework."

Kelsey quickly left the room.

Rachel felt her cheeks flush. She'd been trying to keep it all together, make non-negotiable that the family needed to spend a few quality hours together one night a week. "Tom!" she said. "Why did—"

"She said she has homework," Tom said firmly.

Rachel knew better. Kelsey had things on her mind, but homework wasn't one of them. "We agreed that Saturdays—"

"*You* agreed," he retorted. "I wish you'd just relax, Rachel. Let the kid do her homework. Let us all breathe a little."

Relax? Let you breathe? Rachel suddenly felt exhausted. Feeling her son's eyes on her and her husband's blaring indifference, she rose and walked out of the room.

CHAPTER 27

HE MOVED THROUGH the dank woods listening carefully to any sounds that weren't his own. Restless, he pushed a branch out of his way. He released it a second too soon, and it recoiled. Cool rainwater splashed his face. He stopped and dried his eyes with an elbow.

He needed to clear his mind, to wade through the gloom inside his head. Allie was gone for now. She'd left in another one of her huffs, but not before hurling the usual insults.

He reached up and snapped the branch, sending it flying until it hit more brush and fell against wet leaves. He thought about Allie pressing her body against his the night before.

Lying where the girl had lain.

If she'd only known.

Her visit had been obscene and, for a vile millisecond, disturbingly inviting. Her warm softness, her skin like satin. It had been pitch-black, and he couldn't see a thing, but he could tell she was wearing the black nightie, the trashy one. He was sure of it.

His body had been rigid as he lay on his side, his eyes open, staring ahead, unseeing. Her steamy breath, laced with cinnamon, tickled his neck before he pushed her away, sending her crashing to the floor.

A moment later, loud curses spiked with tears rang from the darkness. Her fists stung his shoulders as she struck him. Then she left the room, the door banging shut behind her. Afterward, all became silent except for the crickets outside his window and the faint whimpers of Ian, the cat.

Now, he stepped out from the woods and peered at the Andersons' home. As always, he had a clear view of the family's living room. Two people were there: the father sitting in the recliner, and the young son on the floor, his body stretched in front of the blue haze of the television set. His upturned face looked pale in the jumping lights of whatever they were watching.

He crouched and crept past the swing set where he had spent hundreds of hours. Tonight, he needed to be closer to the home.

Ten feet away from the big window, he lowered himself onto his stomach and watched. The father was laughing. So was the boy. Then their faces went blank, and they continued to watch their show.

Rachel was nowhere in sight. She was the one who comforted him with her warm smile and silent laughter. He could tell that she loved her family. She was the mother bird of the nest, the nurturer.

But she seemed stressed lately. It tore at his insides for such a beautiful woman to be so stressed. Once, he'd seen her daughter yelling at her. She'd been leaning forward on her tiptoes, shouting into Rachel's face. When his angel turned away, her face was so tight, so upset. It took everything he had not to force his fist through the window, grab the girl by the throat, and tell her that what she had was a rare gift.

He daydreamed of being inside the house—not while she was home, not yet, but when it was empty. What would he see? How did they live? He longed to touch the things she touched. She was a special, special woman. One of very few.

A light shone from the bedroom he knew to be the daughter's. He rose and approached it. Though the blinds were down, he knew she was in there. He could hear her haughty voice and snippets of a one-sided conversation. She was on the phone. She sounded angry.

He slowly circled the home. At the west end of the house, light shone through a small rectangular window: the master bath. He could see the shadow of a potted plant on the windowsill, a sunflower. Once, he'd seen her in the small greenhouse tending to them, her hands moving slowly, deliberately, with more care than he'd seen in his life. Her hands were nothing like his mother's calloused, demanding, greedy hands. He shook her from his head.

Slinking forward, he peered into the window. Through the blinds, he could see someone was moving inside. Water was running. A bath being drawn.

Smiling, he turned away. He pressed his back against the house and stood still. He listened as she walked back and forth. He stood there, close to her, mere feet away.

At that moment, he made his decision. He *would* go inside. And soon.

For now, though, he closed his eyes and relaxed.

CHAPTER 28

THE AFTERNOON SKY was gloomy with the threat of a storm. Erica sat in a red plastic booth, scribbling in her notebook, now half-filled with notes. Everything was finally coming together. Her epiphany had made a world of difference with her writing and left her so excited, she almost felt like smiling.

The diner was fairly empty: one customer lingering at a table, Chris, Kim, Austin, and her. The three workers hovered at the counter, talking. She picked up fragments of their conversation, but only when it interested her.

But for the most part, it didn't.

Lightning shot across the sky, followed by ripples of deafening thunder. She peered out the window, watching the sugarcane next to the diner bend against the screaming wind. Missing-person fliers trembled against the windows where they'd been posted, struggling to win the battle against the hostile and equally tenacious wind.

Erica flipped to the back of her notebook to a clipping from the *New York Times* bestseller list. She ran her finger over the name of a female mystery novelist who could possibly be her mother using an alias. She'd scoured the Internet for a photo of the woman but couldn't find one. The woman's name just popped up one day out of the blue, and Erica had rushed out to get a copy of her book.

There was something about the way the author wrote, the words she chose. They just seemed too familiar. Erica had found articles written about the woman and had learned she was single and from the South, but none of the articles said exactly where.

She closed her notebook and sighed. Her thoughts went to Haley, the only person her age she'd ever liked. She remembered the girl's touch and how easily she had invited her into her house. It was almost as though the girl considered her a friend.

But why her? They were so different. Where Haley was always polite and sweet and—at least before her father's accident—seemed to glow with enthusiasm, Erica imagined herself as being smothered by a black cloud. Besides, friendship was something Erica had never shared with anyone besides her mother. She wasn't sure she knew how to be a friend to anyone besides her.

In the months since Haley's father died, Erica had watched Haley change. The girl's joy for life had faded. Her eyes had slowly deadened. Erica would study her as she sat in the cemetery, mumbling to her dead father. Sometimes Haley would stand in ant piles until little black specks covered her legs. Sometimes she'd cry. That's what had drawn Erica to the girl. She identified with her loss, her need to mask the pain, her secret quirks.

But the two were still so, so different.

Business was slow, too slow. Erica was itching to leave early with the measly ten dollars in tips she'd earned in the four hours she'd been there.

"This investigation of theirs is goin' pretty shitty, if you ask me," Chris was saying, dipping a biscuit into a bowl of étouffée. "The detective's still pokin' around, but I say if they haven't found anything by now, they're not goin' to find nothin'."

"I still say the girl just ran off," Kim piped in, gazing at the weather. "But havin' said that, I spoke with Myrna Adams from the college, and she has some interestin' suspicions about Tom Anderson. Said that some of the staff up at the college has been more than happy to give the detective an earful."

"Just because a man cheats on his wife doesn't mean he's a killer," Austin said from the counter, pouring a cup of coffee.

Kim grunted. "Maybe not, but it does talk to his character. And that's really all you have to judge a man on. Right, Chris?"

Chris nodded, picking up the newspaper.

"That reminds me," Kim continued, plopping back in her seat. "I was talking to my sister in California last night. She asked if Tiffany was the smiling kind. Said there was someone hanging 'round a supermarket years back that seemed to like 'em.

"It was disturbing what he'd do. He'd wait right outside the doors and watch for women to walk out. When they did, he'd smile at them, and he'd wait for the first woman to smile back. That's how he chose his victims. He did it for nearly a year, and my sister said that he would even write letters to the local paper out there and tell them what he was doing. Even so, they never caught the monster. He just quit killin'. Still runnin' loose somewhere. Wouldn't it be somethin' if he's out here now?"

Erica reopened her notebook and pretended to write, not wanting to seem interested in the conversation. *Smiling at strangers*, she mused, shifting in her seat. She barely smiled. She didn't want to be noticed, not yet. Not until she had something brilliant for which to be noticed.

"Anyway, this morning I told both my little ones to never *ever* smile at strangers," Kim said. "You should only be friendly with folks you know because there are all sorts of kooks out there. New Orleans has more than its share, and it ain't that far from here, if you stop and think about it."

Erica stuffed the notebook into her backpack and rose. "It's awfully slow today, Chris. Mind if I leave early?"

"Sure, honey. I think we're all set," he said, one eye on her, the lazy one on the approaching storm. "Another one of them slow afternoons, I'm 'fraid. Not that the weather's helping none."

The cowbells clanked, and Detective Guitreaux walked in wearing a pair of chinos, a blue T-shirt, and a ball cap. He nodded at everyone.

"Storm's a'brewin'," he said, pulling off his cap and running his fingers through his thick hair.

Chris set a fresh cup of coffee in front of him. "What can we do for you today, detective?"

"Would like to have a few words with you, if you don't mind. Let's step out back."

Chris rubbed the back of his neck. "Absolutely. Anything you need."

Erica could swear Chris's face turned pale.

CHAPTER 29

OPENING THE DOOR to her mother's bedroom, Haley was stunned to see that her mother was awake. Crisp, dog-eared black-and-white photos and hundreds of newer color photographs were scattered all over the bed and floor. An empty scrapbook lay on her mother's bureau next to a box of tissues.

For a moment, Haley wondered if she'd had too much to drink and was imagining things. But she'd only had one gin and Coke—so far. Since sharing the wine with Erica and experiencing its exquisite numbness, she had taken to a drink or two each day to cope. Her father had a sizable stash in the bottom of the pantry: gin, vodka, and bourbon. She sampled them all and found that gin was the easiest to get down.

Haley set a bowl on the nightstand. "It's chicken and dumplings. Your favorite."

Her mother smiled. It wasn't the relaxed, genuinely happy expression Haley had grown up with but the detached, obligatory, medicated-looking one she'd grown used to over the last several months. "Thanks, love."

"Scrapbooking?" Haley asked, hopeful, moving toward the window.

Her mother shook her head. The tip of her nose was red, and balled-up tissues littered her lap. "No, just looking at some old photographs, honey." She reached across the bed. "Haven't seen these for a while."

This time, for only an instant, her smile was one of the old, warm ones.

She picked up a photograph and handed it to Haley. It was taken at one of Haley's swim meets when she was ten years old, the one against Chester Elementary, her school's biggest rival. In her red one-piece, Haley was crouched in position, tense and focused, waiting to begin her 600-meter freestyle. Haley still could smell the chlorine and feel the cool pool water. She thought about the University of Louisiana and how she might be swimming right now had she started classes on time.

Her mother set down the photograph and picked up another. In this one, her father was standing at the barbeque grill, a silly grin on his face. He held a slab of meat and wore a white apron that read "Vegetarian," a perfect example of his cheesy humor. "That one was taken at Becky's tenth birthday party," her mother said. She pointed at the top left corner. "See the balloons?"

Haley nodded.

The woman glanced up at Haley. "I don't know why this one didn't make it into a scrapbook. Seems like a lot of them didn't make it. I don't understand why they didn't."

"I don't know, Mama."

Her mother's eyes went to her neck. "That's a pretty necklace. Is it new? Did Mac get it for you?"

Her mother knew good and well that the necklace wasn't new. Haley touched it and thought of Tiffany. "No, it's not new. You bought this for me. And one for Tiffany, too. Don't you remember?"

The woman gazed at Haley's face for a moment, then reached for a pill bottle on her nightstand. She opened it and popped two in her mouth.

Haley's shoulders sagged. Every time she thought her mother was getting a little better, she was wrong. She wanted nothing more than for her to get better and for Tiffany to come home—two situations over which she had no control.

That reminded her of Mac. An entire day had come and gone since she found the pornographic magazine in his truck, and he hadn't called or come over. She wondered if she had been too hard on him, if she had overreacted.

She wasn't angry with him anymore, just confused that he felt he needed to lie to her. Maybe she should be the one to make the first call.

She remembered how loud Becky and Seacrest had screamed when Charles tapped at Becky's window Thursday morning. "Mama, why didn't you come check on us the other night? Didn't you hear the screaming?"

"Screaming? Who screamed? Is everything okay?"

Haley thought of the sleeping pills, but that wasn't an excuse. Her mother couldn't just leave her and Becky alone to fend for themselves, no matter how much she was hurting. They were hurting, too. She needed to stop mourning and become their mother again.

"Did you know that Becky is hitchhiking now?" she asked, desperate for her mother to express some sort of appropriate emotion.

"Hitchhiking?"

"Yes, Mama. You should say something to her."

"Oh, my! I will. It's so unsafe," she said. Then her eyes dulled, and she seemed to look not at Haley but past her, as though focusing on something only she could see. She took several shallow, raspy breaths.

"Have you called Mrs. Perron yet?"

Her mother shook her head.

"You really should call her. Tiffany's still missing."

"My goodness," her mother muttered.

Haley wasn't convinced she'd even heard her. "Mama?"

"Yes, darling."

"You okay?"

"Yes. Your mama just needs some sleep, baby. Why don't you let me get a little shut-eye?"

CHAPTER 30

LATER THAT NIGHT, he lay in his bed, trying not to listen to the sounds coming from his sister's bedroom: laughter, both Allie's and some boy's. He scowled, staring across his room, out the small window.

He wanted to stop them. What were they doing in there?

He hated when Allie brought boys home. She did it to humiliate him.

He could smell her from her bedroom. He'd always had a keen sense of smell. Whether he was detecting Allie's perfume, his mother's mustiness, or the coppery odor of blood, he could do it from a distance that most couldn't.

Allie was so fragrant, just like an oleander, its beautiful pink blossoms disguising its fatal venom. Like the flower, she was poison. Most women were—except for Rachel Anderson, of course . . . and very few others.

He thought of Tiffany, his mother, and the others who lay at the bottom of the pond out back. In life, Tiffany had been attracted to him. She'd wanted him, wanted to be close to him. For weeks, she had come on to him, but he had ignored her—something that seemed to make her want him even more. Then she'd succumbed to his plans and willfully entered his house.

Allie squealed louder. He clamped his palms against his ears. His heart pumped angrily, and his breaths came in ragged bursts.

She squealed again.

Not able to stand it any longer, he sprang from his bed and yanked his door open. He barreled into the hallway and found her bedroom door wide open, candlelight flickering inside.

He moved into the doorway.

They were in her bed. Allie was naked and sitting on the boy's lap. She moved back and forth rhythmically, her arms clasped above her head.

After a moment, she turned and shot him a dirty look. She didn't bother to stop what she was doing. She just gazed at him.

"What the hell do you think you're doing?" he shouted from the doorway, not sure whether he was addressing her or the boy. He took a step forward and saw that the boy wasn't a boy at all but a man, a husky man much older than he was.

He flashed back to all the disheveled-looking men who would stay with their mother for a few hours at night and during many afternoons when he was younger.

"What the hell do you think you're doing!" he repeated. "She's just a kid, asshole!"

Alarmed, the man shoved Allie to the floor and bent to pick up his pants.

Trying to contain his rage, he flipped on the overhead light and walked up to the man. He shoved him, and the man floundered, tumbling back into bed, his pants around his hairy calves.

"I didn't know!" he screamed. "She told me she was eighteen!"

"Eighteen? Christ, does she *look* eighteen?"

"Leave him alone!" Allie screamed, scrambling from her place on the floor. "He's a client!"

He noticed three wrinkled twenty-dollar bills on Allie's night-stand. Trembling, he kicked the man repeatedly, each time harder than the last.

Allie's hands were around his waist now. "Stop! Please stop!"

"What's the money for, Allie?" he shouted, tears stinging his eyes.

She was a whore—an evil, vicious, whore.

She held on to him tighter, her flesh burning his. Their eyes met for a quick moment, and he could tell that she was enjoying this.

Her slow kill.

"What's the money for?" he screamed again, out of breath. "What's it for, huh?"

He had to get away from this place, this house, from her—or they would kill him.

His eyes out of focus and filled with tears, he watched the man rise and fumble with his pants again. He snatched up a cowboy hat and a set of car keys from the floor, then staggered out of the room.

A few seconds later, the front door slammed.

CHAPTER 31

AN HOUR LATER, as he sat on the narrow seat of a swing set studying the Anderson house, a boy walked up. The kid tiptoed through the yard until he reached the daughter's bedroom window. Then, seconds later, the girl poked out her head, and the boy helped her down. The two laughed quietly, then dashed across the yard and into the night.

After they disappeared, he studied the girl's bedroom window. He breathed in the cool rain-cleansed air and tried to decide if it was too risky, if he'd be going too far. He contemplated for a few minutes, the polished stone tumbling violently in his palm, then decided it was worth the risk. He'd seen the girl sneaking out before, and she was always gone for hours. The rest of the house was dark, so the family was sound asleep.

Yes, he'd be safe going inside.

He lifted the window a little wider and pulled himself into the house. Adrenaline flooded his veins as he stepped slowly around the room, taking in the dim surroundings.

There was a bureau with a ceramic ballerina and a jewelry box sitting on its surface. A dresser, untidy with small brushes, makeup, and a large can of hairspray. He picked up the brush, his hand grazing the strands of hair embedded in the bristles. He pulled several out and rubbed them between his fingertips.

The strands were coarse, probably dyed, not the natural, untainted hair her mother had. But it was the closest he'd ever gotten to his angel, so he pocketed them and placed the brush back on the bureau.

He went to the unmade bed. In the murky light, he tried to guess the color of the comforter. A big pillow lay at the foot of the bed. Embroidered within the shape of a heart was the word "Kelsey."

"Kelsey," he mouthed and felt the word roll off his tongue. A word Rachel probably said several times a day. He whispered it again and bent to smell her sheets. They smelled girlish, like Allie's. Perfumed.

He lay on the bed and held the pillow. *This is where her daughter sleeps. These are the things she sees just before falling asleep, the things she hears.*

He glared in the darkness, and his shoulders stiffened. Suddenly, he wanted to grab the girl by the shoulders and shake her until all that was left were the whites of her eyes.

Didn't she know her mother would worry if she caught her sneaking out? This girl was no good, just like Allie, just like the young girls he saw every day.

He ran his fingers over the comforter. It was softer than Allie's, the sheer opposite of the government-issue wool blanket he'd slept with since he was a child. He wondered how soft the mother's comforter would be.

Suddenly, he knew he'd have to find out.

He'd have to know, or the thought would clutter his already-crowded mind. He closed his eyes and reveled in the idea.

Then, he let himself enjoy a memory, one of the few good ones.

Tiffany had been angry when he'd stopped to pick her up from the side of the road. She told him she had lost her keys in the woods. Hopping in the truck, she asked him to take her away. "Anywhere but here," she'd said. So he threw the truck into gear, and they moved up Main Street toward his mother's house.

Soon, her hand was on his shoulder, where it didn't belong.

"We're through," she announced.

"Through?"

"Yeah, we're done for good this time. He thinks he owns me, and I hate it."

"Does he?"

She watched him in the darkness, then seemed to decide he was kidding. "Hell no," she said, and a grin spread across her small face.

He jammed his boot against the pedal.

In the living room, she draped her slim, tanned legs over the side of the recliner as he filled two shot glasses with vodka and twisted the tops off their beers. She complained about her boyfriend as she downed the first two shots.

He kept nodding, not really hearing her, but imagining what he could so easily do.

Once he'd daydreamed of killing her, but that had only been a daydream.

Or had it?

After a while, her eyes began to droop a little. She slipped off the recliner and walked to where he sat.

He tried to stay calm.

The closer she got, the more torment he felt. His breath quickened, and he clenched his fists. He hoped Allie wouldn't come home. He imagined her walking through the door, seeing the girl in the house, then saying something smart—or stupid. But he knew he couldn't stop himself.

Not now.

She pressed her lips to his, and his body filled with rage. He wanted to grab her by the throat and shake her, but instead he leaned back, out of her reach.

"What's wrong?" she whispered, alcohol wafting from her warm mouth.

He stood and took her hand, letting her long fingernails scratch his palm.

She giggled and let him lead her.

"Teeny room," she said as they entered the only bedroom he'd ever known. At that moment, he thought of how well-off her family was, and he hated her even more. "But cozy."

No, it wasn't cozy. In her small way, she was being polite. He pushed her onto the bed. As he'd suspected, she liked it.

She looked up at him, her eyes weary from too much alcohol. "This is so wrong," she said, then giggled.

He nodded.

"But we won't tell anyone. It'll just be our secret, right?"

He nodded. *It will. It'll definitely be a secret.*

She giggled again. Still staring up at him, she brought her fingers to her shirt and unbuttoned it, then pushed it away from her narrow shoulders, letting it fall into a heap behind her. She was wearing a black, lacy bra, and he could make out her nipples through the sheer material.

His body grew warm all over. She had full breasts, not as big as the ones on the models in his magazines, but they were large for her small body.

She laughed as she pulled one of the straps from her shoulder. "You know how long I've wanted to do this?" she asked, her eyes seeming even droopier than a moment ago.

"No."

She laughed again. "A looooooong time." She pulled the other strap down, then reached back and unclasped the bra. Full, pale breasts with taut, pink nipples popped out. The heat grew fiercer. He was getting hard.

She lay back on the bed. "You like what you see?" she slurred.

He stood at the edge of the bed and studied her.

"Well c'mon. Touch me."

Reluctantly, he lowered himself onto the bed.

She reached out and kissed his neck, then guided his mouth to her breasts.

The heat consuming him, he pressed his lips against a nipple, then opened his mouth and pulled it in. His erection pulsing, he shifted his knees forward and reached for her other soft breast and ran his tongue over the nipple.

She arched her back, her long hair cascading behind her. She giggled for the millionth time that night. "You're kinda clumsy," she whispered.

The light went on inside his head, and he jerked away, instantly softening down below. All the heat in his body gathered and climbed into his head. She was teasing him.

She sat up, not bothering to cover her sinful breasts. "What's wrong? Did I say something wrong?"

Blood crashed inside his head, and the room seemed to shift.

"Why are you staring at me like that?" she asked, her eyes wide. "I didn't mean nothing, honestly. It's just . . . it's just that you . . ."

He backed away, disgusted at himself.

She lay back. "Oh, God, I'm getting soooo dizzy," she said, the ugly smile returning to her lips. She giggled, then waggled her index finger at him. "Come back here. I'm not done with you."

When he didn't, she leaned forward and pulled him by the belt loops. She unclasped the button on his pants, then unzipped him.

He was shaking.

As she reached for him, he seized her wrists and held on to them tightly.

"Ooooh," she purred. "You like it rough, huh?"

His head ached, not from the alcohol but from what she'd said, what they were doing. He squeezed harder.

Her eyes widened. "Hey, that's starting to really hurt," she said.

He didn't loosen his grip.

Her eyes darted between his and where her wrists were pinned.

"You don't like pain?" he asked, looking at her hard.

Confusion flooded her eyes.

"Then why would you cheat on your boyfriend?" he asked. "Didn't you think that it would be painful for him?"

"What?"

"Why would you cheat—"

"Yeah, you're one to talk!" she said, glaring at him. "Let me go! Dammit, let go of my wrists!"

He held them even tighter.

"I don't go to bed with whores," he barked. "You should have known that."

When she spoke next, her voice was softer. "I'm sorry," she said, tears welling up. "I'm sorry. I . . . I thought you liked me. I mean, you acted like you did. Look, let me go, and I'll just leave. We shouldn't be doing this anyway."

Blood pounded in his ears. "Do you have any idea how many people you've hurt? Do you even care?"

"I'm sorry. I'm so sorry."

He released her wrists, and she leaned forward, covering her breasts. Fat, pathetic tears streaked her mascara.

He picked up a pillow.

She watched him as she struggled to button her shirt, having forgotten her bra that now lay on the floor.

Ian scratched at the window.

He turned to look at the cat and felt the bed move. One of her legs was on the floor, the other quickly dropping.

He lunged forward and brought the pillow to her face. She kicked and screamed into the pillow, but he pinned her legs with his. She hit him in the chest and clawed at his skin. She tried to turn her head, but his hold was firm.

A powerful titillation filled him, a feeling much more erotic than the one he'd felt earlier when he was tasting her sinful flesh. Every part of him was now alive. He felt fantastic, better than he had in a decade. His rage flowed out of him as though a vent had finally opened.

She clawed at his neck and chest, but he didn't feel any pain.

"It's all right to be afraid," he whispered.

Eventually, her protests stopped, and he moved the pillow so he could see her eyes. They were wide at first, big green crystals of pain. Then they wilted, and she grew still.

At the window, Ian hollered.

He turned and glared at the cat. He'd get rid of it, too. He took air deep into his lungs, then let it out, finally able to breathe freely.

He stared at the girl's lifeless body that was now twisted and still. He'd robbed her of her dignity, her power. The realization was liberating.

The screen door at the front of the house snapped shut.

Allie was home.

He heard a loud crash. It seemed as if his eyes had been closed for only a few minutes. He shot up in the bed, and for a long beat had no idea where he was. The room smelled foreign; the window wasn't where it usually was.

An orange light illuminated the hallway and streamed through the inch of space between the door and carpet.

Then he remembered: he wasn't in his house at all. He was at Rachel's, lying in her daughter's bed.

The footsteps grew closer.

He slipped out of the bed and fumbled to get under it.

The door flew open.

CHAPTER 32

THE SECOND WEEK of July was blistering. The grass was burnt, the plants wilted, and people were unusually quiet. When they did talk, they were irritable.

The AC unit in Becky's room had died. It started with a peculiar noise, metal on metal, every few minutes, like a small animal screeching, its flesh caught in the fan. Haley had been lying in bed in a Nyquil daze, staring at the walls, when a bloodcurdling noise rang through the house . . . then the fan stopped spinning for good.

Becky and Seacrest had taken to sprawling out in the living room, keeping cool with the big GE wall fan humming behind them, old copies of *Cosmopolitan, People,* and *Glamour* stacked on top of the coffee table while MTV blared on the television.

It had been nine days since Tiffany Perron had disappeared. Her black Ford Mustang had been returned to her family and now was secured in the garage. Everyone who had known her had been questioned at least twice. Some, like Charles and Haley, had met with Guitreaux several times, the detective asking mostly the same questions again and again. So far the only evidence that had turned up was Tiffany's car keys. They'd been found in the woods, just a couple of yards from Provost's parking lot.

Haley had no faith in the detective or his abilities, and she had lost all hope of ever seeing her friend again. She'd shed tears until there were none left. The possibilities seemed so limited, so dark, that she refused to think about them.

———

When Haley's shift ended on Monday, she walked out the front door of Luke's to find Mac leaning against her family's station wagon.

Her heart sped up.

It was the first they'd seen each other in two days. She had decided not to call him . . . and he hadn't bothered to call her.

He shielded his eyes from the afternoon sun and smiled uncomfortably, but she couldn't bring herself to smile back.

He grabbed something from the car's hood. Roses encased in a transparent wrapping. "These are for you," he said, when they were face to face. He handed her the roses, looking more ill at ease than she ever remembered seeing him look. He usually looked so confident, but now he looked uncomfortable in his own skin.

"Thanks," she muttered and took them.

He took a cigarette out of its pack and eyed it. "Look, I'm sorry. I know it's not right for me to lie to you. I don't usually . . . I don't usually look at those types of magazines, but sometimes I want to, you know?"

"No, I don't know."

Mac swallowed and studied the unlit cigarette. "I'm a guy, Hale. Do I like my women wholesome? Absolutely. Do I look at pornography from time to time? Well, yeah, I guess I do. I don't know if that's good or bad or maybe neither, but I do know I shouldn't have lied about it.

"I guess I told you what I did because that's what I thought you'd want to hear. I know girls don't like it much." He pushed some dirt around with his boot, then his eyes met hers. "But I want to be straight with you about everything from here on out and tell you that it's something I like to look at from time to time."

He reached out and touched her cheek with one of his strong hands. "Look, I don't want to lose you, Hale. There aren't many women like you out there. I'm a very lucky man, and I know it. I won't let you down again by lying. Cross my heart."

———

Haley had the nightmare again, the same one that had haunted her over the last several months. She thought it had gone away, but it hadn't.

Many times, she'd wanted to ask her mother how accurate it was. It played out like a film, created by her subconscious amid snippets of details she'd overheard about her father's death. If not accurate, it was surprisingly detailed, from the expressions on their faces, even down to the clothes her mother and father wore that night.

Her mother and father were in the car driving down Coontz Road, a windy road on the edge of Grand Trespass. The night was dark, oily.

There was a jarring thump. They'd just hit something with the car.

Her mother brought a hand to her mouth. "Oh, my God, was that a deer?"

Her father calmly reached across the front seat, checking to see if her mother was all right. "You okay?"

"Yes. Are you?"

He nodded and opened the car door.

"Was that a deer?" she repeated.

"No . . . I think it was a big dog."

Her hand covered her mouth again. "Oh, no."

He stepped out of the car and let the door close. She watched him walk behind the car and toward the lump that lay still in the road. Then she saw it move.

"Oh, God. It's still alive," she whispered to herself.

He knelt next to the animal, then stood and took off his coat. He knelt again.

She noticed a light from behind the trees as he picked up the animal. Headlights. Quickly stepping out of the car, she called out to him. "Someone's coming!"

He nodded and moved to the side of the road. His shoulders pitched forward, cradling the wounded animal in his arms.

She shielded her eyes and watched.

The headlights curved quickly around the bend.

"Hey," he called. "See if there's a towel or something in the—"

The truck was hugging the shoulder.

"Move, Daddy! Move!!!" Haley shouted in her dream. "Get out of the way!" But of course, he couldn't hear her.

The truck bounded around the corner, then came the sickening squeal of brakes. It was too late. The truck smashed into her father, then into a tree behind him.

Her mother screamed, standing only a couple of yards away. She ran toward her husband, but he was pinned against a sycamore, dead.

Tyler, whom the Landry family had known since birth and whom Haley once had a crush on, opened his door and stumbled from the truck. He took a few steps toward the tree, bent over, and vomited.

"You okay, Hale?" someone whispered. *Mac.*

Haley opened her eyes. Sweat covered her skin and had pooled into the crevice between her breasts. It was the middle of the night, and she was in her bed with Mac. "Yeah, I'm okay," she whispered, even though she wasn't. "Go back to sleep."

She scooted closer to him and pressed her body against his until her heart calmed down. His skin had always been warm and soft, stable and secure—and he smelled strongly of both soap and beer. She'd always found the combination both sexy and comforting. But although she'd told him she forgave him for his lie, tonight she didn't feel particularly comforted.

Or safe, for that matter.

It was as though the lie had been more significant for her than it should have been. It changed the dynamics of their relationship.

She gazed at his bare back until he began to snore.

A couple of minutes later, she rose. She was going to wake her mother.

They needed to talk.

————

Her mother wasn't sleeping. When Haley walked in, her mother was wide awake—and she was smoking a cigarette, of all things.

She had changed out of the old nightgown and now wore a pair of jeans and a wrinkled T-shirt. She sat Indian-style on the bed with an ashtray and photos scattered all around her. Beneath the odor of cigarette smoke was the scent of perfume. She was even wearing eye makeup and lipstick.

Haley wondered if she were still dreaming. "Mama?" she said in disbelief.

Her mother tore herself from the photos and looked at Haley. "Hi, baby." The muscles in her face twitched. Then she patted the bed. "Come sit here with me. Your mama has something she needs to tell you."

CHAPTER 33

HALEY SAT ON the edge of the bed and watched her mother take long drags from her cigarette. After a moment, the woman set it into the ashtray and exhaled.

"I've never seen you smoke before."

Her mother smiled, and Haley could see that she'd finally brushed her teeth. "*C'est la vie*, baby," she said. *That's life.* "You don't live forever, you know, Hale?"

Wrigley jumped off the bed and went to the water bowl. She lapped at the water, then lay down on the floor next to the door and glanced at Haley.

Haley returned her attention to her mother. "You're dressed."

"Yes, baby. You think I look nice?"

Haley nodded and smiled. "You okay?"

"Yes, baby. Your mama's more okay than she's been in a long time because I have something to tell you, darlin'. Something beautiful."

Haley waited, an enormous weight taken off her shoulders. She smiled both on the inside and outside. It was the first time she could remember feeling so calm since the accident.

"Remember when Nana died? How peaceful her face was when we found her on the kitchen floor, like she was ready to go?" her mother asked. "Remember that, Haley? You saw Nana's face, didn't you?"

Haley nodded. Death had waited impatiently for her grandmother, but it was true. She had looked peaceful when she passed.

"But your daddy, darlin', God bless his soul. No, he didn't look peaceful at all. He was tormented, baby, pinned against that big tree . . ." Her words drifted off. She took Haley's hands into her own. "Is it okay for me to talk about this with you? I don't want to upset you none."

"It's okay," Haley murmured, the smile gone. *Where was she going with this?*

"Hale, baby, I haven't been able to get his face out of my mind, the way it looked the night he died. Every waking hour, I've seen your daddy's face. And all the tremendous pain he felt."

Haley's heart beat so furiously she thought it might stop as she again imagined her father at that moment.

Her mother's eyes brightened. "But he's okay, Hale. He's with us now, and he's okay. I saw your daddy, baby. He was sitting right there," she said, patting the comforter next to Haley. "Just about where you're sitting. He's come back to let us know he's doin' okay. He's not hurtin' anymore."

CHAPTER 34

ON WEDNESDAY NIGHT, he set a box of Triscuit crackers and a loaf of bread in the cabinet above the stove, then opened the refrigerator and filled it with deli meats, fruit, and condiments. As he unpacked the rest of the groceries, he tried to remember Tiffany's small face . . . but the fuzzy memory now did little for him.

He had kept something to remember her by and to set him at ease when he was angry with Allie and the rest of the world. He hid it beside the sandwich bag full of hair he'd taken from Kelsey Anderson's room the night he'd had the close call, the night the beautiful Rachel had opened the door much too quickly.

He hadn't had time to do anything but scramble beneath the bed, and he'd been very lucky to be able to do even that.

She had stood at the doorway for what seemed like ages before crawling into the girl's bed. She cried for a while, soft whimpers that tore at his heart. Then came the sounds of her peaceful breathing. She'd fallen asleep, waiting for her daughter.

He thought about all the arguing he'd overheard the next morning when Kelsey climbed back through the window, all the hurtful words the girl had shouted overhead. The threats the beautiful mother had screamed back.

He was forced to lie beneath that bed for some hours until the last door had banged shut and everyone had gone to sleep. Even then, he feared being seen fleeing the house.

He now set a package on the counter for Allie. The nicotine gum was a small peace offering for screaming at her the previous weekend. He hated shouting at her. She couldn't help who she was any more than he could help who he had become.

He ripped open a bag of cat food, poured some into a bowl, then walked out to the front porch and set it on the decaying wood.

"Here kitty, kitty," he cooed. "Kitty, kitty?" A moment later, a pair of eyes glowed yellow at the edge of the porch. The sickly animal inched its way to the porch steps, then stopped, not knowing whether to trust him.

He looked into the stray's eyes knowing that it, too, was an orphan. Feeling a pang of sympathy for it, he went back inside and, through the window, watched it hurry to the bowl.

He slept almost peacefully that night with the wool blanket balled up at the end of his bed, one of the Anderson girl's soft sheets he'd stolen covering his body and Tiffany's gold necklace cradled in the palm of his hand.

CHAPTER 35

DR. BROUSSARD, THE Landry family's physician, sat in the recliner in the living room with a faded fishing hat between his sun-spotted hands.

"She swears up and down that it's your daddy, *cher*. And this is by far the best I've seen your mother look in a long time." He ran a hand against the gray stubble of his cheeks and chin. "I don't think you girls have a thing to worry about."

"But her sleeping medication might be making her hallucinate," Haley insisted. "She doesn't even believe in ghosts."

"Maybe she's never seen the dead until your daddy, dear. It's not uncommon around these parts for people to see the dead, you know."

Haley thought about Nana and her many tales about the early Cajuns, farmers, and trappers who lived off the land in Nova Scotia. She'd talked frequently of the ethnic cleansing they'd endured by the British, how their land was taken away, how they were separated from their families.

Nana believed that the Cajuns saw many ghosts after living and dying during *Le Grand Derangement* and that their ghosts followed them as they found their way to Louisiana. Nana had even claimed to see the dead while she sat in her rocking chair on the back porch, facing the dark bayou. But Haley's mother never had. She always said that Nana only told those stories because she was getting old.

"Do you think it's possible she could become suicidal?"

"*Cher*, your mother's goin' through a hard time. Do I think she's going to go off and leave her babies by themselves?" He shook his head. "No. No, I don't think so. In fact, I think she's getting much better."

"Would an antidepressant help?" Haley asked, wondering if a pill could really bathe a mind in calm denial and possibly help her mother.

The man shook his head. "Your mama doesn't want to get herself mixed up with any dang antidepressant medications. She's going to grieve it out, just like she should. It's not always a bad thing for the mind to feel some pain. And in your mother's case, it's perfectly normal. She lost the love of her life, you know."

Broussard rose and brought his fishing hat to his head. "I'll be back tomorrow after office hours to check in. Look, death's a sad part of life, but it still has its place. Let your mother get better on her own accord. Her mourning will end when she's ready."

CHAPTER 36

ONE LIE DIDN'T necessarily beget another. Did it? That's what Haley asked herself as she stepped into Mac's truck.

It was a question she'd been asking herself for days. It was Mac for Chrissake. *Mac.* He never intentionally would do anything to hurt her. No one was perfect. Hell, she herself was far from it.

Mac always had been great to her, and their relationship was unlike most. It was unselfish and healthy—certainly not as passionate as her parents' had been, but theirs had been rare, an almost fairy-tale relationship. She had dreamed of that for herself when she was a little girl, but she now understood that was far from realistic.

Her parents had been married for almost twenty years, but they never ceased acting like newlyweds. She could see the extent of their love in the way they looked at each other, the way they treated each other, the way they touched. They had the type of connection you could feel when you were in a room with them.

Mac didn't look at her the way her father had always looked at her mother, but he was very good to her, and they were comfortable together. Although daydreaming about Austin was something she did often, it was only a guilty pleasure.

Mac was her man.

He was the one who loved and wanted her.

As Mac threw the truck in reverse, she managed a weak smile.

"You're smiling," Mac said, sounding surprised.

"What's wrong with smiling?"

He studied her. "I don't know," he said, forming each word slowly, as though he were suspicious. "It's just been a while, I guess. Seeing you smile. But it's nice. It's *real* nice."

He threw the truck into gear, and they headed toward Main Street to the snow-cone stand. Mac had taken the day off to spend time with her, something he rarely did during the week.

"After snow cones, where do you want to go? We can drive to Lafayette and catch a movie. Or we can go fishing? Whatever you're in the mood for. The sky's the limit today."

"Mmmm. Let's see a movie. We haven't done that in ages."

"Then a movie, it is," Mac said, staring out at the road ahead of them.

Haley reached for her purse. She unzipped it and searched for her driver's license. She'd need it to get into an R-rated show. Accidentally tipping the purse at an angle, some loose change tumbled out, falling into the tight space between the passenger seat and the gearshift. "Dang," she muttered.

Mac killed the ignition at the snow-cone stand, then hopped out.

Haley forced her hand into the space to pick up the fallen coins. Her fingers brushed against something smooth. She grasped it just as Mac opened the passenger door for her.

It was a candy tin. Her breath caught in her throat.

"May I, Miss Landry?" Mac said, his hand extended.

Haley recognized the little pink tin where Tiffany kept her breath mints and her marijuana. She turned it over and saw the familiar monogrammed *TP*.

She tried to remember Tiffany ever being in Mac's truck. She couldn't.

"What do you got there?" Mac asked.

She looked up at him. "It's Tiffany's. I found it between the seats."

For a quick instant, Mac looked as confused as she felt. "Oh. She must have dropped it."

"When was she in your truck?"

Mac rubbed the whiskers on his chin. "A few weeks ago. I picked her up. She was walking along Main Street. Said something about Charles dropping her off at the diner, and she didn't have her car to get home."

Thoughts swam through her head. Some made connections that made sense. Some didn't.

Mac squinted. "You okay, babe?"

"Yeah," she lied.

He grinned. "Then let's get us some snow cones."

CHAPTER 37

IT WAS ELEVEN o'clock on Friday evening, and Tom still hadn't come home. The kids were in bed—at least Rachel thought they were.

She tossed aside the book she'd been trying to read, pulled on her robe, and walked down the hallway to Kelsey's room. She opened the bedroom door and waited for her eyes to adjust. When they did, she saw that her daughter wasn't there.

Anger welled up inside her, and she remembered the night when the raccoons knocked over the trash can out back, creating that awful noise. She'd awoken in a panic and raced to Kelsey's room. There'd been a heaviness in her gut, warning that something was terribly, terribly wrong. When she reached her daughter's bedroom, she found that Kelsey had snuck out her window.

That was the first night when she'd gone into Kelsey's room to find her not there, her bed empty. The next morning they'd had it out, both yelling at the tops of their lungs. Kelsey had said she hated her.

Hated.

And that she was a horrible mom.

Horrible.

Her daughter's words had tormented her every moment since.

As she did that night, Rachel crawled into her daughter's bed and awaited her return. Lying against the soft linens, she thought back to a time when she and Kelsey had been best friends.

Had anything happened to them besides puberty? She wanted Kelsey to trust her, to love her, to *like* her, but she knew she was partially to blame for Kelsey's new attitude. She was supposed to be a mother first and a wife second, but for months, she had reversed her priorities.

The room darkened.

Rachel rose in the bed, realizing someone was standing in front of the window, blocking the moonlight. It was Kelsey. She was home.

Her mind raced as she tried to figure out how best to handle this one. Should she be angry again? Or could she manage to be calm with her daughter and simply explain again the dangers of slipping out at night?

Rachel sat on the edge of the bed and smoothed her silk night-gown with her palms. She took a few long, deep breaths. Was now the right time to tell her that she was sorry for not being emotionally available?

Yes, that's what she'd do. Kelsey would appreciate it, and the two would begin to rekindle their relationship.

The room brightened again.

Where was Kelsey going?

Confused, Rachel hurried to the window, getting there just in time to see a figure slipping into the woods.

A figure much too large and tall to be her daughter.

CHAPTER 38

THE FAN HUMMED in the living-room window, but it did little to cool the Landrys' small house. The living room was the coolest room by far and the place everybody congregated, whether they all liked one another or not. And as far as Erica could tell, they didn't.

It was eight o'clock at night and still over eighty degrees, although it felt hot enough to be a hundred. Haley was fixing étouffée in the kitchen, her shoulder-length brown hair pulled into a ponytail and an apron over her sundress. Sasha, having just woken from a late nap, sat at the counter coloring, one of his nostrils crusted with snot.

Becky and Seacrest were in the living room. Seacrest was spread out on the large couch, and Becky was sitting on the smaller one. They were watching a video countdown on VH1.

Erica sat rigidly in a recliner, writing. It was the third time Haley had asked her over and only the second time she'd actually come. Since arriving an hour earlier, she'd mostly kept to herself, but there was something about being there that already felt pretty good. The Landrys were a troubled lot, but they still gave her a sense of what being part of a family was like. A real family.

She jotted down notes as she watched the two younger girls out of the corner of her eye. Mostly she watched Seacrest. The girl would twirl her long, dark hair around one finger, her full mouth pursed as though she were ready to say something. Every now and then, she'd shift on the couch, moving a shoulder back and forth, and she'd sigh.

On the other couch, Becky slouched, her chin upturned and her mouth set, staring at the television.

When she first got there, Erica had overheard the two on the porch. Seacrest had been telling Becky about a boy she'd made out with, and Becky's admiration for the girl had been more than evident.

Haley wet a napkin in the kitchen sink, then reached over to wipe Sasha's filthy nose. The little boy moaned and shook his head from side to side, resisting. The crayon he was using fell from his hand, and he burst into tears.

Erica took a long drink of the Jack Daniel's and Coke that Haley had fixed her, then focused again on her notes. She was glad to be away from her house, away from Pamela and her senseless drivel. The woman had become a permanent, unwanted fixture, always pestering her for information, trying pathetically to be her friend.

Outside, owls trilled on the small bayou, awaiting their nightly hunt. Erica's father once told her that many of the older Cajuns believed owls were old souls. The superstitious ones thought that when you heard an owl at night, you should get out of bed and turn your left shoe upside down to prevent disaster. Her father was Louisiana backward. Of course, he'd believe in ignorant folklore like that. Erica, like her mother, had never in her life turned a shoe upside down—and she never would.

Mrs. Landry's bedroom door opened, and she shuffled out, carrying a silver dog bowl. Her clothes were mismatched, and she was only wearing one sandal. With bleary eyes, the woman took all of them in one-by-one. Sasha gaped at her from the counter, as though a dead person had just entered the room.

"Hi, doodlebug," she said.

Sasha sat silently, the crayon he'd been crying about forgotten. Mrs. Landry moved across the living room and into the kitchen, patting the little boy on the head as she walked by. She filled the bowl with water, then headed back into the living room.

An old, frail dog wandered out of her bedroom, its claws tapping loudly on the hardwood floor. It stretched its long body, and a few of its joints popped. It glanced at Erica with near-dead eyes.

"Hi, Missus Leendry. You steel seek?" Sasha asked, finally finding his voice. His eyes were bug-like behind the thick lenses of his glasses.

Mrs. Landry smiled at the boy, but said nothing.

"Mama, this is Erica," Haley said, walking into the living room and gesturing at her.

"Hello," Mrs. Landry said, not making eye contact with her. She made her way to the screen door and set the water bowl on the porch.

"Want anything to eat, Mama? I'm making an étouffée," Haley said. "I was going to carry some in for you after it was ready."

The woman shook her head. "No, thanks, baby."

Mrs. Landry opened the door a little wider and stepped out. The old dog followed her. Then the screen door slapped shut, and Mrs. Landry was gone.

Erica could see Haley's face was drawn and that there were tears in her eyes. She got up and went to the kitchen counter. "You okay?" she asked.

"I'm . . . I'm not really sure."

Later that evening, after the girls finished dinner, Haley got a prank phone call.

Erica was sitting at the kitchen counter next to her, pouring drinks. It was the third each of them had had that night.

"Hello?" Haley asked. "Who is this?"

"Another prank call?" Becky called from her place on the couch once Haley hung up. "That's like the third one today."

"I'd be pissing my pants if I were you," Seacrest said.

Haley hung up. "It was just a breather," she said quietly, her eyes glassy. Erica had noticed early on that it took the girl less than a drink before she started to get drunk. But regardless, she kept drinking. Erica knew that she was the one who had introduced alcohol into Haley's life. Now she wondered if she'd done a bad thing.

Becky straightened on the couch. "That creeps me out. You know, it could be the guy who kidnapped Tiffany. And he keeps calling us."

"Yeah, it could be a killer," Seacrest said. "He could be stalking you. Holy shit, he could be watching the house right now."

"A keeler?" Sasha gasped, and a blue crayon tumbled out of his hand, onto the floor.

"She's just joking, baby," Haley muttered, and threw Seacrest a nasty look.

Sasha climbed down from the barstool, trotted into the living room, and stood in front of Becky. He screwed up his round face.

"What are you looking at?" Becky demanded.

"Guess!" he squealed.

"No, Sasha. I'm not guessing."

Sasha inched a little closer.

"Get out of my face, dammit," Becky snapped. "Why are you staring at me?"

"Why's yo face that culuh?" Sasha demanded.

Erica looked across the room at Becky. Squinting, she could make out orange streaks across the slouching girl's cheeks and neck, even her arms.

"Go color in your stupid book, Sasha," Becky spat.

Seacrest giggled from her place on the couch. "It's tanning lotion gone wild. She put it on a little while ago. Why'd you put all that cheap tanning lotion on yourself anyway, stupid? I told you not to."

Becky grabbed a bag of Doritos from the coffee table. She stuck one in her mouth.

"You have beautiful skin, Becky," Haley said, stumbling on the words. "You shouldn't . . . mess with it like that."

"I like yo face da otha culuh," Sasha said, his face serious. He took a step closer to Becky and stuck out his index finger. "Does it huht?"

Becky ignored him. "How can you say it's beautiful? It's so pale," she whined.

"Pale can be beautiful," Erica said. "My mother has pale skin, and she's the most beautiful person I've ever seen."

Becky looked at her, uncertain what to say.

"I think she needs more color," Seacrest piped up. "Not orange. But something. Maybe a lot of makeup. Like that pancake crap. Would cover all her freckles."

"Nothing's wrong with . . . Becky being pale," Haley slurred. "And I don't want to ever hear you call my sister stupid again. You understand me?"

Seacrest shrugged. "It doesn't look healthy. And I was only joking when I called her stupid. You know that, right, Becky?"

Becky nodded, but she looked unsure.

Erica studied Seacrest. There was something in the girl's eyes that bothered her. It wasn't just her uncouthness or the fact that she seemed to be a bully, the haughty way she carried herself, or even the anger she could tell the girl kept inside. There was something else.

"I mean it, Seacrest," Haley repeated. "Whether you're kidding or not. Don't call her names."

"Don't cawl huh names!" Sasha squealed, his finger now pointed at Seacrest. He giggled, thinking Haley's words were hilarious.

Seacrest raised an eyebrow. "Whatever." She reached into her purse, pulled out a pack of cigarettes and a lighter, then stood and stretched. Her low-rise shorts dipped low on her hips, exposing a long, olive torso and silver belly ring. Opening the screen door, she stepped into the sticky evening air.

"You hate her, don't you?" Becky asked her sister when she was gone.

"Yes," Haley said. "And I don't understand why you put up with—" She hiccupped loudly. "Put up with her. She's mean."

"Yeah, I guess," Becky said quietly. "Sometimes I don't like her, either. She seemed really cool at first, but I think she lies a lot."

"Then why do you waste your time with her?" Haley asked.

Becky shrugged. "Because I don't have any other friends."

Erica went outside and found Seacrest sitting cross-legged in one of the two rocking chairs on the small porch. She dragged on a cigarette, and its cherry glowed in the darkness.

Erica sat in the chair next to her and silently lit up, a warm breeze hitting her bare shoulders. She thought of how her mother used to sit out on their own porch and rock, facing the water.

There were nights she'd caught her crying uncontrollably.

Erica looked out at the bayou and wondered about Seacrest. *What is this girl all about? If I was a real writer, I'd find out.* There was no room for shyness or discomfort when your happiness completely depended on your success as a novelist. She'd have to suck it up and talk to people, even if some were vermin.

Setting her cigarette on top of an empty Coke can, she cradled the glass of Jack Daniel's between her hands. "So, where do you live?" Erica asked.

The girl was quiet for a long moment. "Weston," she said finally.

Erica nodded. "Seacrest is a different name. Kind of odd."

"Yeah? Well, if you knew me, you'd probably say it fits."

Erica rocked in the chair, wondering where she should go from there. Sasha was crying inside the house, screaming something about not being allowed to go outside. Becky was shouting for him to be quiet.

"Your mother drive you out here?"

Seacrest shook her head. "I usually take my bike. Sometimes I hitch."

"Your mother doesn't mind that you hitch?"

"She doesn't know. She's always working."

"So why do you come all the way out here?"

"There's no one in Weston," Seacrest said, tapping ash into the can. "The place is a ghost town."

Erica had been through Weston plenty of times because it touched most of Grand Trespass, but she'd never stopped there. There'd never been any reason. It was a town not much different than Grand Trespass. Blink a second too long, and it's gone.

"What does your mother do?" Erica asked.

"Sells Avon."

So she was one of those women: loud, pushy, always trying to sell you something you didn't need.

"Your father?"

"Salesman."

"Any brothers or sisters?"

Seacrest shook her head.

"They happy together?"

"Who?" Seacrest asked, and snubbed out her cigarette.

"Your parents."

Seacrest's eyes shone against the night. "Why are you asking me all these questions? Can't you see I'm trying to relax?"

It hit Erica that Seacrest reminded her of herself in some ways: The anger. The sarcasm. The unwillingness to be like everyone else.

"You have a hard time being nice to people, don't you?" Erica said.

"No."

"Think it was nice making Becky feel bad about herself tonight? Embarrassing her? Telling her and Haley that someone could be watching this house?"

Seacrest looked at Erica, her eyes slits. "I was telling Becky the truth. I don't just say what I think other people want to hear. I happen to think Becky's pale, and she has too many freckles. So what?" She kicked off her sandals and stood. "And some sicko keeps calling this house and hanging up. I think it could be a killer. Becky thinks so, too. She's just too afraid to say it. The girl's too freakin' afraid of everything, including that sister of hers."

She sauntered down the concrete steps to the pier.

Erica stood so she could see Seacrest over the tall bushes. When the girl reached the rotting wood of the pier, she stopped and pulled off her T-shirt and her shorts. Then, fearless of the alligators and snakes that overran the dark water, she dove in.

CHAPTER 39

IT WAS MIDNIGHT, and Mac had just shown up.

"Jesus. You're falling into a trap, Hale," he said when he realized she was drunk. "The same damn trap just about everyone in this town's fallen into. You're too smart for that. You get too dependent on that shit, and it's a mighty tough road gettin' back."

"Back to what?" she asked. She threw her arms in the air. "Oh, you mean this? My oh-so-happy reality? My father's dead; my best friend is . . . um, probably dead. My mother is losing her mind, and I just find out that my dependable boyfriend, my *rock*, who I felt I could always count on and would never lie to me—" She stopped to catch her breath. When she spoke again, her voice was barely a whisper. "Anyway, I don't know if I care too much about living in reality right now."

Haley heard the words she'd said, but she hadn't meant to say all of them. Mac had already apologized for the lie. But an unfamiliar anger had snowballed inside of her, an anger so intense, it crowded out the hurt and sadness and made her want to lash out.

Mac stared at her.

"Having a drink or two brings me some peace," Haley said softly. "Sometimes I just can't bear to feel any more pain."

"You'll feel it no matter what. Hell, you're *supposed* to feel it so you can get past it. Besides, this isn't you, Hale. I don't know who this is."

Earlier in the night, she'd thought back to her conversation with Tiffany at Provost's before she disappeared. Her friend had said she had a crush on someone.

She knew Tiffany's type. Unavailable.

And she knew how her friend flirted. She also knew that Tiffany loved it when someone was hard to get.

Could Tiffany have made an advance on Mac at some point? Could there be more to their relationship than she knew about? Is that why he had seemed so uncomfortable talking about her since she'd disappeared?

Maybe what she was saying in Provost's was her way of talking about Mac without *really* talking about Mac. Tiffany never had been able to keep a secret. She'd always told Haley everything, even stuff she wished she'd never heard. Maybe she felt the urge to share and was going to leave the fact that it was Mac out of the equation.

Of course, it all sounded far-fetched and ludicrous to her, but Mac's one lie had opened a can of worms. Besides, she was drunk, and she knew it.

"You ever flirt with her?"

"Flirt with who?"

"Tiffany."

Mac flinched. "For Chrissake, why would you ask me that?"

"Why wouldn't you? She's gorgeous. Any guy would be attracted to her. She's my best friend, but I know who she is and what she's capable of."

Mac glared at her. "I never flirted with her because you're my girl. Besides, she's nothing but trouble. You can see that a mile away. Look, I told you, I just gave her a ride. I don't like where this is going, Haley. You sound like you don't trust me."

She flashed back to the cover of the pornographic magazine and laughed. But it came out meaner than she'd intended.

A vein in Mac's neck pulsed.

"So, you're telling me I *should* trust you?" she asked, her words tumbling out sloppily.

There was an odd, unfamiliar expression on his face. "You want me to leave, Haley? Because if you do, just say the word."

Her head ached. She rubbed her temples. "I don't . . . know what I want. I don't know anything these days."

"What's that mean? You sayin' you're not sure you want to be with me?"

"I don't know."

"Christ, you don't *know?*"

The room fell silent. She was sure Mac was waiting for her to say something to the contrary, to take it all back. But she didn't. Part of her wanted to because she knew she wasn't in the best state of mind, but the other part—the one that won out—couldn't.

When he broke the silence, there was fury in his eyes. "Fine, I'm not goin' to beg you to be my girl if you don't want to be. You just let me know when or if you change your mind."

Before she could fully process everything that had just happened, he was gone.

CHAPTER 40

RACHEL WAS TIRED of Detective Guitreaux's impromptu visits and his endless string of questions. It had been three weeks since Tiffany's disappearance, and he was still interested in her.

Why was that?

What were people in town telling him?

When he responded to her call late Friday evening, she explained what she had seen outside Kelsey's window, but she didn't like his reaction. He just studied her, as though trying to gauge whether he believed her.

He had walked out to the backyard and trained his flashlight on the tree line for no more than two minutes before leaving.

Some detective work.

Before he left, he'd said to her, "I find it disturbing that you let your daughter run the streets at night. Don't you remember that a girl went missing?"

Let? She hadn't *let* Kelsey do anything. What did he expect her to do? Chain her daughter to her bed? Didn't he know that teenagers had minds of their own, that she was doing all she could do?

Or was she?

Tom was another story. He didn't seem fazed about Kelsey sneaking out. He had told Rachel to *handle* it. She understood that he didn't care about her anymore, but didn't he still care about the welfare of his children?

Tom didn't even seem concerned by the detective's countless visits. He simply would hand Guitreaux a beer, invite him into his office, and close the door.

Secrets.

What secrets was he telling the detective that he didn't want her to overhear?

Grimly, Rachel realized that things always had a way of changing. She just never imagined Tom changing, not this much.

After her classes Monday afternoon, she worked on the house. She was determined to have it spotless each and every time the detective came by unannounced so he'd see her as a well-put-together family woman, not the scorned wife she'd been made to feel she was.

Rachel picked up Tom's khaki shorts, underwear, and a golf shirt that he'd worn the previous day from the floor. She checked the shorts' pockets, then went into the bathroom and ran a rag over a small mound of crusted toothpaste he'd left on the counter.

After the master bed and bath, she decided to check the children's rooms. Kelsey's room was a zoo. Rachel stood in the middle of it and looked around. A ceramic ballerina lay toppled over on her vanity table. A can of hairspray lay on its side on top of her bed, and clothes were strewn all over the carpet. The room smelled moldy. Wondering if there was a wet towel in Kelsey's closet, Rachel walked across the room and opened the door.

"What are you doing in here?" a voice demanded.

Rachel jumped. She hadn't heard anyone enter the house. "Dammit, Kelsey. You frightened me!"

"You were snooping!" the girl snapped, standing in the door-way. Her blue eyes shined behind thick black eyeliner. Despite the July heat, she was wearing all black: a black T-shirt and long, black baggy shorts. Her bare legs appeared unusually pale against all the dark material.

"I was *not* snooping!" Rachel cried, then realized how defensive she sounded. *Calm down*, she told herself.

"I saw you!"

"Kelsey, do not raise your voice to me," Rachel said as calmly as she could.

"Don't snoop in my room!"

"You know you're grounded, and you're not to go anywhere but the library until school starts, young lady. So where've you been?"

Her daughter pressed her lips together. "The library."

Like hell, Rachel thought. Kelsey was rebelling. Rachel remembered rebelling, too, at her age. Hell, she wanted to rebel now.

Maybe she was in a lot of ways.

"Kelsey, we talked about your punishment for sneaking out at night. I was serious about—"

But before Rachel could finish her sentence, Kelsey spun on her heel and charged down the long hallway. Seconds later, the front door slammed shut.

Rachel hurried to the front window and watched her daughter dart across the lawn. She watched until she disappeared behind the next-door neighbor's house.

She sighed. She'd always imagined a much different life for herself. These days her life was no different than a prison—for her and her children.

She caught a glimpse of herself in a wall mirror. Her blond hair looked like uncared-for wheat. There were fine lines on her forehead and circles beneath her eyes. She shuffled down the long hallway to the kitchen and grabbed the last bottle of wine from its rack. While uncorking it, she looked out the window above the kitchen sink.

Mac, the young man who had cut their lawn for years, was walking to the shed. She noticed, not for the first time, that he'd grown into quite the handsome man. He was also very polite. She hoped little Tommy was as polite around people as Mac was.

Mac had always had a certain charisma, even when he'd barely been a teenager. She thought of the cute little girl he dated, Haley Landry, the one from the diner. She'd bet Mac made Haley very happy. He didn't seem the type to stray.

No, not all men were like Tom.

She downed a glass of wine and watched Mac until he was out of view. She poured another glass before walking back to the kitchen table where she sat, thinking, sipping, and pouring for a long while.

Rachel's eyes were moist when there was a knock on the back door several minutes later. Kelsey still hadn't returned. She had been wondering if she should hunt her daughter down, then realized that she'd had too much wine.

She was an awful mother.

There was another knock.

"Come in!" she called, wiping her eyes.

The door opened, but no one stepped in. She stood and saw it was Mac. He held his ball cap between his hands, and his T-shirt was soaked with sweat.

"Just wanted you to know I'm about done. Just some edging to do, then—"

Rachel suddenly realized she needed some company. Another minute alone, and she'd probably snap. "You look worn out. Would you like to take a break and have some sweet tea?" she asked.

"No, ma'am, but thanks for offering." His short bangs were soaked with sweat. They stuck straight up in a comical, but very cute sort of way.

She needed him to stay, just for a few minutes. That was all it would take to regain some control. "Take a break. Come on, have a glass of tea with me."

Mac ran a hand through his damp hair. "No, thank you, ma'am," he said. "I really should—"

"I insist."

"Well, okay then. Sure."

Rachel was lightheaded as she walked to the fridge. Taking out a pitcher, she carefully filled a glass. "Now don't just stand there in the door. Come on in," she said, trying to sound light. And sober.

He took a step inside.

"You like Luzianne Tea?" she asked, careful not to slur her words. Years ago, she could fake soberness perfectly. These days, she was rusty.

"Yes, ma'am."

Rachel made the return trip to the table, careful not to let any of the tea slosh out of the glass. "Have a seat."

"I'm pretty sweaty, Mrs. Anderson."

She slid the tea in front of a chair. A little sloshed onto the table. "Rachel. Please call me Rachel. And don't worry about it. Have a seat. Get comfortable."

Rachel sat down and smiled. Now, what would they talk about? What, if anything, did they have in common? "How long have you cut grass for us, Mac? Four, five years?"

"Yeah, five, I think. It was my first job. I've always appreciated the opportunity."

Five years. Where did all the time go? Rachel wondered. She poured another glass of wine. "You realize that in five long years, we've never really talked before, adult to adult? Or taken the time to have tea together?"

Mac set down the glass and looked at her politely. "No, ma'am. Guess we haven't."

"Then it's about time, isn't it? How's that girlfriend of yours? Haley, right? You two have plans of getting married anytime soon?"

Mac studied his glass. "No, not really."

"Oh, I see. Well, I hope things are okay."

Mac was quiet before he spoke. "To be honest, we're having some problems. Looks like we're not doin' too good these days."

CHAPTER 41

LATE TUESDAY AFTERNOON, Erica sat beneath a shaded area of her carport, writing fervently. Every once in a while she'd look up, in deep thought, and stare unseeing at the overgrown patches of grass, the yard's many burnt spots, the old green fishing boat resting upside down with no motor, and the dirt-encrusted flowerpots that had remained empty since her mother had left.

She didn't focus on any of these things. Instead, she focused on her mind's eye. These days she didn't need to use her mother's rituals as much. Writing seemed to have become natural to her overnight. But she wrote quickly, in fear that the crippling writer's block would return.

The writing had progressed a great deal. Her notebook was full of excellent notes, and she had forty pages written, the words coming quicker than she could write them. She jotted down notes during her shifts at Luke's, while on the pier, sitting in class, at the cemetery, everywhere.

She was looking forward to the detective coming by again. So far, he'd come by twice to ask her questions. Both times he had irritated her, but he wouldn't now. Now, she had too much to learn. She even considered asking the detective if she could help him with the investigation in some sort of small way. It would allow her to gather more information.

She heard footsteps behind her. "Why, hello, *cher*."

Erica tensed. It was Pamela.

Pamela stood next to her father's rusted tackle box, holding a faded beach towel. She wore only a black-and-white polka-dotted bikini. Her bony shoulders were sunburned, and her sunglasses were too large for her small face.

"Why are you sitting in the shade? You should be out getting some sun, darlin'."

Erica's grip tightened on her pen. "The sun's not healthy."

"Neither's cigarettes or voodoo. But at least the sun makes you look prettier," Pamela said and winked.

Erica looked away, toward the bayou. Two teenage boys had appeared on the opposite side, wearing swimming trunks and carrying a blow-up raft.

Pamela plopped down next to her and situated herself. "Seems your writing is goin' better. You're doin' more of it."

"How would you know? You spying on me again?"

Pamela let out a little laugh. "No, not at all. Guess I just notice things. My mama always said I was the most observant child in the family. Not that I learned to put it to any good use." She sighed. "Well, not yet, at least."

Erica pushed at some dirt with her bare toe.

"I'm happy for you. You seem much more at peace when you're doin' good writin'." Pamela pulled out a pack of cigarettes. She held it in front of her. "You want one?"

Erica hesitated. She breathed in deeply, and the odors of motor oil and mint flooded her nose. The cigarettes were appealing. The tips at Luke's had been more meager than usual, and she had been forced to ration her own cigarettes, most days smoking butts wherever she could find them. Every spare nickel and dime went into her New York City fund.

She reluctantly accepted a cigarette, and the two sat, smoking in silence.

"Your daddy tells me that you were friends with the missing girl."

Erica shook her head.

"You didn't know her?"

"I knew her, but we weren't friends."

"Did you know her well?"

"No. We just worked together at Luke's."

"Luke's?"

"The diner on Main Street."

"Oh, yes. Your daddy told me that's where you worked. Well, if you worked with her, then you should know her pretty well. What was she like?"

"Bitchy. Rich. Head stuck up her ass."

"Well, she doesn't sound too nice now, does she?" Pamela said. She dragged on her cigarette. Setting it on an old Coke can, she looked thoughtful. "I knew a girl once that went missing. Turns out she just ran away."

"Tiffany didn't run away."

"How do you know, *cher?*"

"It doesn't make any sense. She would have done things differently if she had run away."

"Your father doesn't seem to think that boy Charles, the boyfriend, had anything to do with it."

Erica hadn't realized that her father knew anything about what had happened. But of course he would, right? The whole town knew. Erica still found it odd that he hadn't mentioned anything about it to her.

"Big news gets around in small parts like this," Pamela said, as though reading her mind.

Pamela probably thought she was a big-city girl because she'd lived in Dallas once. A couple of nights earlier, she'd overheard Pamela and her father talking. Pamela had been bragging about the year she'd spent in Dallas as though it were as exotic a place as Europe.

"I give great pedicures, if you're ever interested," Pamela said, pointing to Erica's calloused feet and filthy toenails.

Erica stole a glance at Pamela's feet. A French pedicure.

"And I won't even ask for nothin' in exchange," Pamela said, snuffing out her cigarette and getting up. "I'll do it because I'd really like to be your friend." She stood and brushed off her backside. "I'm going in to shower and make a jambalaya for your daddy. Want some?"

Erica shook her head.

"Okay then. But I'll tuck a little extra in the icebox just in case you change your mind," she said and gave her another annoying wink.

After Pamela had gone, Erica gazed out at the bayou. *Friends?* Why would she want to be friends with a woman like Pamela? *Never*, she thought. Not all the cigarettes or pedicures in the world could help her stomach that woman.

She dug her toes into the dirt again and watched the boys across the bayou try to balance on their raft. She watched until sunset, even after their mother called them back into the house.

She watched until the headlights of her father's new silver Ford F-350 bounced off the driveway, then she gathered her things and headed to the cemetery.

CHAPTER 42

HE SQUIRTED THE conveyor belt with window cleaner and scrubbed it clean with a fistful of paper towels. A child had just pitched a fit and slammed an opened bottle of juice onto the conveyor. The juice had splashed all over the tabloids, copies of *TV Guide*, and booklets that held the never-before-printed secrets to losing weight fast.

The kid's mother had been apologetic, but blood was pounding in his ears, and he had refused to look at her. She wasn't the real problem, though. Neither was her kid. He just hadn't been feeling well lately. He craved the calm he'd felt after Tiffany.

He was anxious again, plagued by the realization that only one thing could calm him these days—the thing he mustn't do again. He thought of crack cocaine and what it did to its users between fixes. Killing was just as addictive.

"Clean up on aisle ten," a voice rang out. He looked up to see Henry, the store manager and the worst, red-faced alcoholic he'd ever met, looking at him through the smudged glass window of the office, speaking into the microphone.

He thought of his father, whom he hadn't seen since he was a little boy. For some reason he thought a lot about the man these days. His memory of his father was hazy at best, but he did recall that he had been kind to him. His mother cursed his father's last name over the years. Although it was listed on both his and Allie's birth certificates, she would never acknowledge it. She went by her maiden name and insisted that Allie did, too.

She never insisted that he did. For as long as he could remember, his mother had hated everything about him. She didn't care whether he lived or died, never mind whether he had a decent or despicable name.

Lately, everything seemed to bother him more than usual. The television, all the images of women. Horrible, trashy women. The women he abhorred. He didn't want to hurt anyone. He really didn't. But he did. Yes . . . oh, yes, he did.

His mind was a jumble of pent-up energy—confused, dangerous thoughts, unmentionable urges. That morning, he had ripped out the last pages in the filthy magazines. He ripped most of them to shreds—the pages, binding, everything. Maybe if he burned them after his shift. Yes, that might make him feel better. If it didn't, maybe he'd take a trip back to the Andersons'.

Someone tossed items on the belt. He glanced at them: a box of condoms, a can of SpaghettiO's, a pack of cigarettes, and a tabloid magazine. He looked up and nearly screamed.

"Why, hello, handsome."

It was Allie.

"The nicotine gum you left on the counter doesn't work too good," she said, now standing in front of the credit-card scanner. She reached in her pocket and popped a white square of gum in her mouth. "But the thought was nice. My big brother buying me gifts. My savior has reappeared in the form of a crazy screw-up."

She flashed him a toothy grin. He had the urge to fly over the conveyor belt and strangle her. Now was not the time for her to ridicule him, not in front of other people. She was crossing the line. His life with her was supposed to be separate, could *only* be separate.

What was she doing here?

A kid in a cart done up as a red-and-yellow plastic buggy wailed. He glared at the kid, then quickly returned his focus to his sister. She was wearing too much makeup. Her blue-red lips blared at him beneath the fluorescent lights of the store.

An older woman walked up behind Allie and placed a box of kitty litter on the conveyor, then picked up one of the juice-splattered tabloids.

"You wouldn't be trying to get into my panties, would you, big brother? Giving me thoughtful gifts so that you can molest me?" Allie said, loud enough for the woman to hear.

"Shut up," he snapped.

The woman's jaw dropped. She picked up the kitty litter and walked to the next open register.

His blood boiling, he rang up his sister's items and shoved everything into a plastic bag. The *blip-blip* of the scanners in the store was driving him mad. He wanted to jam his fist through the smudged rectangular panel of glass. "Eleven sixty-six," he said.

"I think I forgot my wallet," Allie said, smirking. "Can you, you know, *take care* of me?"

He glowered. Shoving the bag at her, he leaned in and hissed: "Get the fuck out of here."

After his shift, he jumped into his truck and drove home. The evening was calm; he was not.

On Coontz Road, he passed a girl who looked to be Allie's age, hitchhiking. She was wearing next to nothing, her thumb in the air. A sitting bird for predators like him.

Without thinking, he jammed his foot against the brake, and the truck lurched to a stop, leaving a cloud of dust in its wake. Seeing his taillights, the girl jogged up to the passenger door, her breasts nearly bouncing out of her tube top. He lowered the passenger window halfway.

"Where are you headed?" he asked.

"Grand Trespass."

His mind manufactured a scenario not unlike the one with Tiffany: snuffing out the life in this half-dead girl. The opportunity to take another evil out of the world and quiet his rage.

His eyes left the girl's and settled on a dried-up, flattened bullfrog on the road ahead of him. How dare his sister show up at the grocery store? How dare she humiliate him when he was outside the house? She knew the rules. Giving her the gift had been an unwise move, and he wasn't even sure why he had in the first place.

Yes, he felt responsible for her. And yes, in a twisted way he guessed he might even love her. But that didn't mean he had to be nice. She just would see it as a weakness and use it against him. She always had.

He'd learned his lesson.

The hitchhiker lifted the handle on the door. Discovering it was locked, she looked up and scowled. "You givin' me a ride or what?"

CHAPTER 43

HIS EYES FLEW open, and he found his naked torso slick with sweat.

Sitting up in the small bed, he struggled for air. It was five o'clock in the morning. The stress had brought on the nightmare of the last moments with his mother. Sweat chilled the sides of his face, and he let out a sob before lying back down.

He looked out the small window, listening to the faint crooning of Bob Dylan. He'd set the CD on loop the night before, and now Dylan's "Lay, Lady, Lay" played softly on the floor beside his bed. The sky outside was splattered in shades of gray and pink, the beginnings of dawn.

Ian brushed against the window, mewing loudly. Wickedly.

In the nightmare, her face had been so vivid. Her features true to that night, even down to her smeared eye makeup and the mole above her lips. Her words as sharp as they had been in life still echoed in his head.

She had regarded him with eyes that knew he would be just as twisted as she was. She was wearing one of her many wigs and speaking in a voice he hadn't heard before. He knew the night would be bad, even worse than the others.

The door to the basement stairs had been open, and she'd balanced on her bare, calloused heels in the doorway for a bottle of liquor. Her red nightgown was too sheer, too short. "We're going to have us a little quality time tonight, boy," she said.

He'd been trapped, standing next to the recliner, trying to find a way back to his room. He'd glanced at the carpet. Allie had been gluing leaves to a sheet of pink construction paper. A bottle of paste lay on its side next to his feet.

Sashaying into the kitchen, his mother reached into the cabinet and pulled out two shot glasses and filled them with whiskey. Hugging the bottle beneath her armpit, she walked into the living room carrying the glasses.

They drank in silence for the next half hour. He knew better than to say no to the alcohol. He just prayed he'd be able to outlast her, that she'd pass out on the couch before being able to do much harm.

As they drank, she looked past him. "I never wanted a boy. Men are manipulators. No good." She smirked. "Look at you," she said, venom in her voice. "You're pathetic. You'll always be pathetic. Ruled by women."

His erratic heartbeat, the wind outside, his mother's smoker's cough, the liquor trickling into his belly, all roared inside his head. His fists clenched.

Allie appeared in the living room, rubbing her eyes with the back of her hand.

"Go back to bed, girl," the woman ordered.

Without question, Allie scurried back to her room.

When she was gone, his mother leaned forward and ran a rough hand down the side of his face. "You think your mama looks pretty in this little nightie?"

He studied the carpet, knowing that if he looked full-on at the nightgown, he'd be able to see the evil beneath it.

"I thought you would." She took a long sip of her drink and set the glass down hard. "You know better than to let me down, don't you, boy?"

Yes, he did. But in that instant he felt something inside his head click. He'd finally learned to transform the terror into anger.

Not two minutes later, he shoved his mother down the basement stairs. When he charged down after her, carrying the foot of rope he'd kept hidden beneath his bed, he made certain she wasn't getting back up.

CHAPTER 44

AS HE JOURNEYED through the woods to the Anderson house later that evening, he thought of the girl hitchhiker he'd almost picked up a few days earlier. It had been a near disaster. He'd come so close to inviting her into the truck, possibly doing what he had to Tiffany.

He'd floored the gas pedal as she'd tried to open the door. It had been amusing to watch her through the dust the truck kicked up. She flipped him the bird, her hand no doubt stinging from the truck's sudden movement.

Now he was at the opening of the woods, but the Andersons' windows were dark, and neither automobile was parked in the driveway. Cold fingers of disappointment tugged at his heart, the familiar stir of despair.

Then he had an idea. One that both excited and frightened him.

Minutes later, he felt so alive, tiptoeing through the murkiness of Kelsey's room with his flashlight trained on the carpeted floor. Clothes were strewn all over the place—tops, jeans, shoes, a dirty dinner plate, and a fantasy paperback.

He entered the family's hallway, keeping the flashlight trained on the floor, then wandered into another bedroom. Her son's. Posters of rock bands covered the walls. School books, a laptop computer, a CD rack, twisted bedsheets.

He wondered if the boy was anything like him, but he doubted it. The boy would go places. He was wondering if he'd ever really get to see Nevada.

Walking into his angel's room, he breathed in the soothing scent of lavender and let the flashlight shine across her king-size bed. His mind racing, he walked into the master bathroom. Cosmetics and lotions were arranged neatly on a shelf above the toilet. He picked up a few, imagining her holding them. Squirting a perfume on the back of his arm, he sneezed as quietly as he could manage.

He went to her bureau and saw something that interested him, a gold bracelet. He stuffed it in his jeans. Being in her room both excited him and calmed his nerves in a way that only one other thing did. He drew air into his lungs and allowed himself a few moments of complete ecstasy.

He left the master bedroom and moved through the front of the house where the living room and kitchen were. There were so many shadows, but everything was still, calm. Wandering into the living room, he paused by the huge window. He looked out, marveling at how many times he'd been on the other side, staring in.

Then, headlights bounced off a wall, and he heard a car approach. Someone was coming up the driveway. He hurried across the room to the back door. In less than fifteen seconds, he was back in the woods.

Winded, he stopped for a moment to gather his breath. It had been a close call. Too close. He glanced back at the driveway and saw the front of Rachel's vehicle. A door slammed. Then another. He heard the young boy's voice.

Leaves crunched behind him. He swiveled around, and that's when he saw her—first her outline, then a few features. He knew exactly who she was.

Rachel's daughter, Kelsey. She was probably trying to beat her mother home.

She was frozen in a crouch, staring at him.

His heart hammered in his chest as he tried to figure out what to do. But before he could, she darted out of the brush and to the safety of her home.

CHAPTER 45

WHEN HER AFTERNOON class ended, Rachel dodged Myrna and the other teachers who routinely stayed late for afternoon coffee. She wanted to go straight home and use the time alone to look over a manuscript. She needed desperately to focus on something besides Tom, and she needed a drink.

Maybe two.

Strong ones.

Tom had taken a few days off and was going to take the kids to his sister's for a couple of days. Lately, he'd made a point of spending more time with them. Though she was relieved he was finally making an effort, she couldn't help but notice that he scheduled special outings without considering her calendar.

It's probably best, she thought. They needed time away from each other, time to cool down and figure out where their relationship was headed. Having the kids with him during that time at least brought her some peace.

As she turned into the driveway, she saw Mac pulling the Weed eater out of the shed. Surprised by the tug she felt in her chest, Rachel climbed out of the car and walked up the little path that bordered the house. She grinned at the young man. "I'm going to have a glass of wine. Care to join me?"

Mac shielded his eyes from the sun. "Ma'am?"

"Let's have a glass of wine."

"Mrs. Anderson . . . the edging and the weeds. I really oughta—"

"Rachel. Call me Rachel. And don't worry about the weeds. They'll be here later."

Mac hesitated.

"Is there somewhere else you need to be?"

Mac shook his head. "Nope, nowhere other than here."

"Well, c'mon, then."

CHAPTER 46

ONE GLASS OF wine turned into two, then three.

After the first glass, the two ended up moving from the kitchen table to the couch. Rachel asked Mac more about his relationship with Haley, and he told her how strange she'd been acting since Tiffany disappeared, how she'd pushed him away.

"That's horrible," Rachel said, her fingers going to her wrist, then she remembered it was bare. *Where could my bracelet be?* she wondered. "Relationships are difficult enough without all of the stress she's going through. Maybe she'll feel differently once Tiffany's found."

Mac shrugged. "If she ever is."

Rachel had the urge to talk to him about Tom, to ask if he'd heard anything about the affair or heard their names spoken in reference to Tiffany's disappearance. But she didn't. It would be inappropriate. Maybe even more so than having a few drinks alone with him.

Several moments later, Mac lifted his half-empty wineglass in front of his face. "I don't think I've ever drank this much wine before." He grinned, his words slurring ever so slightly. "I'm a beer guy."

"Going to your head?"

He nodded.

She was relieved to see that he finally was relaxing around her. At first he had seemed tentative, almost cautious in her presence, something she chalked up to their age difference. Now he seemed at peace. He even seemed as though he was enjoying himself.

They talked until two o'clock in the morning, until they'd finished a pot of coffee and Mac felt clearheaded enough to make it home.

She had had a nice time. In fact, it was the best conversation she could remember having with anyone for nearly a year. She had almost forgotten what it was like to have a decent adult conversation.

CHAPTER 47

ON SATURDAY EVENING, Rachel and Mac sat on the couch, finishing up a bottle of Merlot. Tom and the kids weren't due to return until the next afternoon, and when Mac came by to finish the lawn, he'd seemed happy that she invited him inside again.

This time he wasn't the least bit hesitant, and they found much to talk about between four and six o'clock. After the last drop of wine had been poured, Rachel failed to remember her problems or fears—or the nagging feeling that told her that this new friendship with Mac was inappropriate. After all, Mac was of age to do anything he wanted, and he wasn't a student.

She just focused on the way Mac looked at her and how handsome he was. She had always thought him to be especially good-looking, but only lately had she noticed how much of a man he had become.

She thought it interesting how relationship troubles could do that to a woman, make them notice such things.

Plus, Mac understood what she was going through with Tom. He'd listened intently to every word she'd said. *Really* listened. He'd sat silently, taking in everything. He'd been interested in what she was going through, and even seemed angry that Tom had been treating her the way he had. Finally being understood made her feel relieved. She'd desperately needed someone to understand.

Rachel set down the empty wine bottle. "Shall I uncork another?"

"You know, I probably shouldn't be doing this, Mrs., uh, Rachel."

"Why? We're not doing anything wrong. We're just—"

"No," he interrupted. "It's not that. It's because I gave Haley a lecture about not drinkin' so much. She's goin' through a really hard time, and she's hitting the booze too hard. Even though we're not together anymore, I'm still really worried about her, and this kinda makes me feel like a hypocrite, you know?"

Rachel wasn't sure what to say.

"Besides, I really oughta take a shower," he said. "I could come back after—"

"Don't be silly," Rachel exclaimed, patting the air. "You can't drive in this condition. Just take a shower here. You can change into something of Tom's."

After a little more prodding, Mac took the shower. Then, afterward, midway through their second bottle of wine, they began to kiss. In her drunken state, Rachel was unsure who had kissed whom first. All she knew was that it felt better than anything had in a long while.

The first kisses were clumsy and wet but also warm and exciting. Rachel tasted wine and a hint of spearmint chewing gum on Mac's tongue. Then she found herself leading him into the back of the house to her bedroom.

There, she ripped back the purple comforter, unbuttoned the shorts Mac was borrowing from Tom, and pulled down the zipper. She began unbuttoning her own blouse and watched Mac as he stared at her. He seemed a little nervous. Thinking that was sweet, she gently pushed him down and pressed her body against his.

They kissed for a long while, their mouths hot and soft. The temperature inside her chest and between her legs spiraled as she kissed his neck and ran her hands through his short, thick hair.

She stroked him.

His breathing grew louder.

Pulling Tom's T-shirt from Mac's back, she gazed at his wide, tanned shoulders and muscular abdomen. She ran her finger across his nipple and watched it stiffen.

These days, Tom was too quick, too removed. He acted as though sex was a chore, as if the experience was just his own, like she wasn't there—or at least didn't need to be.

She thought about Haley and wondered if Mac were thinking about her, too. How different was her body from nineteen-year-old Haley's? Naked, did she seem that much older?

Mac was the whole package, manly but still warm, gentle—things Tom never would be again and hadn't quite been in the first place.

He rose above her and threaded his fingers through her hair. "You sure you want to do this?" he whispered.

"I'm sure," Rachel whispered back. She was. Why not? Tom had. Why couldn't she? Revenge would help mend her heart.

Suddenly, Mac's hands were all over her. She was pleasantly surprised by how hard he was. She stroked him harder, faster. Wondering if his girlfriend had been sensitive to his needs, she lowered herself, her face softly brushing his chest, then his stomach, his hips. Then, finally arriving at her destination, she made him moan even louder.

The second time was different, less tender. Rachel could tell Mac was no longer nervous. He was better than Tom had ever been. He took more time, moved with much more precision.

Mac pinned her hands behind her shoulders. He kissed her neck, her collarbone, then worked his way down to her chest. He stayed there for a while, his tongue tickling her cleavage, her nipples. The desire was intense, as intense, if not more so, than their first time.

He rose to kiss her again, and she wrapped her arms around his back. His skin was smoother than Tom's, even when Tom had been his age. Tighter, more supple. His breath was now warm and heavy next to her ear. He started to move lower, and Rachel laughed.

His mouth was by her ear again. "You okay?" he whispered.

"Yeah," she said, having no idea why she'd laughed. She hadn't meant to. It had something to do with the cloud the wine had made in her head that cushioned her thoughts, dulled their razor-like talons.

Mac lowered his body, kissed her abdomen, and slowly worked his way down below. Using long, hard strokes of his tongue, he thoroughly explored her with his mouth. When she began to squirm, unable to stand it any longer, he lowered his hips against hers and entered her.

Afterward, they slept on their sides, their legs entangled, Mac's arm draped over her. They slept long and hard. Rachel's slumber, for once, was peaceful and uninterrupted.

She awoke to a ray of sunlight dancing across her eyelids. Mac was snoring softly, his smooth back to her. She sat up and stretched.

She startled.

Someone was standing in the doorway.

It was Tom.

CHAPTER 48

BY THE TIME Rachel pulled on her robe and made it out of the bedroom, Tom was in the kitchen, opening a cabinet. He casually pulled out a glass and took his time filling it with water.

"I guess we're even," he muttered.

Rachel's eyes narrowed. "I have a feeling we're far from even, Tom."

The two stood in the kitchen in silence. She waited for the guilt, the remorse to hit her. But there was none. If anything, she felt better than she had in a long time. Sleeping with Mac had opened her eyes in an odd sort of way. He'd been kind to her, gentle, caring. She felt desirable and feminine again and realized that the lack of desire in this marriage hadn't been her fault.

What *was* her fault was that all of her focus had been on Tom. Somewhere along the line she'd stopped loving herself.

"You must be wondering why I'm back early and without the kids," Tom said.

Yes, she had. "Why?"

"Because I wanted to talk to you."

"About?" Rachel asked, folding the robe over her thighs and taking a seat at the table.

"Well, seeing that I come home to find you bedding a sixteen-year-old—"

"Twenty-one," she interrupted. "Two years older than the little whore you were screwing."

Tom smirked. "Fair enough. Anyway, I came home so we could have a discussion. One that's long overdue. But now," he said, filling his glass again, "I'll just let my lawyer handle the discussions. Fair enough?"

Rachel didn't react. Without emotion, she said, "You just do that, Tom. And ask him to expedite things. I've wasted way too much time as it is."

———

Seven hours later, Rachel dropped to all fours on the ceramic tile. She'd dropped a glass, and it now lay in jagged pieces in front of the sink. She hurriedly picked up the bits, tossing them in the garbage can. The kids had just returned home, and she didn't want them to see that she had been drinking.

She knew the trick to drinking was knowing when to stop, but she'd been unable to master the trick her whole life. The only way she didn't drink too much was when she didn't drink—period. She wasn't even sure why she drank today. She'd felt so strong after the conversation with Tom.

The drinking was a problem she would deal with soon. One thing at a time.

She was shaking out the blue houndstooth rug when Kelsey walked in and stared at her.

"What?" Rachel asked defensively.

Kelsey had been acting oddly, even more than usual. She'd been hanging out in the living room with her brother when usually she escaped to her room unless forced to spend time with everyone.

Had Tom told her anything about what he'd seen? He was a pig, but surely he wouldn't do that.

Kelsey moved closer. She eyed the open garbage can and the shards of glass on top.

Rachel readied herself for a quick comeback should Kelsey remark about her drinking again. Lately, that had been Kelsey's argument of choice.

"I saw a man in the backyard, Mom," Kelsey said finally.

Rachel dropped the rug. "What? When?"

"The other night."

"What? Where were you?"

Her daughter hesitated. "In the woods. He was coming from our yard."

"Why were you in the—" Rachel stopped. Kelsey was talking to her for the first time in weeks. She couldn't put her on the defense. She needed to know about this man. "Did you recognize him?"

"No. It was too dark. All I could tell was that he was tall," her daughter said, rubbing the back of one of her arms. "Mom, this guy was creepy."

Rachel reached for the phone on the wall. She was livid. She was calling the sheriff again. She'd file a lawsuit against the department for not doing more the last time she'd called.

"Mom?"

"What, darling?"

"I, uh . . ." she said, then stopped. She gazed into Rachel's eyes, her eyes almost soft.

Almost.

"There's something else."

Rachel noted that the usual anger in Kelsey's eyes had vanished. In its place was what appeared to be confusion.

Rachel put down the phone. Was this about Mac? So, Tom *had* told her? Suddenly, she felt ashamed.

"What, baby? Go ahead, you can tell me," she said, preparing herself.

Kelsey's voice was gentler than it had been for over a year. "Why are you staying with Dad?"

Rachel blinked. "What?"

"I know what he did. Everyone knows what he did, Mom. And he treats you like shit. He doesn't come home. He won't even talk decent to you. So why do you stay with him?"

Rachel was at a loss for words.

Kelsey dug her hands into the front pockets of her jeans and looked down at the floor so she didn't have to meet her mother's eyes. "You used to be so strong, Mom. What happened to you?"

———

Rachel watched the blood swirl down the drain. There was a lot of it. Too much.

She'd cut the inside of her hand picking up a missed sliver from the broken wineglass. Now she was running cool water over it. The sheriff was on his way over to take a report from her and Kelsey. All the windows in the house had been checked, and she'd instructed the kids to keep the doors locked. She still felt they were unsafe in the house.

She was ashamed. Kelsey's words had hurt her worse than she'd ever been hurt, even by Tom. Her daughter was right. She was no longer as strong as she'd once been.

No wonder the family had grown so far apart.

Now there was this strange man. He wasn't a product of her imagination. She had to protect her children. She had to do so many things differently.

She quickly bandaged her hand, then picked up the phone. Her hand trembled as she dialed a phone number she hadn't dialed in a long while. After a few moments, someone picked up on the other end.

"Mom? It's Rachel," she said, sniffing back tears. "The kids and I . . . we're going to come out to Phoenix for a while, if that's okay."

CHAPTER 49

THE NEXT AFTERNOON, Erica sat on the sidewalk outside Luke's with a grilled cheese sandwich and a cold Coke. She pressed the chilly can against her forehead and neck.

Red ants swarmed in the cracks of the sidewalk and in the gravel, busying themselves with a sandwich crumb. She watched them for a while, until the white glare of the sidewalk grew so intense, she felt it burning her eyes through her cheap sunglasses. She spread her slender legs out in front of her and squeezed her eyes shut.

She still was confused by what she'd seen two evenings earlier. When she'd stopped at Mrs. Anderson's hoping to ask her a question, Mac's truck had been parked in front of the house. She had been mildly curious when she first saw the truck, but as it grew later, she thought it even more bizarre for him to be there, especially since Tom Anderson didn't appear to be home.

While she waited, she found a swing set in the backyard. It was bathed in darkness, and she was confident she wouldn't be seen. She sat on the swing and watched the house long after the lights had gone off.

Were they having an affair?

No, they couldn't be.

It just didn't make sense. She thought about Haley.

The rumble of an eighteen-wheeler grew closer, and she opened her eyes. The rig pulled into the gravel lot, and after some rattling, the engine cut off. The trucker stepped out into the dust the rig had kicked up. He grinned at her.

Through her sunglasses, she glared back.

Why were men such children? Especially truckers, who would flirt with anything that moved. Had they always been such horrible flirts? *What came first,* she wondered, *the urge to flirt or to drive big trucks?*

"Howdy," the man said, walking up to the building. He tipped a baseball cap and smiled.

She kept her eyes narrowed until he walked past, her lungs filling with diesel exhaust and dust. She closed her eyes again and wished to be in the city, where her mother was. There, the air burst with exotic food aromas blending with the exhaust of stop-and-go traffic. There wasn't an ounce of back-road country dust in sight.

Everyone would be different there. They'd even be celebrated for it.

And Erica knew that she'd finally fit in.

CHAPTER 50

HALEY GRABBED A cane pole for fishing from its place in the overgrown, wasp-infested monkey grass and stepped cautiously onto the small rectangular pier behind Erica's house.

Most of the families in Grand Trespass lived on lots that backed up to the bayou. Most had small piers, splintering and warped from decades of Louisiana sun, the wood jutting up in odd places from rot. Erica's lot was no different.

The yard was neglected. A row of dead bushes, burnt from the summer sun, lined the front of the house. Moldy pecan husks lay everywhere in the tall grass, and Haley had counted four wasp nests in the few minutes she'd been there.

"Does your father ever cut this grass?" she asked, wiping sweat from her brow. It was past six o'clock in the evening, and the air was still heavy with heat and humidity. As she sat down, the heat from the dry wood stung the back of her bare legs.

Erica sat in a lawn chair, bent over a notebook. She had on a faded yellow bikini top and a pair of cutoff sweat shorts. Beads of sweat glistened on her tiny copper shoulders. "Sometimes. Depends on whether he has a floozy or not in his life. When he does, the grass gets pretty tall."

Haley watched Erica. She liked the way the girl bent over her work, sometimes scrunching up her forehead, deep in thought, silently moving her lips as she pored over what she'd written. Haley found her intensity and simplicity to be stunning.

Tiffany had been gorgeous, but she was often dolled-up: hair meticulously done, makeup skillfully applied. To Haley, the au-naturel girl next to her, with her razor-sharp wit, focused frown, and glistening sweat, was just as beautiful. Perhaps what was most attractive about Erica was that she knew who she was—like, *really* knew. Haley envied her for it.

"I don't know why we've never hung out before. We've always lived so close," she said.

"Tiffany," Erica said flatly. "She's why."

Haley didn't say anything, knowing Erica was right. She reached into a plastic cup to corner a plump cricket and pull it out for bait. She laid it on its back and jabbed a hook into the tough armor of its chest, watching white goo ooze onto her ragged thumbnail. Staring at its writhing body, its antennae twisting in what could only be fear, she felt a wave of guilt. Quickly, she swung the line into the water, sending the cricket below the murky surface.

Out of sight, out of mind.

She wiped her thumbnail along the edge of the pier and watched the red-and-white bobber bounce gently on the water. After a little while, she moved her line closer to the seawall. "Mac and I broke up," she muttered.

Erica looked up from her notebook and tilted her head as if curious, but she didn't look surprised.

Haley set her pole on the pier and shifted to face her. "A week ago, I caught him in a lie for the first time. It was a stupid one, really, but still a lie. And knowing he lied about one thing makes me wonder if he lies about other stuff, you know?" She sighed. "Then I find something of Tiffany's in his truck the other day, and I flipped out. He said that he'd given her a ride a week before she disappeared and that she must have dropped it. You'd think that with that explanation, I'd feel fine, but I don't."

Haley thought again about Mac and Tiffany together, alone. She cringed and shook her head. "I don't know if I can trust him anymore."

Erica listened in silence, letting her talk.

"He always said he didn't care for her. I'm so confused. Everything's just so crazy. First, my dad. Then, my mom and Becky. Then Tiffany. The prank phone calls. Now Mac. I feel like I could go insane at any second. Just snap and go completely crazy."

Erica uncrossed her slender legs and let her feet drop to the pier. She leaned forward. "So, what did he lie about?"

"Porno magazines."

"Yuck. My father has some of those, too," Erica said.

"But Mac always told me he liked his women wholesome and that he *hated* pornography. Yet, I found one in his truck. A really filthy one. It just makes me wonder all kinds of things. Maybe I'm just paranoid, but I'm wondering if something could have happened between him and Tiffany behind my back. I mean, I've never had a reason not to trust him or to think he'd cheat on me, but now . . . I don't know. I can't get the idea out of my mind."

A family of ducks glided by. Wary of the girls on the pier, the mother duck quacked shrilly at her ducklings, warning them to stay close.

Haley looked at Erica and saw an odd expression on her face.

"What?" Haley asked.

Erica was quiet for a minute, watching the ducks. "I think I should tell you something. Something you're not going to like," she said. "It's about Mac."

It was two-thirty in the morning, and as always, Haley couldn't sleep. With a steaming cup of tea in hand, she flipped off the kitchen light and went out to the porch.

Pale moonlight bathed the center of the bayou. She curled up on a rocking chair and tried to sort out everything. The anxiety she'd awoken to had been insistent. Erica said she'd seen Mac at Rachel Anderson's when it was late at night and her husband wasn't home.

Were the two having an affair?

If so, when had it started? Weeks ago? Months?

The thought made her stomach queasy—and she was beginning to feel as though she'd never really known him.

A barn owl called out, and she glanced toward where the sound had come. She stiffened as she saw something move in the darkness of the carport. Someone was walking toward her.

Unable to move, she held her breath as he came closer, now only a few feet from where she sat. An unbidden image of Tiffany's face passed through her mind's eye.

Then a familiar voice cut through the darkness: "Hey, it's just me."

———

A few minutes later, Haley was staring at Charles. He sat on the porch swing, his shoulders sagging, his hands clasped together. Instead of appearing overly anxious as he had been the last time she'd seen him, he just looked exhausted.

Resigned.

Dark circles framed his eyes, and he looked much thinner than he had during his last visit.

"How are you holding up?" he asked, the bug zapper behind him incinerating a mosquito.

Haley laughed, surprising even herself.

"That good, huh?"

She wasn't sure how to respond.

"You don't look so good," he said.

"Well, that makes two of us."

There was a long silence.

"I still look for her, you know," he said. "I can't sleep not knowing."

Haley studied him. The pain on his face seemed real. "She was my life, Haley. My entire *life*. I guess the joke was on me, huh?"

Haley was tired and wanted nothing more than to just crawl into bed and pass out. Even so, she knew she wouldn't be able to.

"This is really taking a toll on my mom," he said. "Between her being worried to death about Tiffany and the shitty way folks have been treating her at the college. The comments behind her back, the stares . . ." Charles's mother was part of the custodial staff at the community college. "People stopping in front of the house and yelling nasty things. Hell, someone even threw a brick into our living-room window last night. My little brother got hit with some glass. This is getting to be too much. Way too much."

He leaned back and sighed. "She's a wonderful woman, Haley. You know, she left everything in New Orleans to move us here. Her friends from childhood, her sister, a good job. Just to make sure my brother and I were okay. And *this* had to happen," he said, a tic appearing above his left eye. "Sometimes I think things would be much better for her if I wasn't around."

Three bolts of heat lightning pierced the sky like silent screams. Everything about the night became still, even the crickets.

"I don't know how much Tiffany told you, but I was getting myself into a shitload of trouble in New Orleans. Going down the wrong path. Running with the wrong crowd. Creating a lot of havoc in her heart. My mom's always loved me. You know, *real* love. And I've always been such a huge disappointment.

"What's funny is that I've been clean for over a year, and now I'm suspected of doing something much worse than I ever even *thought* of doing. It just doesn't make sense."

"I'm sorry to hear that," Haley said, realizing that sounded hopelessly empty but not knowing what else to say. Inside the house, the ice maker in the kitchen released cubes of ice. Haley could hear them clink into their plastic tray. Her eyelids began to droop.

Charles leaned forward, and the chains that supported the swing protested. "Want to know why I came here tonight?" he asked.

Haley turned to him.

"Because no matter if no one else in the world does, I need for you to believe me. To believe I would never, ever hurt Tiffany. You were her best friend, Haley. I need that from you."

CHAPTER 51

LATER THAT EVENING, he was having one of his head-aches. There were too many thoughts in his head, all competing for his attention.

They beat at the soft, fragile walls of his mind, pounding so forcefully, his skull felt as though it were changing shape. His mother kept screaming at him, more and more each day. He wasn't far from coming apart at the seams.

He'd bought new magazines and couldn't tear the pages quickly enough. Grabbing as many of the glossy pages as he could, he ripped them from their binding: pictorials, advertisements, cartoons, ads for cologne. He ripped until the binding was bare.

He picked up another magazine and began shredding it. Images of red-lipped, doe-eyed, filthy women littered his floor, their faces and bodies torn to pieces. They peered up at him with dull stares; they had the eyes of the dead. When his hands began to cramp, he stopped and lay against the wall opposite his bed. He tried to remember being inside the Andersons' house and how nice it had felt, but he couldn't. His mother was screaming too loudly.

There was scratching above his head.

The window.

Ian.

He squeezed his eyes shut. The urges had become undeniable. He'd felt so calm after Tiffany, so calm after his mother. After their deaths, his headaches and nightmares had quieted . . . for a while. He'd felt almost normal.

But he wasn't normal. He'd *never* be normal.

He'd begun losing it on the outside, his mask slowly slipping away. The woman's daughter had seen him in the woods. It was dark, so he hoped she didn't get a good look at him. But it was possible she had.

Tiffany had begun screaming, too. Every night from the pond, her cries were so loud, he could hear them from his bedroom. They were trying to get him in trouble—and they would. After all, it wouldn't be too long until the law figured out for sure just who he was. They probably had a good idea already.

The small room was cramped, and its mustiness suffocated him. Ignoring Ian, he went to the kitchen and grabbed a beer from the refrigerator. Then he moved to the living room. Hoping the beer would calm him, he gulped it down.

The pipes clanked in the walls. Allie was home. He would have to leave. He lunged for his truck keys, but it was too late. Allie's footsteps sounded behind him, and a blaring odor filled the room. She'd sprayed on perfume. He tried to stifle a sneeze, but it came out anyway.

"May God bless you," she said sweetly. She walked around the couch and stood in front of him. A blue towel speckled with motor-oil stains was draped loosely around her. Her hair was dripping, and she had on bright red lipstick.

She pursed her lips. "So," she teased, "think your little girlfriend has a better body than me?"

He wouldn't look at her.

Ian had followed him to the front of the house and now perched outside the living-room window, scraping a flea-ridden paw against the smudged glass.

Her tone turned chilly. "I asked you a question."

"Stop it."

"What if I don't want to?"

He was silent.

"I'm only doing you a favor, you know. It's because I feel sorry for you. Mama was right. You're pathetic."

He shot a quick glance at her and saw that she was grinning again. For a quick moment, he remembered her as a little kid, dirty-faced and tomboyish in her pigtails and little striped bikini, snorkeling in the ditch in the front yard, catching crawfish and tadpoles.

She used to follow him out to the pond and into the woods. She used to be his little admirer. That was so long ago.

That Allie was dead and gone.

"Look, this is for you. All of it." The towel fell before he could look away, and he took in her naked body: her bare breasts, full and taut; her tiny waist; and flat, smooth stomach. "You can have this, you know," she said. "It'll be the best you'll ever have."

The beer quickly soured in his stomach. "Christ!" he yelled, hurling his beer across the room. The bottle smashed into the living-room window and glass shattered.

She screwed up her face. "I know you want me!" she shouted. "*Everyone* wants me! They all say I'm beautiful! Don't you know that?"

Fighting the urge to shake her until she could no longer breathe, he shot out the front door. He had to get away . . . far, far away from everything.

Branches snapped as he snaked through the dank woods. Owls screeched above him. He cursed the owls and the voices from the pond.

"How can I hear you way out here?" he screamed into the night. "Leave me alone!"

His mother was angrier than ever. She wanted to be found. She wanted to get her revenge. Tiffany was frightened. She kept screaming, asking where she was. She cried that she needed to go home.

Sometimes, rare times, he was able to smile at their pain. Pain was something they'd never known until now. But he wasn't smiling now. He picked up a pinecone and hurled it into the air in a vain attempt to quiet the owls' screeching.

Something rustled behind him. He turned and crouched, prepared to twist Ian's neck if he had followed him. He'd left without his flashlight, and the brush was so dense, the night too dark for him to even see his own hands.

He waited for a long while and heard nothing, so he moved forward again, his jaw clenched. If only Allie knew what he could do, how close he was to doing something unspeakable to her.

Fifteen minutes later, he was at the opening in the woods. His heart fluttered beneath all the noise in his head. The Andersons' house was lit, and someone was in the living room, just as he'd hoped. It was frustrating when they went to bed early and when they were away from the house. He needed them. Didn't they know that?

He crouched and moved past the swing set. The father was in the living room, talking to someone. A woman who didn't look much older than Allie. They were standing, facing each other.

He lowered himself to the ground, the night earth cool against his T-shirt. He watched as they embraced and then began to kiss.

His body tensed.

Rage ripped through his skull. Tom was cheating on Rachel . . . hurting her yet again.

He sprung up. "No!" he shouted, his wail bouncing off the trees. He stood in the darkness, trying to gather air into his lungs.

Two faces now peered out the tall, rectangular window: Tom and the teenager.

The yard flooded with light. Tom stepped out the back door.

"Hello?" he said. "Someone out here?" Tom stepped forward tentatively. One step, two steps. "I know you're standing there," he said, his arms by his sides. "Do I know you?"

He tried to breathe. Air trickled into his lungs as if it were being tunneled through a straw. He knew he should run before the man got a good look at him, but his muscles wouldn't cooperate.

"I'm going to go in and call the sheriff now. You can't be doing this, you know. Standing in people's yards. Looking through their windows. That's what you were doing, right?"

"Do you even know what you're doing?" he screamed.

"Pardon me?" Tom said.

"How could you do this to her?" he bellowed.

The man went silent. When he spoke next, his voice had lost its accusatory tone. "Who are you?" he asked soberly. "Do we know you? Do you know Rachel?"

CHAPTER 52

HALEY WAS SURPRISED to see a blond-headed woman sitting in Erica's living room on Thursday evening when they walked into the house.

The room was sparsely furnished. Aside from a butter-colored leather couch and a coffee table, the only other fixtures were a stuffed buck's head in the corner and an empty fish tank on a wooden stand.

"Why, there," the woman exclaimed, looking up from a paperback. Her face broke into a warm smile. "You brought home a friend!"

Erica ignored her and led Haley down a hallway. Haley smiled uncomfortably at the woman and followed.

"Who was that woman?" Haley asked once they were in Erica's room.

"No one important," Erica mumbled, setting her backpack on the floor. She unzipped it and pulled out two wine bottles and a Styrofoam box that contained a fried oyster po'boy and a heap of crinkly fries they'd taken after their shift at Luke's.

Haley looked around the small bedroom. It was about the size of Becky's, and there was a small window covered by a bisque-colored shade. Brown shag carpet covered the floor, and an ancient computer sat atop a walnut desk.

"You have a lot of books," Haley said, staring at a wall-long bookshelf.

"Yeah," Erica said. "I read everything I can get my hands on. My mom did, too. Most of those are actually hers."

The other wall was covered with newspaper clippings. "What are those?"

"*New York Times* bestseller lists," Erica said.

"Wow. That must be a year's worth."

"Five. Five years."

Haley sniffed and made a face. "The house smells like . . ."

"Paint?"

Haley nodded. "Yeah, paint fumes."

"The bimbo can't quit painting. I think she's getting bored of my father."

An hour later, Haley stumbled into the hallway, looking for the bathroom. She'd been laughing hard at something Erica had said, something she couldn't even remember. It might not have even been funny.

In the bathroom, a book for learning how to cook Mediterranean food lay closed with a pen stuck in its middle. Two overstuffed cosmetics bags were propped against the toilet.

She and Erica had finished off a bottle and a half of the wine and had shared countless cigarettes as they'd talked. Now she was paying for it. Everything was beginning to spin.

As she stumbled out of the bathroom, she saw the pretty blond woman leaning against the wall in the hallway.

"She hates me, doesn't she?" the woman asked, her face kind.

Haley reached out to hold on to the wall. "Uh . . . I don't . . . I don't know," she said as evenly as she could.

The woman smiled sadly. "I try to be her friend, but I guess there's only so much someone can do to make another person like them. And it probably don't help that I'm dating her father. Especially with her mother skipping town and all when she was so small. Probably don't help either that she loves her mother like nothing else in the world."

"Probably not," Haley agreed, and leaned harder into the wall. "I'm . . . Haley, by the way," she said, trying hard to sound sober.

"Pamela," she said and extended a soft hand.

"You girls hungry? I have a roast and some dirty rice in the fridge I can heat up."

"No, thanks. We . . . just ate."

"Oh, okay." She smiled. "Well, if you change your mind . . ."

"Thanks."

The two stood in silence, smiling dumbly at each other.

"Well, I better get back."

"You do that. Nice meeting you, honey. Real nice."

Haley tottered into Erica's bedroom, which was dark except for three lit candles and a small book light attached to one of Erica's books. Erica turned to look at her and the book light moved, too, throwing a long shadow across the room. A floor fan oscillated at the foot of the bed.

Haley dove beneath the cool sheets.

"Were you talking to her?" Erica asked.

"Yeah. She seems nice."

"Well, I wouldn't talk to her too much if I were you. You could catch stupid."

Haley laughed and wrapped the comforter around her. She reached over and grabbed a cold crinkly fry from the Styrofoam box, then rolled over to face Erica. "Do you ever wonder if it's possible that everyone in our lives are really strangers?" She sat up. "I mean, like, you don't really know people although you think you do?"

Erica lit another cigarette.

Haley went on. "I know, it probably sounds stupid. It's just, I wonder if it's ever really safe to love someone . . . or even get close to them." She hiccupped, then started again. "Like my mom. I never would have thought she'd be capable of abandoning us. And Mac. I never thought he was capable of lying to me. Or cheating."

Erica licked her lips. "My mother always said that love is an entanglement. If you get too tangled, you lose yourself. It's just a distraction. A way of escaping into someone else because you think that'll be what finally makes you happy. Like a drug." She studied her cigarette. "Besides, we're not meant to be happy. Not really. It's just a concept someone made up to make us miserable."

Haley mulled over her friend's words.

"To answer your question, I guess you can't ever know someone unless they want you to. And even then, they don't want you to know everything. Everyone has secrets."

Haley started to feel woozy.

"So, what's going on with Mac?" Erica asked. "I hope it was okay to say what I said. I just thought you should know."

Haley felt even woozier.

"We haven't talked since you told me. He hasn't come around. But I'm glad you said something. It's something I needed to know."

The two sat in silence, listening to the crickets outside. After a while, Erica broke the silence.

"Here, I think you should read this," she said, handing her notebook to Haley.

Haley took it and struggled to read what was on the page. It was difficult. The words bounced around, playing games with her eyes. After a few minutes, she managed to catch them all. It was a character description of sorts, and the character it described seemed like someone who she would like to be.

"Who's this about?"

"You."

211

"Me? Are you serious?"

Erica shrugged, and there was a flush in her cheeks. "I don't know. Just felt like writing it, I guess."

Haley's brows knitted together, and she looked at the page again. "But this doesn't sound like me at all."

"Trust me. It's you."

"But how can you think that I'm responsible?"

"You are. You're just going through some shit. But this won't be you for long."

"But how do you know? Before this summer we didn't even talk."

"You don't need to talk to someone to know them. All you need to do is watch."

Erica kept talking, and Haley fought to keep her mind in focus. She knew her friend was saying something deep, and she tried to grasp all she could, but there was too much alcohol in her. A cloud had descended, and everything suddenly seemed impossibly distant.

After a while, Erica stopped. "You don't look too good, Haley. You're green."

"Huh?"

"You don't look so great," Erica said more slowly this time, her voice even more distant than before, as though she were underwater. She leaned closer, looking concerned.

Haley tried to ask Erica what she had just said, but she was sinking into a dark, balmy pool. She noticed Erica staring at her. She tried to ask her why, but her mouth wasn't obeying. Neither were her eyes. Every time she managed to open then, they'd slam shut again. And after much futile effort, finally, they remained shut.

CHAPTER 53

HALEY CLUNG TO the darkness behind her eyelids, the remnants of a comforting dream still heavy in her mind. She was dreaming about Austin. They were standing on her porch, and he was leaning over to kiss her.

Feelings she hadn't felt in a long time washed over her. The weak-in-your-knees, tingly, *electric* feelings she'd witnessed vicariously through movie love scenes or through Tiffany and her string of boys. She'd had similar feelings for Mac—just not as intense— and that had been wonderful, but that was long ago. Now Mac was gone.

"Haley?"

Someone was calling her name. Without opening her eyes, she felt around. Her hand closed in on her pillow. Yes, she was at her house. Tiffany . . . no, Erica's father's girlfriend, had driven her home.

She knew that if she opened her eyes, she'd lose the moment, so she willed herself to sink back into the dream. Her body began to relax again, and Austin's face returned. He thought she was pretty, not plain.

He really liked her.

She sank deep, deep, deeper.

Now she was at Luke's. Her mother was walking around in a uniform, smiling and serving coffee. Her hair was done up, and she looked happy. Austin and Mac were talking to her father at the bar. Her father threw his head back and laughed.

That laugh.

She hadn't heard it for almost a year. It was one of those wonderful, comforting parts of him she had forgotten.

Erica walked up to the two of them. "My mother snuck out in the middle of the night," she said. "She wasn't meant to grow old with a used-car salesman."

Now Tiffany was standing next to her: "I can't stay with the same boy forever. I want to leave this backward town. I want . . . I want . . . Haley, do you miss me? Haley?"

The voice was louder this time. Becky's. "Haley! Wake up. Erica's here!"

Haley tried one last time to hold on to the dream, but Becky kept calling out to her and the kaleidoscope quickly melted away. Haley opened her eyes.

Becky and Erica were standing next to the bed, staring at her.

"You okay?" Erica asked. "Guess we overdid it, huh?"

"I thought you had a shift today?" Haley whispered. She winced. It felt as though something was squeezing her head.

"Um, I did," Erica said. "It's already five o'clock."

———

Two hours later, the sky was a deep shade of blue, the color of dusk. Haley gazed out at the bayou, a cup of coffee in her hands. She reached into her pocket, then dropped an aspirin on her tongue. She still tasted last night's cigarettes.

The Smiths next door were firing up their grill, something her father loved to do when he was alive. Mrs. Smith spotted her on the porch and waved. Haley waved back, then closed her eyes.

Her head was pounding. *I'll never drink again,* she told herself. *At least not that much.* She was starting to black out when she drank, not remember things. Erica was right. She was losing herself. She'd always been responsible, and she took pride in that. Mac had been right, too. Numbing the pain wasn't going to make it go away. It was only prolonging things. They'd already been prolonged long enough.

She set the coffee cup on the table next to her and started to rock. She needed to make some changes in her life, whether her mother got better or not.

Major ones.

She couldn't just wait for others to do so.

It was time for her to take control of her life.

Hearing shouts, Haley's eyes popped open. Becky and Seacrest were running across the Smiths' yard. Mr. Smith, in front of the grill, glared at the two girls as they bolted through.

"Haley!" Becky yelled.

Immediately Haley sensed something was wrong. It was so very out of character for the two to be running when they usually just sat around trying to look cool for each other.

Becky started to say something, but she couldn't seem to get it out. Seacrest was running equally as fast just behind Becky, her dark hair whipping around her shoulders.

The girls reached the carport. "Did you hear?" Becky asked, standing in front of Haley, out of breath.

"Hear what?" Haley asked.

"Oh, Jesus, you didn't," Becky said.

Seacrest stopped and blew air from her lungs. Her cheeks were beet red.

When she heard her sister finally spit out the words, tears filled her eyes.

"Charles . . ." Becky repeated, as if stunned by her own words. He killed himself."

CHAPTER 54

THE MORNING OF Charles's funeral was drizzly and gray. As Haley and Erica plodded toward the dusty green canopy over the casket, Becky and Seacrest silently trailed them.

Sweat beaded across Haley's forehead, and her mind raced. She thought of his last visit. He'd been so concerned about his mother.

He also had told her that he needed for Haley to believe in him.

She felt sick at the realization that Charles was about to be lowered into the ground. She envisioned his poor mother finding him in the backyard, hanging, lifeless, from a pecan tree.

She stroked the pendant around her neck. Maybe she'd had a hand in this. If only she'd tried harder to understand what he had been trying to tell her, to believe without question that he had nothing to do with Tiffany's disappearance.

Because he hadn't, had he?

Haley sighed, still not completely sure.

She and Erica stood in silence while four tall black men lifted the casket from the hearse and walked toward Charles's final resting place.

A dog barked somewhere in the distance.

Charles's mother and little brother, Joshua, made their way to the graveside, hand in hand. The crowd was small, but Haley wondered why most of the people who had shown were even there. Three black women and the four men, no doubt family members, stood next to Mrs. Johnson and Joshua. One, an elderly woman, whispered to them.

A preacher stood several feet behind them. Then there were Sheriff Hebert, Kim Theriot, and a handful of townspeople—some she recognized from Luke's and a few she didn't.

Opportunists, she thought, glaring at them. Most of the townspeople were there because of their curiosity over what had happened to Tiffany, not because of their feelings for Charles. She was sure that Mrs. Johnson knew it.

Haley wanted to scream at them, to tell them to leave his family alone.

Someone appeared at the mouth of the woods. Detective Guitreaux. He wore a black suit and a pair of sunglasses with mirrored lenses.

Haley walked closer to the family. She wanted to give her regards to Charles's mother. She hadn't been able to at the church. But when Joshua started talking, she stopped in her tracks.

"Where's Charlie going, Mama?" he asked in a high-pitched voice.

The woman lifted her head. "In the ground, Joshua."

His jaw dropped. "Why?"

"I explained it to you, baby."

Joshua's little face screwed up. "When's he coming back to live with us again?"

Mrs. Johnson took his small hand, and the two stepped closer the coffin. "He isn't, honey."

"But won't he be scared down there?"

When she didn't answer, he ground the heel of one of his palms into his eyes and sobbed.

Haley stepped back to allow them privacy and remembered the scene at her own father's funeral, how her mother had thrown herself against the casket.

"No, David!" she'd screamed. "No! Please, don't leave us, David!" She'd turned to her horrified daughters. "This isn't happening, girls," she'd cried. "Your daddy's okay. There's been a mistake." She had wept as they carried her away. "I should have told him to stay in the car. I should have warned him sooner!"

Haley felt tears on her cheeks.

There was a familiar voice behind her. "Haley."

She turned, puzzled to see Mac.

"There was a four-car accident on I-10 I got called in for. I'm sorry to have missed the service."

Mac nodded to Erica, who Haley had forgotten was even standing next to her.

Haley's instinct was to reach out to Mac and hug him. It was *Mac*, for goodness sake, the man she'd slept with for over a year. But she couldn't bring herself to touch him. It was strange how much a relationship could change in the course of such a short time . . . how much two could grow apart.

"Hey, Mac," a soft voice behind them said. Becky.

Mac gave her a hug. "You doin' okay, kid?"

Becky nodded. "Where've you been?"

Mac looked at Haley.

Sweat had formed at the nape of Haley's neck and at the backs of her knees. "Charles came over just the other night," she said. "He was so upset."

Mac's face darkened, and he nodded. "It's a damn shame," he said. "For someone to cut their life so short. He must have been miserable." He cleared his throat. "Anyway, you okay these days?"

Haley nodded.

"Well, then, I should go pay my condolences. You take care of yourself. Say hello to your mama for me."

———

The next morning, Haley drove to Trespass Gardens and dropped off a basket of orchids and homemade pecan pralines. She recognized the old woman on the other side of the screen door as the one comforting relatives at the funeral.

"Hi, I'm Haley. I was a friend of your grandson's," Haley said meekly, unsure of whether Charles had ever mentioned her to his family. "Just wanted to bring these over."

"Oh, you didn't have to do that," the woman said and unlatched the door. She held it open with her hip. "We've gotten more pretty flowers today than we have space, I'm afraid."

Haley handed her the tray and bouquet, then reached into her back pocket. "I wrote my name and number down. Can you give this to Mrs. Johnson and tell her that if she needs anything, anything at all, that she can call me?"

"Sure, baby, I'll do that," the woman said. "Want to step in for some coffee? Louise is taking a little cat nap right now, but you can come in and wait for her if you'd like."

The late-morning sun blared down on Haley's shoulders and the top of her head. She wiped the sweat from her temple and shook her head. "No, thank you."

"Charlie wasn't no killer," the woman said softly. "He was a good boy. You know that, right?"

Before she could answer, the woman patted the air with her hand and smiled warmly. "Why, of course you do. You and Charlie were friends."

CHAPTER 55

A FEW MOMENTS after the girl climbed into the truck, the weather intensified from a light drizzle to billows of clean, cool rain. "You would have been stuck in that," he said, as if nature had been his accomplice. He flashed the most trusting smile he could muster. He'd have to be very careful with this one.

She smiled at him, and a dimple lit up her left cheek. Her teeth were the whitest he'd ever seen. "I'm Sarah," she said, stretching out her legs, allowing the hems of her shorts to creep into the insides of her thighs.

Sarah. Sarah Greene. Oh, yes, he knew. The teenager who was a threat to his Rachel. The Andersons' former babysitter and apparently the current lover of Rachel's husband, Tom.

It had taken four days for this opportunity to present itself. He hadn't been certain she would be dumb enough to get into a truck with a stranger. He thought he'd be forced to take her some other way.

But now here she was in his truck.

It was almost too easy.

It took all he had not to reach over and grab her by the neck. *The Andersons. How could she? Did she know what she had done? Did she even care?*

She wasn't pretty, and it wasn't because she was dressed in clothes that were so tight, they could have been painted on her. She had other flaws. Her eyes were a brilliant blue, but her teeth were crooked, and her bottom lip was thin and chapped. Even her nail beds were ragged.

She raised her arms above her head in a stretch, and he could see the generous profile of her chest. She was flirting, flaunting her body for a total stranger. Playing girlish games. If he hadn't had plans for her, he'd be furious. But for now, he had to stay calm.

He looked over and saw her staring at him.

"I'm Charles," he said, rolling the stone in his palm. He thought about the real Charles and what had become of him.

She smiled at him. "Nice to meet you, Charles."

"Where am I taking you?"

"Just a quarter of a mile. I live on Piney Branch."

Yes . . . I know.

He glanced at the time on his dashboard. Nine o'clock. "Turning in this early?" he asked pleasantly.

"I guess. My friend had to be home early tonight. Grounded or some shit. But it sucks because my parents aren't home. They're in Biloxi."

"Yeah, that sucks. Hey, I'm headed to a party. You wouldn't want to go, would you?"

"A party?" she exclaimed, her eyes lighting up. Then quickly, she seemed reluctant. She straightened in her seat and appeared to be mulling it over.

"Or not," he said, careful to gain her trust. He was going to destroy her no matter what, but it would be much easier if she trusted him. "I should just take you home."

"Is it in town? The party?"

"It's just off Whiskey Road."

Still looking straight ahead, she grinned. "Yeah, I'd love to go to a party. I would just need a ride home. If I knew that I had one, then . . ."

He squeezed the rock. She was falling for it. His plan would be easier than he had thought. "Sure, but I need to change my shirt first. Mind stopping at my house?"

"Um, where do you live?" she asked.

"Close."

She nodded.

They drove in silence for a minute. "You know that it's dangerous to be walking along the side of the road at night?" he said, pressing his foot against the brake for a stop sign. "To let strangers pick you up . . . bring you home?"

She snorted. "You're not dangerous, are you? You don't *look* dangerous. Besides, it's not a long walk to my house from Maria's. I do it all the time. And I never hitch. It's just that with the rain and all."

Her eyes were on him again, and his flesh crawled. "How old are you anyway?" she asked, all hint of nervousness out the window.

She was just a stupid animal.

An animal. A girl. An animal. A girl. A beast.

Gravel crunched beneath the tires. "Why? Do you like older guys?"

"Sometimes. If they're cute." She cut her eyes at him. "Hey, you have beer at your house?"

———

She sat in the dimly lit living room, running her fingers through her long blond hair.

Earlier, Allie had strolled out of the house with an overnight bag, so he was pretty certain he had the house to himself.

Hopefully . . . he could take as long as he wanted.

She took a sip of the Miller Lite he'd given her. "Maria's parents are such morons," she said. "Really, if my parents were like hers, I'd be so much more miserable than I already am. And you won't believe it: One time, when we were driving home from the movies, her father put his hand on my thigh. I almost puked."

He wished she'd drink more and quit babbling. Her words were carving a hole in his head. The beer was laced with his mother's haloperidol, a sedative the doctor prescribed for her schizophrenia. She had been too easy, she herself suggesting they stay at his house and drink beer after he'd changed his shirt.

By ten o'clock, they were in his room.

"Eww, how many magazines do you have?" she asked, eyeing the collection he'd left out. He wanted to read her reaction, to see a little of himself through her shiny blue eyes. To see if there was anything worth redeeming.

Or if there wasn't.

She opened one and flipped through it. "Why did you tear so many pages out?"

"You like magazines like that?" he asked, rubbing his chin. "Dirty pictures of other girls?"

She hesitated before answering. "I don't know. I think they're . . . kind of gross, I guess."

"I do, too," he said honestly.

She sat on his bed with the magazine on her lap. Her eyes kept flopping closed, and it looked as though she was struggling to hold her head up. Suddenly, she took in a deep breath and straightened.

Setting the magazine aside, she looked up at the small bedroom window. "Is that your cat?" she asked.

He looked up at the window and grimaced. After he'd fed Ian, the animal had decided to hang out at the window even more, sometimes screaming his mangy head off in the early morning hours.

The gifts to both his sister and the cat had been a very bad idea.

She lay back and rested her head on his pillow. Her blond hair splayed out, and her lips parted. "What did you say your name was?"

He told her his name again, but this time he told her the real one. Now there was really no going back. His heart kicked into high gear, and his voice turned gravelly. "How long have you been sleeping with Tom Anderson?"

Her eyelids fluttered. "What?"

She started to sit up.

"Oh, you didn't hear me? I said: How long have you been fucking a married man?"

Her expression quickly turned to disbelief.

Then fear.

She tried to get up from his bed, but he could see she was weak from the alcohol and haloperidol.

And he was anything but weak.

CHAPTER 56

THE SUN WAS a sharp afterglow in the western sky when Haley returned home from her shift at Luke's. When she turned onto her street, she was shocked to see the sheriff's cruiser parked in her driveway.

Her heart sped up.

Mom. Something's wrong.

Jumping out of the station wagon, she hurried to the carport. There, she found the sheriff sitting on one of the rocking chairs facing the bayou. Guitreaux sat next to him.

The sheriff looked up from his coffee, fine beads of sweat coating his hairline. "Why, hello, Miss Haley," he said.

"My mother. Is she okay?"

"Now, now, this isn't about your mother. I'm sure she's fine," he said, straightening in the chair. "Just need to ask you a few questions."

Haley nodded.

"You know a little girl named Sarah Greene out of Truro?"

Haley shook her head. "No, I don't think so. Why?"

"Her parents have reported her missing. They returned home from a trip to Biloxi, and she wasn't there. She was with a friend until Sunday evening, but no one's seen her since."

Haley's hand went to her mouth. "Oh, my God."

Another girl had disappeared.

The detective stood. "You said that you don't know her?"

Haley shook her head. "No. I don't think so. I know an Olivia Greene—at least, there's an Olivia Greene who comes into Luke's sometimes. I've seen the name on her credit card. Is Sarah her daughter?"

The detective nodded, thumping his notebook against a bent elbow.

"Do you think she could have run away?"

"No," the detective said.

"Who is she?" Haley asked.

"She's a sixteen-year-old junior at St. Theresa's. On summer break like the rest of the kids. Does some babysitting for folks."

The springs on the back screen door snapped, and Haley's mother stepped out.

"Mrs. Landry," the sheriff said. "I didn't know you were home. We knocked, but . . ."

Haley's mother glanced at the lawmen, then at her daughter. One eye was made up nicely with makeup. The other was bare as though she'd forgotten what she'd started. She was also wearing a sundress, but it was Becky's and a few sizes too small. "Another child went missing?" she asked. "Did I hear that right?"

"Yes, ma'am."

"Oh, my, what's the world comin' to?" she asked of no one in particular. Then her gaze fixed on Hebert and his Styrofoam cup. "Come on in for some *real* coffee. You can ask my daughter questions inside, where it's cooler."

She held the screen door open.

Haley followed the men indoors.

CHAPTER 57

JUST HOURS AFTER the news broke about Sarah Greene's disappearance, the media descended on Grand Trespass in a way it hadn't when Tiffany had vanished. Camera vans, reporters, and people with maps and radios congregated at public meeting places.

Sheriff Hebert drove Sarah's parents into Lafayette in his police cruiser to make their tearful statements on television, then quickly drove them back to Truro. The sheriff told the community to keep an eye out, lock their doors, and watch their children extra closely.

Two FBI agents, Special Agent Denise Jones and Special Agent Leon Adashek, were called in from the New Orleans office to work with the local law on the case. The agents showed up at all of the residents' homes for statements, made certain the woods were combed thoroughly and that Grand Trespass Bayou was dragged.

The two worked much differently than Guitreaux had. They weren't interested in wasting any time. They were out to find someone and quick, no matter what it took . . . and they seemed particularly interested in one Grand Trespass local.

Haley, Erica, and Austin were on the clock and Chris was reading the *Daily Advocate* at the counter on Wednesday when the two agents showed up. They sat at the counter and ordered pastries and coffees.

Erica found the female agent riveting. She looked pulled together and polished in her starched khakis and a lavender polo shirt. A thick black belt with a gun holster cinched against her small waist. She was forty-something and beautiful, another woman who reminded her of her mother. She was calm, cool, collected, and self-possessed with a type of toughness that was uncommon in most women—at least the ones Erica had known.

Odd as it was, Jones even reminded Erica a little of Pamela. Though her father's girlfriend was simple and uneducated, she, too, had a strong sense of herself. She knew who she was, something that puzzled Erica.

"How long did you say you've lived in these parts, Chris?" Jones asked, bringing her cup to her lips and blowing on the steaming coffee.

"Twenty years, ma'am," Chris said, looking up from his newspaper. One eye was fixed on Jones, the lazy one on the front door of the diner.

Jones nodded.

"In a small town like this, you're bound to know nearly everyone. Isn't that right?" Adashek asked.

Erica saw a muscle in Chris's cheek jump. He shot a quick glance at the portrait of his dead daughter. "That ain't so," he said, his weary eyes focusing again on the agent. "Like I've told you before, several times actually, people 'round here are scattered. Spread out. We go to other towns to do our shopping, mostly. Just 'cause you own land in Grand Trespass don't mean that you know all the other townsfolk."

"You saying you don't know many people here, Chris?" Jones asked, feigning surprise.

Chris scratched his head. "You're puttin' words in my mouth. Of course I know people. Didn't say I didn't."

"Well, that's what it sounded like you said," Jones said.

Chris gazed out at the family of four who were seated closest to them. A boy in a WWE T-shirt was picking apart a ham-and-cheese sandwich while a smaller boy in a NASCAR shirt was pleading with his mother for another milk shake.

Haley shuffled toward Chris and the agents with customers' orders, her face blank. She pushed open the door to the kitchen trailer and disappeared in the back.

Jones interjected. "Okay, well, let's try this. How well did you know Tiffany Perron?"

Chris's shoulders sagged, and his voice was as low as a whisper. "How many times are you goin' to ask me the same dang questions? Seems as though you think I have somethin' to hide, and I don't."

Jones smiled. When she spoke, it wasn't a whisper. "Nothing? You call a record for peeping in innocent folks' windows nothing?"

Chris's face went red. He stole a quick glance around to see if anyone was listening. Then he looked down at his hands.

Erica was listening intently. She knew she should busy herself somewhere else in the diner, but she wasn't about to go anywhere. Chris? Peeping? She pretended to wipe down the counter.

"How about Sarah Greene?" Adashek asked.

"I don't know nothin' about a girl named Sarah Greene."

Jones flashed a photo of Sarah, and Chris looked away. "You already showed me that," he said. "Look, Tiffany Perron worked for me. She came in, she worked, and she went home. That was it. This Sarah Greene? I haven't a clue who the girl is."

Jones spoke this time. "Would you say the rumors are true? That you had a crush on Tiffany Perron?"

Chris's grip tightened on the paper. "The kid was nineteen, for God's sake."

"And that you were a little too touchy-feely with her? Probably creeped her out?"

Erica's eyes narrowed. Chris was touchy-feely all right, but he was like that with everyone. It was just his way of being personable. Yes, it was a little creepy if you didn't like to be touched, but he didn't mean any harm.

And him having a crush on Tiffany? What man didn't at some point? Did that make every man who knew her a suspect?

"I don't know what you're talkin' about," Chris snapped.

The door to the trailer opened, and Haley walked back in. She tiredly poured herself a cup of coffee.

The sun had become harsh outside, and its rays coursed through the diner. Chris scooted his stool back loudly and got up to adjust the blinds.

"You've got some scrapes on your forearms," Adashek called to Chris. "You like the woods? Spend much time in them?"

Chris's snakeskin boots clicked against the tile as he went to the front doors. He flipped the sign that read "Open" on the door to "Closed." Then he turned to face the agents.

"I don't appreciate this line of questioning. Especially in public and in my place of business with my employees around. There has to be a law against this shit. I've been an upstanding member of this community for years now," he barked. Anger flashed in his eyes as a ray of sun bounced off his face.

The family stopped eating.

"Upstanding?" Adashek said with a laugh, the edges of his lips curled into a grin. "Peeping is considered upstanding in this town?"

Chris's eyes flickered. "Someone's probably out there killin' girls, but the law keeps hasslin' me. Have I made mistakes in the past? Yes, sir, I have. But I've paid for them. You're wastin' your time here tryin' to drag my name through the mud." He pointed toward

Main Street. "Wastin' precious time that you could be using tryin' to find out what's happenin' *out there*."

Chris's neck was as red as a crawfish, and he looked about ten years older than he actually was.

His eyes landed on Haley and Erica. "We're closin' early for the day. I'll have Kim come out to help close up, so after these customers are done, you gals can go on home. But business as usual tomorrow." His eyes went back to the agents. "And if you two are through, I'm leavin'." He waited for a response but got none. "So, am I excused?"

"Have a good day," Adashek said pleasantly. "If we have more questions, we'll just swing by."

"How long ago did they leave?" Detective Guitreaux asked, his voice too even not to be perturbed. Erica could tell from the first time she'd seen Guitreaux with the FBI agents that he wasn't crazy about the fact they were there. His face now was a blank slate, no emotion registering across his features. He looked as political, hard-to-read, and inept as always.

"About ten minutes ago."

Guitreaux scratched his neck.

"They're really getting around, those FBI guys," Erica said, hoping to elicit a reaction. If she knew anything about men, she knew they couldn't stand being outdone by another man, especially when it came to their jobs. The fact that a man *and* a woman might outdo Guitreaux probably was even worse.

The detective looked toward the window. "I'd like a coffee and one of those chocolate Danishes, if you don't mind," he said, scratching his neck some more.

"They were questioning Chris," Erica added.

"Is that so?"

She set a cup and saucer in front of Guitreaux. She filled the cup with coffee. "Made him so upset, we're closing early for the day. You're the only one I've let in since he left."

She pulled a Danish from the pastry bin and served it to him. "Seems like they know something they're not sharing," she prompted. "Think they do?"

Guitreaux dipped the pastry into his coffee, then took a big bite.

"Chris, a Peeping Tom. Really. Now how weird is that?" she said.

Guitreaux almost choked.

"Where'd you hear that?" he said, wiping his mouth.

"From the agents. They talked about it here at the counter like it wasn't a secret or anything. Is it?"

Guitreaux didn't answer.

"You know anything about this Sarah Greene girl?" Erica asked. "I mean, have any clues turned up that *you* know about?"

He quietly chewed.

"She take anything with her when she disappeared? Like a runaway would? Clothes? A toothbrush?"

Guitreaux took a long drink of his coffee. He set down the cup. "You're full of questions. Thought you didn't know the kid."

"I don't. I just want to, you know, learn about what y'all do. Investigations stuff."

"You're kiddin' me. A pretty little girl like you?"

Erica tried hard not to glare at him. She needed something from him, something important.

"Just doesn't seem like the kind of work that pretty little ladies like you would be interested in is all," he added.

Erica lowered her voice. "I'm writing a book. A mystery. So I'm, you know, doing some research."

For a second, his eyes filled with what looked to be curiosity. "No shit? School project or the real thing?"

"The real thing," Erica said between clenched teeth. The guy turned her stomach with his incompetence, but she knew the sheriff wouldn't give her the time of day, much less the FBI, so she had no other option.

"What's your book about?"

"Can't really say," she said. "Anyway, think I could tag along with you a little? Watch how you investigate?"

Guitreaux shook his head. "Oh, I don't know about that. You may be a little distracting, honey, if you know what I mean."

"No. I don't. What do you mean?"

He looked her over for a long moment. "How old are you?"

"Nineteen."

"Hmm . . . yeah, I don't know. I'll think about it."

CHAPTER 58

"YOU SLEEPIN' WITH him?" Mac asked, his eyes shiny against the dull glow of the porch light.

"What?" Haley asked incredulously. The dust hadn't even had a chance to settle since Austin and Erica had driven off. It felt strange to find Mac waiting for her.

"I've noticed he's been taking you home an awful lot," he said. It was the first time she'd seen Mac's eyes look so cold.

"Mama's been leaving with the car lately. We work together, so Austin's given me a few rides."

"Wasn't Erica working tonight? She could have taken you home."

"Austin took her home, too, Mac. Her truck won't start. Besides, we closed early today. What is this about exactly?"

He took his gold lighter from his pocket and snapped it open, then shut. "You didn't answer my question."

Haley stiffened. "No, I'm not sleeping with him. He's got a girlfriend. But even if I were, I don't think you and I would be discussing it."

Mac said nothing. He snapped the lid of the lighter open and shut again. Then he looked down at his muddy boots.

"And how did you know Erica was working tonight? Are you checking up on me?"

"I watch out for you." The vein in his neck trembled. "You know that."

"But that's not your job anymore."

Swallowing hard, he looked out at the bayou. "Yeah, guess not."

Haley suddenly wondered if he was more sad than angry. It was difficult to tell. She noticed a sack next to the rocking chairs. "You brought crawfish?"

Mac nodded. "Ordered extra from Comeaux's. Thought about your family." He pulled his cap from his head and looked at her, his hair disheveled and plastered against his skull. He ran his fingers through it. "So, you like him like that?"

"What?" she asked.

"Austin."

"Like what?" she countered. "Like the way you like Rachel Anderson?"

CHAPTER 59

HE HURLED THE large rock, and the big window shattered, slicing through the still night. What he was about to do was risky, riskier than anything he'd ever attempted. But he had no choice. Rachel was gone, and this might be his only chance.

He had given Tom the benefit of the doubt with Tiffany, thinking that if he destroyed her, the family would have the opportunity to go on happily. He'd given Tom a chance, but he had failed miserably.

Now he'd suffer the consequences for his actions.

A light blinked on in the bedroom. A moment later, one in the living room. The back door swung open, and Tom Anderson stepped outside.

"What the hell?" He shuffled toward the broken window, stood in his bathrobe, and scratched his head.

The crickets had quieted those first few moments after the ear-splitting noise of the shattering window, but now they began chirping again.

In a flash, he rushed up to Tom and struck him hard in the head with a metal bat. Tom cried out and immediately dropped to the ground, writhing in the damp grass and cradling his head in his hands. He raised the bat and struck several more times in the kidneys, the backs of his thighs, and his shoulders. Then he cuffed the older man.

He pulled Tom to his feet and pressed the hunting knife to his throat. Tom groaned.

"Fuck with me just one time, and that'll be the last thing you do. You clear on that?" he said from behind the wool ski mask.

Tom nodded.

"Get movin'," he ordered and pushed Tom toward the woods. He needed the man to cooperate for the trek to the pond. Once there, he would finish him and dispose of the body.

Shivers coursed up the back of his neck as he kept the hunting knife jammed into Tom's back through the dense brush. An owl screeched, its nocturnal hunt interrupted. The moon, fat and furious, sliced through the trees to light their gloomy path.

Suddenly, he had difficulty breathing. His breaths came ragged and shallow behind the itchy wool ski mask, and he knew it was the beginning of a panic attack. The more he walked, the more ragged his breath became. He tried to think of something else, something comforting to ease the anxiety.

As they moved single file among the shapes and shadows of the murky woods, he forced himself to think of Sarah Greene. Her kill had been different from Tiffany's. With Sarah, he'd spent a fair amount of time scrubbing blood from the walls and carpeting of his bedroom.

The rush was more intense than he'd experienced before. But the calm didn't last for long. After only a few hours, his mother's horrifying presence had made it back inside his head. He wondered when it would ever end, if it ever would.

"Why are you doing this?" Tom asked, snapping him back to the present.

"Shut up and walk," he warned.

"Does this have anything to do with Ray—"

He yanked the handcuffs upward, and Tom screamed. "Quiet! I said don't fuckin' talk, and I meant it." He applied more pressure to the knife pressed against Tom's back.

The man went silent.

Just a hundred yards into the woods, the itching from the mask became so fierce, he couldn't stand it. He reached to readjust it, and Tom suddenly sprinted.

It took him a second to realize what was happening. Quickly, he was on the man's tail. He chased Tom as he zigzagged through the tall trees, screaming for someone to help him. Tom was fast, but handcuffed, he had trouble keeping his balance.

Catching up with Tom, he sank the knife deep into Tom's spine. Tom let out a thunderous yelp and tumbled forward, smacking into a tree. Then he fell to the ground with a loud thud.

He hovered over Tom, who lay wheezing and stinking of urine. Pale moonlight had made its way through the tangle of giant trees to light the area just enough for him to make out the terror on Tom's bloody face.

"Please. I'll do anything. I . . . I have children."

"You should have thought of them while you were screwing their babysitter," he said, taking the bat from its harness.

"No, please," Tom pleaded, wide-eyed. He inched backward on his rear end as though there was hope of getting away. "Please. I have money. I can pay you."

The killer raised the bat above his head.

"Oh, God, no. Please. No!"

Tom screamed the first few times the bat made contact with his head. Then the screaming stopped.

He stared at Tom's body, his head nothing now but blood, bone, and tissue. An exquisite calm entered him. Oddly, as the calm came and the rage dissipated, so did his energy.

He became lightheaded as something bright flickered meaninglessly behind his eyes. He yanked off the mask, but it did nothing to help. He felt drunk and desperate for rest.

Stumbling a couple of yards from the body and its offensive odor, he sank to the ground.

———

He awoke to daylight and instinctively wiped the dried saliva from the edges of his lips. He squinted, trying to get his bearings. There were trees. Birds were singing. Above him, a chattering squirrel leaped from one tree to another.

He tensed as he remembered. He was in the woods, lying a short distance from Tom's body. He'd fallen asleep.

He'd fallen asleep!

He glanced at his watch, and his heart pounded. This was dangerous. Very dangerous. The woods were too well-traveled with the FBI in town.

He heard a rustling and rose to his feet. He looked around woozily, his neck snapping left to right. He turned in a circle, his eyes darting every which way, taking in everything possible.

Then he discovered what the noise was. On the ground to his right lay a martin bird. Its wings and beak were squashed as though it had been stepped on, but it was still alive. Its beady black eyes were open, and it gazed up at him, quivering.

He knew some believed that seeing a wounded bird up close was as unlucky as shattering a mirror or having a black cat cross your path. They believed it was an omen for something bad about to happen, an unfortunate turn of luck. He'd never had luck in the first place.

Spooked by his presence, the bird began to flail its better wing. It managed to scoot around in a semicircle, but after a few seconds, it stopped. It watched him and began to tremble again.

He couldn't stand it. Its helplessness. Its pain.

Gazing up at the sky, he pleaded for forgiveness, then took a step forward, thrusting his foot hard into the bird's skull. Its suffering ended immediately.

Tears filled his eyes, and his insides screamed. As far as he knew, the bird had been innocent.

He averted his eyes from the dead bird and started toward Tom, who *hadn't* been innocent. He'd need to work quickly. If someone along the way saw him . . . A branch snapped close by. He stopped, and his body went rigid. Someone stood a few feet away from him. His hand shot to his back pocket to rest on his knife.

"Hello," he said, as casually as he could when he saw who it was.

"Howdy," Chris replied, looking dumbfounded.

He'd seen Chris, the man who owned Luke's, in the woods twice before. "You're out awfully early."

Chris glanced around but said nothing. He waited for Chris's eyes to land on Tom's body, which was less than a yard away, but they didn't. He was looking in the opposite direction.

He eyed the binoculars hanging from Chris's neck. "What are the binoculars for?"

Chris's face went red, but he didn't answer.

"Don't you worry. I won't tell anyone that I saw you out here with those."

Chris closed his eyes.

Sweat formed at his temples. The only option he had sickened him. "You lonely, Chris?"

Chris's eyes opened. At first, it looked like he was going to argue, but then he just looked resigned. "I . . . yeah, I reckon I am.

241

But I'm no killer. That's not me. I just have me a little problem. Since Luke Anne died and all, I've—"

"Been peeking into folks' windows, right? Since your daughter died, you haven't been able to help yourself."

Chris's forehead creased with worry. "Yeah, but that's all. I have nothin' to do with those girls goin' missing."

"I understand. See, I'm lonely, too." His grip on the knife tightened.

"You?"

Chris studied him and seemed to notice the bloodstains on his arms.

He went for the knife.

Chris turned to run, but he didn't get far.

CHAPTER 60

ERICA TRAILED FAR behind Guitreaux. Far enough away, and he'd think her sounds were nature's, she reasoned. But five minutes after she began following, Guitreaux abruptly stopped.

He stood still for a second. Then, without bothering to look back, he called, "C'mon, Agatha Christie. You'll get hurt out here by yourself. Might as well join me."

Erica felt her face flush as she walked toward him. But she knew she'd have to play along to get what she wanted: the experience of the investigation firsthand.

"What are you doing?" she asked by his side, hoisting her backpack higher on her shoulders.

"Now, I don't want you blabbering to the FBI like you did with me. Got it?"

Erica nodded.

Guitreaux grinned. "Okay, then. Know the Anderson place?"

"We're going there? Why?"

Erica thought of Rachel. Did he suspect her, like those girls in class had said? Her husband, Tom? Rachel hadn't been home for days. She'd left shortly after Erica had seen Mac's truck at her place overnight.

"The missus reported seeing someone in her backyard on a couple of occasions. And her kid saw someone in the woods near the house. So I've been watching their property. If someone's been out there, he'll come back."

Erica remembered sitting on the Andersons' swing set that night and watching the house herself. "Who do you think it could be?"

"Dunno. I reckon there's a killer out there. Don't you?" he asked. "That's why you're wanting to follow me and all, right? To see how I track killers?"

He pulled a low-slung branch out of the way and motioned for her to go ahead.

Track killers? So far, no one knew of him tracking a thing.

"You ever catch anyone?" she asked.

Guitreaux laughed. "You kidding me? In the three months since I made detective, you mean?"

"It doesn't bother you that everyone thinks you're really bad at this? All this time not being able to figure out what happened to Tiffany?"

"Sweetie, not much bothers me. Besides, I didn't ask for this job. Not really. It just kinda landed in my lap."

"But don't you want to find out what happened?"

"Sure I do. More than anything. But if there isn't anything to go on besides a set of keys, what can I do? I've exhausted many an avenue. All I can do now is keep my nose close to the ground, continue to talk to folks and wait to stumble upon something. If there's foul play, something'll turn up. These things don't keep secret for long."

"Think the FBI'll figure out what happened to Tiffany first?"

"Maybe. Look, am I a great detective? Hell no," he said, "never said I was. But would I have been able to find out what happened to the Perron girl if there were any signs of foul play? Sure as shit I would have. Hell, if there were any signs of foul play, I could've gotten more boys from Lafayette down here to help me. But funding don't grow on trees, sweetheart."

"So you think Tiffany could have just run away?"

"She could have, I suppose. But it's doubtful. Now c'mon. If you're coming, zip up those lips of yours. Don't slow me down."

Erica followed Guitreaux as he moved through the woods. Several times he stopped and looked around. Erica looked around, too, not seeing anything out of the ordinary but at the same time knowing better than to ask more questions.

Rays of sunlight coursed through the endless web of branches, casting shadows on the far sections of the woods as they plodded along. Locusts buzzed loudly, absorbing the last of the day's sun.

As Erica reached to pull a branch out of her way, a slender moccasin darted in front of her, then scurried beneath the leaves. Erica flinched but kept pace behind Guitreaux.

Not two hundred yards from the Anderson house, Guitreaux stopped dead in his tracks once again. Erica waited patiently, now familiar with his pattern. She waited for him to start again, but this time he bent down.

He reached out and touched a leaf. Then his head shot up, and he looked straight ahead at a tall oak. Erica's eyes followed his. Her breath caught in her throat.

Blood was everywhere. Splattered across the tree trunk, painting the surrounding leaves. The ground also was barren in spots as though something had been dragged across it. Her eyes moved another foot to the right. She saw a pair of legs, the feet bare and bloodied on the bottoms.

Guitreaux made the sign of the cross over his chest and whispered, "Lord Almighty, look what we got here. A clue."

CHAPTER 61

HE WAS BECOMING unraveled, undone. Half-dragging, half-carrying Chris's body through a thousand feet of woods had been pure horror. Chris, from what little he knew, was a good ol' boy, someone who would never hurt anyone.

Killing him had been more than unplanned. It had been evil, the same kind of evil that he'd practiced when he'd killed for his mother as a little boy. Senseless, brutal murder wasn't a part of his soul, as dark and twisted as it was.

He wondered how his mother had managed to do it time and time again. He knew for a fact that the man that night hadn't been her first—or her last.

He quickly wrapped Chris in lawn bags, careful not to look at the man's eyes. He waded into the water. Several feet out, he let go.

Chris's body disappeared instantly.

Back on land, he gazed up at the sky. Blood covered his clothes and skin, and tears ran down his cheeks. "Please . . . I was forced to," he said, pleading to the God he feared. He knew he was getting closer to the end, and it frightened him as much as his mother did.

"Forgive me. Please," he pleaded again. "I . . . I didn't have a choice."

The sun set, and the sky became a radiant, peaceful blue. But there was a storm brewing inside him, one that he knew would never die down.

It was *the* storm.

The one that would finally end him.

———

For hours, he paced the woods near his mother's house, paralyzed with fear. He couldn't bring himself to go back for Tom's body. It was too dangerous. He was almost certain it had already been found. People were still combing the woods for Sarah Greene.

He looked down at the blood on his clothes. The pond water had done only so much to cleanse them.

Shivering, he walked to the house. A light was on inside. Had he left it on? Or was it them? Had they already come to get him? Allie couldn't be home, could she? No, he told himself. She'd be out somewhere sinning with truck drivers. Her clients. Industrious little girl that she was.

The FBI agents were much more thorough than the detective, and they seemed to be able to see right through him. Earlier that afternoon, they'd stopped by the house. His mother had screamed inside his head, and he could have sworn they heard her and saw the fear in his eyes. Sweat had formed along the length of his back, and many times during the interview, he'd felt like running through the house and out the back door. But he stayed, and at the end of the questioning, they got up and left.

But he was certain they had put two and two together by now.

He reluctantly entered through the back door. Allie stood in front of the stove, her back to him. She wore a purple half-shirt and a short denim skirt.

His heart hammering, he wondered if he could get by without her seeing. But after two careful steps into the kitchen, she whirled around, holding the spatula out as though it were a knife. "You nearly scared the piss out of me!" she screamed. She turned back around to stir her brew. "Shit," she muttered.

He studied her back, knowing she'd know what he had been doing. The damp clothes, the blood stains—she'd put everything together and run for help. She'd love to be the one to tell. She'd revel in watching them lead him away. His heart crashed against his chest so hard, it felt as though it was tearing at the bone.

"I'm making sloppy joes," she announced. He could see her profile from where she stood. She had a grin on her small face. "Enough for both of us. Want some? It's kind of a gift to you for the one you gave me. I know I'm not Martha Stewart or anything, but you should at least have some. I made it sweet."

As she licked tomato sauce off the spatula, she turned to face him again. Her eyes took him in slowly from head to toe. "Holy shit. What happened to you?"

He didn't have an answer, so he just stood there. He knew he should move, but he couldn't.

"Cat got your tongue?" she asked.

There was a rustling next to her. She looked down, and his eyes followed. Ian emerged from behind the counter and wrapped his matted tail around her slutty platform heels.

"What the—" he gasped.

"It likes me," Allie beamed. "I've been giving it the spoiled milk from the fridge. It even likes beer."

Ian watched him, a murderous look in its eyes.

"How . . . how long have you been feeding it?" he demanded, his voice wavering.

"Couple of months, maybe? It's so skinny, I felt sorry for it. Too bad all we usually have is beer and old take-out. I know it can't be good for him."

He fumbled in his pocket and pulled out the stone. He rubbed it fiercely.

Ian stared even deeper into his eyes and mewed.

He wanted to grab it and twist its neck. Couldn't she see that this animal was evil?

"It needs a bath. Can you give cats baths?" she asked.

He had nurtured Ian as he did his sister, feeding it the evening he had bought the groceries and the kind of gum that was supposed to make her not want to smoke cigarettes.

"I asked you a question. Can you give cats baths?"

He laced his fingers behind his head in order not to strike out and hurt the cat or hurt Allie—*really* hurt her.

"Why aren't you answering me?"

"Yeah, if you want your eyes scratched out," he said.

She screwed up her face and started stirring the food again. Then she looked thoughtful. "Why do you have books on Ted Bundy in your room? Don't they scare you? And those magazines with the naked chicks. The pornos. It's gross that you have so many of them. But you know what freaks me out even more? How you rip them up. Why do you do that?"

Lightning flashed behind his eyes. He leaned into the counter.

Allie looked startled for a moment. "You okay?"

He did his best to pull air into his lungs . . . to calm down. He looked up and saw she was angry.

"What's wrong with you?" she snarled. "I wanted to make up with you tonight! Quit being such a freak, so we can get along for once."

The air came in trickles, but he needed more. The room started to spin, and he clutched the counter more tightly.

"You walk in here looking like you're some crazy person," she said. She pointed at his shirt. "And what's that all over you? For all I know, it could be someone's blood."

It IS someone's blood, he thought. *I made a horrible mistake.*

"I try to look past it all, to be friends with you, because I know you need one, but you won't even talk to me!" she snapped, tears in her eyes. "You're more interested in your piece-of-shit cat than you are me!"

She lunged for Ian and grabbed him firmly by the shoulders. Then she pulled open the screen door and flung him into the darkness.

He was gone by the time she turned back around.

CHAPTER 62

THE NEXT MORNING, Haley spent an hour at Mrs. Perron's. The two talked out on the porch while contractors worked inside, installing an addition to their living room. Haley wondered why the Perrons would add on to the house now that only two people lived there and figured Mrs. Perron was looking for something to do.

Unlike her own mother, who coped by doping herself with sleeping pills, Mrs. Perron survived by cleaning and keeping busy. She'd installed new floors in their two-story home, repapered most of the walls, and had the roof reshingled. Now she was paying for an addition. The only part of the house that seemed unchanged was Tiffany's room.

"Be careful out there," Mrs. Perron told her as she left. "He's goin' after the pretty ones."

———

Once Haley arrived home, she stopped at her mailbox. Seeing that it was empty, she loitered for a moment, closing her eyes and resting a palm on the warm metal. She was tired, very tired. But for the first time in a long time, she was determined. That felt good.

"Where've you been?" a voice called.

Haley opened her eyes and shielded them from the sun. Her mother was standing under the carport. Sasha stood next to her, wrapped in a bath towel.

"The Perrons," she said, walking toward them.

"Where's Becky?" her mother demanded.

"I don't know. Why?"

Sasha ran from the carport, toward her. The towel dropped to the concrete driveway.

"Hay-wee! I falls into da water and sees a gatuh!"

"What?" Haley exclaimed, staring up at her mother. "He fell into the bayou?"

"He could've drowned. I found him at the shallow end by the dock," Mrs. Landry said. "But what if he hadn't been? What if he would have fallen from the pier?"

Haley's heart pitched.

"I dids. I dids see a gatuh. He had sharp teeths! He almost gots me, but Missus Landry got out o' huh bed and sayfed me."

The damp-haired little boy hugged Haley. He had no idea of the magnitude of what happened, what *could* have happened. Haley's stomach tumbled.

"If it hadn't been for your father waking me up to tell me he was out there . . ." her mother said and stopped to hug her sides.

Haley's face began to burn. She ignored her mother's words. She wasn't going to make this all about ghosts, death, the past. They needed to live in the present, once and for all. She had made the decision earlier, and she was going to stick to it, no matter what everyone else chose to do.

"This is *your* fault!" Haley screamed. "Becky's fifteen, Mom. *Fifteen!* If you're not looking after her, no one is. What's it going to take to get you to come to your senses? Sasha falling in the bayou again and actually drowning?"

Sasha let go of her waist and took a couple of steps backward. He peered at Haley, his eyes wide.

Haley's voice grew louder. "How about Becky getting snatched up by some freakin' lunatic while she's out there taking rides from strangers? Or happening across the *lunatic* who took Tiffany? For one of us to die like Daddy did? It really seems like that's what it'll take for you pay attention to us again!"

The woman's face crumbled. "Oh, God. I'm . . . a horrible mother."

Haley hadn't meant to scream, but she wasn't sorry she had. Months of built-up hurt and frustration needed unleashing.

She watched a lizard scale the front of the house, and her eyes filled with tears. "Yes, you've been horrible. Becky's impressionable, and she needs you. We both do. This has to stop, or you're going to ruin her."

Her mother gazed into the distance.

"Daddy's been gone for nearly a year," she added. "But we're still here. We're still here, and Becky needs you. Be here for her. Be here for *us*. If you don't, you'll regret it. We all will. You've not only lost him, you'll lose us, too. We'll hate you, and then you'll have nobody."

Tears in her eyes, the woman nodded. But for the first time since the accident, her eyes were open. *Really* open.

CHAPTER 63

ERICA HURRIED THROUGH the front door and sneezed.

Pamela was in the living room, wearing denim overalls, a paintbrush in her hand. "Oh, dang it, I wanted this to be a surprise!"

Ribbons of tape were everywhere, and the once-white walls of the living room were now a cool, navy blue.

"Does my father know you're painting in here?"

Pamela's smile spread. "No, he's still at work. It's his surprise, too. Don't it look nice?"

In a way, it did. It was the type of look she imagined many New York City apartments boasted. Contemporary. A little airy. Cozier somehow. Erica had the suspicion that her mother would have thought the color gave the room more character.

She shrugged. "It's okay."

"You don't mind, do you? I wanted to talk to you, but you haven't been home much. I thought I'd just surprise you."

No, she didn't care. She wouldn't care if Pamela had painted the living-room walls black. This was her father's house, not hers. Besides, she had much more important things on her mind than Pamela and her silly redecorating.

Through the fumes, Erica could smell Pamela's perfume. It was new, better. She'd also taken notice of the books the woman left around the house. Some were romances, but most were nonfiction. From the titles, it was apparent Pamela wanted to learn how to cook more ethnic food and had a fascination with self-help. The woman liked to learn.

"Any news on the missing girls?"

The memory of the dead man flashed in front of her eyes. She shuddered. It had been beaten unrecognizable, a large chunk of it stuck to a nearby tree. He'd been dressed only in a robe, so there had been nothing immediate to identify him. Her mind hadn't stopped racing since the discovery.

For some odd reason, Erica wanted to tell Pamela what she and Guitreaux had found, to just blurt out the news. But she didn't.

"Not that I know of," she said, then took off down the hallway.

"Erica?"

Erica turned. "What?"

"You goin' back out?"

Erica frowned. She didn't have to answer to her.

"Because if you are, I want you to be very careful. Those girls didn't just run off. No," she said, shaking her head. "They met with someone bad. I sense these things. I have since I was a little girl. And I haven't been wrong yet." Pamela sighed. "They're gonna be found . . . and real soon. And not just those two, either. There'll be more."

CHAPTER 64

RACHEL OPENED THE front door and walked in. The house still smelled the same, although she knew her life would never be.

The four nights at her mother's had been therapeutic. Her mother had listened as Rachel filled her in on her life. It was the first time in almost a year that she felt she could be honest about her marriage troubles, but once she started talking, it all came pouring out effortlessly. When she finished, her mother hugged her and told her that she and the kids weren't just welcome but were expected to stay with her until Rachel could find a teaching position and get on her feet.

Oddly enough, Kelsey had softened a lot during their days in Phoenix. Rachel knew she'd scored brownie points by finally standing up to her situation with Tom. Little Tommy, on the other hand, was angry and wanted to go back home. He hated Phoenix, and he missed his dad. Rachel told him they'd work everything out in due time. For now, she had to return to Louisiana alone to see to their affairs.

Now, she called out for Tom, but there was no reply. Without bothering to set anything down, she walked upstairs to talk to him, to tell him her plans. His keys and wallet were on the bureau in the master bedroom, but he was nowhere in sight.

"Tom?" she called.

Nothing.

She checked the bathroom and the kids' rooms. No Tom.

She was confused. The car was there, his keys, wallet. Maybe he was in the living room and hadn't heard her.

She went downstairs. When she stepped into the living room, her hand flew to her mouth. One of the big windows was shattered, and glass was everywhere.

She hurried to the phone and dialed the detective's line, then got his voice mail. She dialed the sheriff. Again, voice mail. As she began to dial 911, there was a knock on the door.

She hurried down to the foyer, but when she opened the door, no one was there. An envelope lay on the porch step. She gazed at it for a minute, a sense of foreboding blossoming deep inside her gut. Then she bent and picked it up. A crow cawed from the side of the house. Rachel quickly glanced its way, then returned her focus to the envelope. She opened it and unfolded the message inside.

Your husband will never hurt you again.

———

Detective Guitreaux showed up at Rachel Anderson's within seconds of her call. It was almost as though he'd arrived too quickly.

They stood in her kitchen. "And you don't know who dropped this off?" he asked.

For the first time since she'd known him, he didn't look so calm and cool. In fact, he looked disheveled with his shirt untucked and his sleeves rolled up in a hasty fashion. His thick hair was even mussed, as though he'd spent hours running his fingers through it.

"No. I answered the door, and no one was there," Waves of nausea washed through her stomach. *Had someone hurt Tom?*

"And you have no clue what happened to that window? Or where your husband is?"

She shook her head and glanced at the windowsill. Her sunflowers were limp, their leaves dehydrated. Tom hadn't taken care of them. He hadn't nurtured *anything* in a long while. Still, he didn't deserve to be hurt.

"And you said you just got back from Arizona."

"Yes, Phoenix."

"Right, Phoenix. And you've heard nothing from the FBI?"

Rachel's brow furrowed. "FBI? Why would I hear anything from the FBI?"

"You know a Chris Guidry?" Guitreaux asked.

Rachel was confused. "Doesn't he own Luke's Diner?"

He nodded.

"Then, yes. I know who he is."

"How about a Sarah Greene?"

Rachel narrowed her eyes. Of course, she knew Sarah. She'd known Sarah since she'd been a baby. "Yes. Why do you ask?"

"You're telling me you don't know that she went missing? Chris Guidry, too?"

Her heart leaped into her throat. "Missing? Oh, my God."

"Don't look so surprised. It's not becoming."

But she *was* surprised. She'd always loved Sarah. And she certainly didn't want to hear that Chris . . . or anyone for that matter . . . was in danger.

What's going on?

"And I suspect you'll tell me next that you had no idea that Tom and Sarah Greene were having an affair?"

Her mind raced. "An aff—?"

Guitreaux shook his head in disgust.

Rachel felt as though a bus had hit her.

"Your husband doesn't seem to keep to himself very good," he said. "I'd think you would be very angry with him. Possibly very angry at the girls with whom he transgressed."

Her voice came out as a squeak. "And you wouldn't?"

"Oh, of course I would. Anyone in their right mind would. Hell, I may even go as far as having murderous thoughts. After all, we're only human. Wouldn't you agree?"

Blood rushed into Rachel's cheeks. She was beyond exhausted. But she had to regain her composure. She'd deal with the shock and the pain later.

"I don't like what you're saying, detective, or how you're saying it. I didn't do anything to Tom, and I didn't do anything to those girls. I'm beginning to think I should have a lawyer here."

"Two of your husband's lovers have disappeared, ma'am. Not one. Two. And this ain't a big town like Washington, DC, *cher*. This is Grand Trespass."

Lovers. Tom's lovers.

"And we have a body at the morgue now," he added, "about ready for identification."

"Body? Who? One of the girls?"

Guitreaux stared deeply into her eyes as though he were trying to pry something from them. It infuriated her.

She took in a deep breath. "Are you arresting me?"

"No . . . not yet."

"Then get the hell out of my house. Now. I don't have time for your games, detective. I need to find my husband."

He opened his mouth to say something, but his cell phone rang.

He answered it. "One second, sheriff." He covered the receiver with his hand and said, "Looks like you got your wish for now. I'm goin' now. But you might want to stay put. I'll be back real soon."

CHAPTER 65

ERICA'S HAND JERKED open, and the fruit fell, splattering against the moist earth. The taste of decay rocked her taste buds, the not-so-subtle taste of the tomato's slow death. She spit twice to help rid her mouth of the rotten taste, then quickly finished the page she'd been writing.

A few minutes later, she snapped the notebook shut and grinned at the cover. *Never Smile at Strangers* by Erica Duvall—an account of what had transpired in Grand Trespass that summer. Of course, it was far from finished. But with the information she'd gathered thus far, the discovery of the body and Guitreaux's feeling that it would be the key for unveiling the murderer's identity, she figured she was a good portion of the way through it.

She peered across the cemetery. Chris hadn't shown up to open Luke's that morning. No calls, no messages to anyone. It was a first in the three years she had worked for him and the first time the diner had been closed for a full day.

Could he have been involved in the disappearances? The one who beat that man's head to a bloody pulp?

No, it was impossible to imagine he could hurt anyone. He wasn't the type. But there wasn't a specific type for killing, was there?

She was pretty sure that with the right reasons, most everyone was capable of it.

She spit again, hoping to get rid of the nasty remnants of the tomato. That's when it happened. Fifty feet from the clearing, just a hundred yards from Harper's Road, she heard movement. She fell into a crouch and scanned the woods.

She saw someone. A man wearing a black ski-mask stumbled toward her. As he approached, he let out a bloodcurdling scream that made her want to cry out herself.

It was *him*.

Startled, she withdrew into the shadows, her back against a large oak, the rotten taste in her mouth quickly forgotten. As he grew closer, she curled into herself, trying to make herself as small as possible.

Her heart beat so furiously, she was afraid he could hear it.

Muttering to himself, he pulled off his mask and took in several labored breaths.

Although she could only see the side of his face, she knew exactly who he was. Haley's words echoed in her mind: *These days it just doesn't seem like people even really know each other . . . or what they're capable of.*

He stumbled forward again in her direction. He was closing in on her.

She sucked in a breath and prepared to run.

Suddenly, their eyes met. His eyes widened, and he froze.

Her heart hammering, she tried to run . . . but was horrified to find that she couldn't move.

She was frozen, too.

CHAPTER 66

HALEY FINISHED WIPING down the kitchen counter. The house was quiet, almost too quiet. She dropped the dishrag in the sink and walked to her sister's room. She knocked and immediately heard whispers. "What?" an irritated voice cried from the other side.

"I'm putting dinner up. Sure you don't want any?"

"I'm not hungry," Becky called out.

There were more whispers. Then Haley heard hushed giggles.

Careful not to turn on any lights, Haley went to her own bedroom. Becky had pinned two blankets to the wood planks separating their rooms, but there were a few areas that still were exposed. Haley found one and peered through.

Seacrest was in the room with Becky, and so were two boys Haley hadn't ever seen before. A half-emptied bottle of Southern Comfort and an empty two-liter bottle of Coke were on Becky's dresser.

Seacrest was sitting topless.

"Truth or dare," one of the boys said.

Becky's voice was wobbly. "Uh, dare."

"I dare you to take off your shirt, too."

Seacrest laughed. "Are you serious? And see what? Fat rolls?"

Haley's breath hitched in her chest.

"That's a pretty shitty thing to say," the boy said.

"It's the truth," Seacrest said defiantly. "Why are you so interested in seeing Becky's tits anyway? It's not like she really has any yet."

Seacrest turned toward the makeshift wall. It looked to Haley as if the girl were staring right into her eyes. "It still creeps me out that your sister could be in there, watching us," she said. "She's the type of freak who would."

Haley stared back at the girl, then noticed something. She gasped and brought her hands to her mouth. "Oh, my God," she whispered.

Her heart pounding, she jumped out of bed and hurried to her sister's door. She tried to open the door, but it was locked. "Becky! Becky, let me in!"

"Haley, wait!" Becky cried.

When Becky finally opened the door, the window was open and the boys were gone. The room reeked of spilled liquor. Seacrest was standing at the end of Becky's bed, adjusting her tank top.

Haley pointed at the girl. "Show me what's on your neck."

Her dark hair wild, Seacrest threw Haley a piercing glare. "Excuse me?"

"Show me. Show me what's on your neck!" Haley shouted.

Becky gaped at her. "Haley? Are you okay?"

Seacrest brought a hand to her neck, then seeming almost surprised that it was there, she touched the necklace. She pulled the heart-shaped pendant from beneath her tank top. "This?"

Haley ripped the necklace from the girl's neck.

"What the hell's wrong with—" Seacrest protested.

Haley turned it over and saw the monogrammed *TP*. She held the necklace in front of the girl's face. When she spoke, her voice came out as a hiss. "Where'd you get this?"

Seacrest took a step backward, and fear crept into her eyes. "Why? What's wrong?"

"Where'd you get it?!" Haley screamed, stepping toward the younger girl.

"I . . . I found it. So what?"

"Where?"

A loud, throaty moan rose from another part of the house. Wrigley was howling.

Seacrest's lower lip trembled. "I . . . I just found it, okay?"

"This necklace is Tiffany's! She was wearing it when—"

Feet padded on the hardwood. "What's going on?" Mrs. Landry asked, walking in. Her eyes took in a bewildered Seacrest.

"Mama, Seacrest was wearing Tiffany's necklace!" Haley exclaimed.

Mrs. Landry looked confused.

"She was wearing Tiffany's necklace! The one you bought for her. Don't you see? Tiffany was wearing it when she disappeared!"

Her mother seemed to be putting the pieces together slowly—too slowly—in her head.

Haley turned back to Seacrest just in time to see her climbing out the window. Losing her balance, her chin smacked against the pane, and she let out a sharp cry.

Haley darted across the room to stop her.

But the girl was gone.

CHAPTER 67

THUNDER RIPPLED THROUGH the sky as he replayed the scene in his head. His angel had looked at his note for a split second before wilting in front of his eyes. Seeing her pain made the terror swell inside of him, but what hurt even more—and was almost too much to handle—was the realization that he'd never see her again.

On the way back to the house, he'd been seized by a panic attack, one so intense he thought he'd suffocate. In the midst of it, he'd seen Erica Duvall crouched down in the woods. She'd seen him, too, but that didn't concern him much.

There was nothing she could do to him now.

At the house, he went to his bedroom and grabbed a second note from under his mattress. Then, in the kitchen, he focused on steadying his hand. Five minutes later the more important note—the one he had worried over for a month but hoped he would never have to send—was completed. He slid it into an envelope and dropped it in a small box . . . then he walked out to the mailbox. Sliding the package into the metal box, he raised the red metal flag to let the postman know that there was outgoing mail.

Back inside the house, he went to his mother's private bathroom. The bottom shelf of the medicine cabinet held a skinny tube of toothpaste covered in dust and two orange plastic vials half-filled with haloperidol. The labels were faded and peeling away from the plastic, but he could still make out his mother's name: *Dariah S. Thibodeaux.* The *S* stood for *Seacrest,* her precious maiden name.

He opened the first bottle and turned it upside down. Four small round pills with white crosses etched across their centers fell into his shaking hand. The second vial held nine. Gripping the thirteen pills in his sweaty palm, he shuffled out of his mother's room and into his own.

Earlier that afternoon, he'd carried the television into his bedroom, then filled a bowl with a mixture of cat food and rat poison. He had set the bowl on the front porch for the evil Ian.

Now he flipped the television on and tuned in to an old episode of *Leave It to Beaver.* He turned the volume down and grabbed his CD player. He slid in a Bob Dylan CD and set the volume to medium. He could no longer bear silence. He needed to feel as though someone was with him. He didn't want to die alone.

He sat on his bed. It should only be a matter of hours before they found him now.

This was the end.

Finally.

He hoped the world outside his head was the real one. He wasn't sure if it was, but he decided to be hopeful. It was all he had. He thought about Chris and felt even more frightened. Killing him had been a mortal sin.

He wondered if God would find a way to forgive him.

He closed his eyes.

Darkness.

Is this what death would look like? How would it feel? Peaceful? Safe? Would there be love? Families? A chance for a new, normal beginning?

Deciding anything was better than what he was living, he opened his eyes and twisted the cap off a bottle of Budweiser. He took three pills at a time until he'd swallowed them all.

He lay back in his bed and peered out the window, listening to Dylan croon "Lay, Lady, Lay." The sky had darkened so much with the storm that he could no longer see outside his window. Ian had come and gone moments ago. His eyes had looked especially red and cruel against the stormy evening as he glared at him through the window.

He'd mewed weakly and pressed his scrawny body against the dirty glass. Then the cat had left, perhaps to retrieve the food from the porch.

The killer now lay in the small room under the sheet, his body curled into a ball. The heavier his eyelids felt, the more frightened he became. He fought going to sleep, dying and going to an unknown and possibly more terrifying place. But it was getting difficult to stay awake.

Dylan crooned to him as he drifted off.

CHAPTER 68

IT HAD BEGUN to storm, and the sky was now a purplish-black. Erica had waited what seemed an eternity to leave her hiding spot against the big oak, worried that he might be waiting in the shadows close by, ready to spring. But once she was somewhat certain he'd gone, she jumped up and ran.

It was difficult to navigate the woods through the darkness. Branches tore at the bare flesh of her arms and legs, and pinecones ripped at her feet. But she kept running, oblivious to the pain. All too obvious to her was the fact that she had an excellent idea who was responsible for the missing girls and the dead body she and Guitreaux had found.

A wall of Spanish moss whipped into her face, temporarily blinding her, but she kept running. He wasn't who they all thought he was—and she had to let the detective know before someone else was hurt. Headlights appeared as Erica cut through the tree line at the edge of the road. She reached the pavement and frantically waved her hands.

An SUV pulled onto the narrow shoulder and slowed to a stop. A crow cawed from the near distance, then flew across Whiskey Road, its wings beating in the stormy night air. Running to the passenger side, Erica peered into the window.

"Mrs. Anderson!" she screamed. She opened the door, and a bewildered, red-eyed Rachel stared back at her.

"I need your help," she started, out of breath. "I know who he is."

"Who? My God, are you okay?" Rachel exclaimed.

Erica looked down at her bloodied arms and legs. "Yeah, I'm . . . I'm fine. I just saw—"

"It's too dangerous for you to be standing out there. You could get hit by a car. Come on, get in."

She climbed in the truck and slammed the door.

"Okay, now slow down. Who are you talking about?" Rachel asked.

"I think I know who took Tiffany Perron and Sarah Greene—and who killed the guy in the woods!"

"Guy in the woods? I don't—"

"We found a body."

"We? *Who* found a body?"

"Guitreaux and I—"

"Erica, you *must* slow down," Rachel said, talking very slowly as though she were dealing with a crazy person. She touched Erica's shoulder. "Just take a second, and gather your thoughts. Then tell me what's going on."

"Okay, okay," Erica said, then took a few long breaths. She told Rachel what she had seen just minutes ago. Once she was done, she felt the need to clarify.

"Look, I'm not positive, but I'm pretty sure," she said, her voice a little calmer. "If he's the guy, he lives a quarter of a mile from here by road. Please, just take me there so we can know for sure."

Rachel pulled a cell phone from her visor, hit a number on the keypad, then put the phone to her ear.

Finally, the SUV slowly inched forward.

CHAPTER 69

THROWING THE STATION wagon into park, Haley jumped out of the car and ran to Erica's front door. Fat rain drops pelted Haley so hard, they felt like balls of hail.

There were vibrations coming from inside the house. Loud Cajun music blared. A surprised Pamela answered, a can of Miller Lite in a well-manicured hand.

"What's wrong, *cher*?" she asked, her eyes wide.

"I need to talk to Erica," Haley said, out of breath. "Is she home?"

Pamela's eyebrows arched. "She's not here, darlin'. But you're gettin' all wet. Come on inside."

Haley shook her head. "Do you know where she is?"

"No tellin', she goes off so often by herself. Probably in those woods, even though we've warned her about them."

Haley ran back to the car. As she drove, the windshield wipers protested, jerking and screeching as they stuck and unstuck from the windshield. There was a truck behind Haley, but through the clouds of rain and the sticking wipers, she could barely make out its headlights.

Lightning leaped from the sky. Unable to catch her breath, Haley rolled the window down for some fresh air. Rainwater and the wet, sour scent of manure trickled in.

A few minutes later, Haley turned onto a dirt drive.

She wondered if she should have called the sheriff or Guitreaux to tell one of them about Tiffany's necklace.

But it was too soon, right?

Maybe her negative opinion of Seacrest was clouding her judgment. Maybe she wasn't thinking straight.

She wanted to think everything through before implicating the teenage girl in the disappearances of Tiffany and Sarah, no matter how appalling the girl was.

CHAPTER 70

HE OPENED HIS eyes, but his vision was blurry, so blurry. Strands of hair tickled his back, and he felt fingernails trail across his neck.

He stiffened.

Was it a dream? Or had he passed already? What was—?

He blinked in the darkness.

Slowly, his eyes adjusted, and he saw his window. He wanted to close his eyes, but he knew this was important. What was going on? Was he still alive?

"Don't speak," a voice next to him said. A warm hand moved from his bicep to his chest.

His heart jumped. Big jumps, little jumps. He tried to pull himself up.

"Lay with me," she whispered. "Please. I'll give you what you look at in your magazines . . . but I'm the real thing."

He felt her smooth skin against his. The cinnamon on her breath seared his neck. It was Allie. He was still alive. His skin turned to gooseflesh.

Beneath the cloud of cinnamon, he could smell her cosmetics and the tobacco on her breath. He could also smell something equally as foul: vomit. He must've vomited in his sleep.

He stumbled out of his bed, and pain sliced through his body. It was so sharp, he winced and doubled over. His mother had been right: He *was* pathetic. After all, how difficult was it to kill yourself?

Allie got up and stood in front of him. In a sliver of moonlight, he could make out her naked body. "What's wrong with you?" she wailed.

A memory droned inside his head. His mother's long, cold fingers on his frightened skin, invading, humiliating him. The memory was enough for a second wind. He staggered to his bedroom door and pushed it open.

Then he stumbled toward the back door.

"Why's the television in here, anyway?" she snarled. "That's all I really wanted. To watch the TV. It wasn't about you. It's *never* about you!"

As he pulled open the back door, he heard her bare feet on the kitchen floor.

"Quit ignoring me. You hear me, you son of a bitch?" she screamed. "Just stop because I know what you did! You killed those girls, you sick freak! I *know* it was you!"

———

The clouds had grown thicker since he'd fallen asleep, and the outside world had taken on a somber grayness not unlike the cramped space inside his mind. A heavy rain now pounded against his back in a mad frenzy, mingling with the electricity that blared in his head.

He stumbled from the shed, back to the house with the old army-issue .45 his father had left behind. Over the years he'd handled it sparingly, but he always knew that one day he'd be forced to use it.

He looked up to see Allie glaring at him through the back window. She was wearing one of his T-shirts, her bare legs dark against the blue-white fluorescent lights of the kitchen. Her eyes looked wild.

He rounded the house and arrived at the front porch.

Ian had taken the bait.

He was now curled up on the second-to-bottom step of the porch, asleep for good. He felt a pang of sadness, but he knew that what he'd done had been the right thing.

The cat had been miserable and had wanted an end to its wicked existence. That's why it had trailed him all summer. Animals could sense unkind people, and this one had sensed unkindness in him.

He stepped over the animal, feebly kicked opened the screen door . . . and found himself face-to-face with his sister.

Her face screwed up as though she were ready to shout. Then she saw the gun and shook her head. "You've got to be kidding me," she said. But her voice shook a little, betraying her.

His eyes drifted in and out of focus.

There was one Allie.

Two . . . Allies.

He wondered about the longing that swelled inside of him, the uncontrollable desire to kill his sister. Was it evil? Or would God see it as an acceptable means of justice? Would God understand him at all?

Lightning ripped through the sky, and rain battered the windows. He took a step forward.

Allie took a step back. He could see that her chest was heaving.

The roof began to creak, and Allie's face crumpled. Her full mouth pulled into the shape of a square. She was crying, but there was no sound.

Now *he* was the one in control. He looked into his sister's terrified eyes, appreciating that she felt it, too. With his free hand, he reached into his pocket and withdrew the polished stone.

Her eyes were glued to the gun. "I won't do it again. I . . . I promise. It was just a joke," she pleaded. "It *all* was. I'm so, so sorry." Her lips quivered, and he could see goose pimples on the bare flesh of her thighs. Her red fingernails flew in front of her face, and she wiped away tears.

Crocodile tears.

Lies.

"I said I'd tell them about what you did to the girls. But I won't," she cried. "I wouldn't do that to you."

He shook his head, and his vision blurred. When he spoke next, his voice boomed. "You made my life a living hell, Allie. Why the hell would you want to do that? What have I ever done besides try to take care of you?"

"I'm sorry! I'm so sorry! Really!" she said, taking a timid step toward him, then thinking better of it, stepped back again.

Sheets of rain crashed against the living-room windows. The screen door out back banged shut, opened, banged shut.

He blinked.

Now there were three Allies.

CHAPTER 71

THE SKY OPENED wide, and rain shot down so viciously, Haley had to strain to see in front of her. But after minutes of searching, she finally found what she was looking for in Weston: Austin's truck. The license plate reading LUVINBETH sat stone-like under the tumultuous sky, down a long dirt driveway in front of a small house. She stopped and dialed Mac's phone again. But again, he didn't answer.

A bluish-white sliver of the moon peered down at the woods, competing against the cloudy sky. It reflected ominously off the overgrown front yard as the station wagon bumped along the soaked gravel drive and pulled next to the blue Ford F-350.

Since she couldn't find Erica or Mac, she'd decided to confide in Austin. He was intelligent, and she trusted that he'd be able to shed light on the situation, help her make sense of it all. He'd tell her just where her logic about the necklace was flawed.

Not bothering to shut her car door, she dashed across the yard. But once she reached the porch, she froze. A dead cat lay curled up, the tip of its tongue clenched between its teeth. She gasped and took a step back.

Through the downpour, she thought she could hear voices in the front room, arguing.

Could Beth, his girlfriend, be in there with him?

Maybe this is a bad idea, she thought, blinking rain from her eyes. After all, aside from several weeks of idle small talk and a few rides home, she hadn't really had any meaningful conversations with him. Not really.

But this was important—and who else was there for her to talk to? Erica and Mac were nowhere to be found.

Biting her bottom lip, she climbed the porch steps. Once she reached the top, she peered through a broken window and caught a glimpse of who was in the front room. Her heart pounded even harder. Austin's back was to her, and Seacrest was facing him. They appeared to be having some sort of argument.

These two *knew* each other?

What? Why?

Were they . . . sleeping together?

She frowned, knowing that the scene in front of her was very wrong.

She backed slowly down the stairs and away from the house, trying her best to process what she'd seen.

Then she heard the roar of an engine.

A moment later, headlights appeared. Someone was bouncing up the drive in an SUV.

She shielded her eyes and peered at the truck, her eyes stinging and her clothes soaked. Before it came to a complete standstill, the headlights blinked off. Someone jumped out of the passenger side and ran toward her.

Erica?

"Oh my God, what are you doing out here?" Erica gasped, her arms and legs covered in what appeared to be blood. "Haley, are you okay?"

Haley was really disoriented now. Nothing was making sense.

Am I dreaming?

I have to be dreaming.

Haley pinched her arm as hard as she could, and winced.

CHAPTER 72

THE HALOPERIDOL WAS making him nauseous. His head was suddenly too heavy for his neck, and the image of his sister's tear-stained face faded in and out of focus.

"Please," she pleaded, her voice soft. "Please don't do this. I'll change. I will. Really. Just wait. You'll be *so* surprised at how nice I can be. How *normal*." Suddenly, she looked as though she were eight years old again, powerless and innocent.

Free of their mother's evil.

Wanting nothing more than to catch crawfish and fireflies, and laugh at anything remotely funny. Sneaking into his room not for sex, but because she loved him . . . looked up to him.

A cockroach dropped from the wall behind her, and he shivered. "No," he said, shaking his head. "You'll never be normal."

"I will. I cross my heart. I . . . I *love* you."

His grip on the stone tightened. "Don't say that to me!" he exploded.

"I do, Austin," she cried. "You're all I've ever had. Mama was sick. I hated her for what she did to you. For what she did to everyone, but *especially* you."

Thunder crashed inside his skull.

She's trying to trick you. She's my daughter. She's me.

"I guess . . . I guess I just didn't know any other way to act."

"Fuck you!" he screamed, not certain if he was speaking to his mother or to Allie. *Or both.*

Allie was bright, more intelligent than most. He'd recognized that when she was very young. But over the years he'd seen her use her intelligence to manipulate people, which was exactly what she was doing now.

He remembered the animals, too, the ones his mother had questioned him about. They had been tortured and killed, then posed in odd, grotesque positions in the backyard. He'd suffered horrific punishments for those animals even though he swore he knew nothing about them.

Strangely, it had taken him a while to realize it had been Allie in a quest for power of her own. Then she'd grown a woman's body, and the dead animals were a thing of the past. She'd learned to be cruel in other ways.

Allie studied him now, terrified. The power had finally shifted.

"Quit causing people pain," he whispered. "Just stop it. It's wrong." He blinked a few times. "And don't think this is about you, because it isn't. It's me. It always has been."

Ice crept into his blood as he made his decision, and he whispered to himself. "God, please forgive me."

CHAPTER 73

"ERICA, PLEASE GET back in the car!" Rachel shouted from the driver's seat, her voice competing with the downpour.

She was parked on a long, dirt driveway. Up ahead was a small white house. The porch light was off, but a light shone from inside. She could see shadows in the front room.

Lightning struck, revealing an old car on concrete blocks and, behind it, a shed. The night became dark again, and she began to feel even more ill at ease. She shouldn't have let Erica talk her into stopping. She should have driven directly to the station.

Erica had jumped out of the car as soon as Rachel had slowed down, and now she was talking to someone in the yard. Through the dense shower, Rachel couldn't make out who it was.

She looked up in the sky to see if there was a full moon, because nothing was making sense. To think, just that morning she was having a nice, quiet breakfast in Phoenix with her mother and children.

She thought of the broken window and Tom somewhere without his keys, car, or wallet. The man she and Kelsey had seen in their yard. Tiffany Perron and now Sarah Greene. The mysterious body to which Guitreaux and Erica had alluded. Could Tom be hurt? Or could he possibly be a murderer? She had no idea. After all, she was a horrible judge of character.

She dialed, trying the sheriff and the detective again. "Pick up your damn phones!" she yelled.

Guitreaux had told her to stay put. *Stay put, my ass.* She'd needed to figure out if something had happened to Tom. But then she intercepted Erica.

Her cell phone rang. Her hands trembling, she fumbled for the power button. "Hello?"

It was Guitreaux. Within thirty seconds, she filled him in on what Erica had told her and where they were.

"Get her back in the vehicle and drive away. I don't care where you go, but get the hell off that property," he barked. "We'll be there in five minutes."

She tossed the phone on the passenger seat. "Erica!" she shouted. She slid out of the SUV and hurried out into the rain. Not until she was upon the girls did she realize who the other one was. Haley Landry. Mac's ex-girlfriend.

Haley blinked at her, looking confused.

"Girls, get in the truck. Detective's orders," Rachel said, shielding her eyes from the driving rain.

"Guitreaux?" Erica exclaimed. "Did you—"

Rachel interrupted, her tone firm. "I'll explain in the car. Let's go."

As the three ran toward the SUV, a deafening crack of sound split the night air.

———

The three turned toward the house.

Rachel gasped. "Oh, my God."

"Was that a gunshot?" Haley cried.

Screams erupted from inside the house. Haley and Erica raced to the porch and stopped short at the steps. There was more scream-ing . . . feral, mournful cries that forced Haley to cover her ears.

Ignoring Rachel's orders to get in the truck, she slowly climbed the porch steps, then peered in the window.

Seacrest was hunched over on the floor, her head bowed. A cheap-looking painting had been blown off of a wall. Blood was splattered everywhere, the wall, the carpet. It glistened in Seacrest's hair.

"Austin, no!" Seacrest wailed. "Oh, God! I don't have anyone else! Don't you understand? Don't leave me. Pleeeeease! I was telling you *the truth*!"

Swallowing hard, Haley looked down and could see Seacrest's bare, bloodied legs.

Then she saw what was left of Austin's head in her lap and vomited.

CHAPTER 74

ALL NIGHT AND into the morning hours, Weston was alive with local, state, and federal law enforcement, reporters, and their crews.

Confused, numb, and exhausted, Haley stood at the edge of the Seacrests' property, breathing in the damp morning odors. It was nine o'clock, about twelve hours after Austin's suicide. She hadn't left the property since the previous night. Neither had Erica, who now sat next to her, writing furiously in a notebook.

Half of Grand Trespass had shown up. Everyone peered from the property line at the east side of the Seacrests' house, hoping to get a glimpse of the excavation that was taking place in the pond.

Guitreaux had told Haley and Erica to go home a countless number of times. But when they'd refused, he'd found them blankets and told them they could nap in his car until he had more news.

Instead of napping, though, they poured cups of coffee and sat cross-legged at the entrance of the woods, a few yards from the pond, the blankets tight across their chilled bodies.

The sky broke every now and then, a light drizzle falling, thumping against the leaves of the tall oak trees, soaking the blankets.

Haley just sat next to her friend, her lips pressed too hard against the Styrofoam cup.

They hadn't talked much since the previous evening. They spoke only when they had to, to the authorities and to their families, who had shown up an hour before dawn. Becky and Haley's mother stood near Rachel, Pamela, and Erica's father on the side of the small house. There was a deputy standing guard, keeping the spectators at bay.

Haley still was in complete shock at what had happened, and at what was happening now right before her eyes. She wasn't even completely sure what kind of news she was waiting to hear.

When one of four divers pulled out the first corpse, dread slammed into her body. She wished for miles of scorching pavement or a grove of anthills in which to escape. When the body was safely on the embankment and the plastic bag encasing it had been sliced open, the sheriff called out: "It's a man!"

Mrs. Perron, who stood next to her husband a few yards away from Haley and Erica, began wailing. Haley supposed it was from relief.

She stood and squinted to get a better look at the body, but she was too far away and didn't dare walk closer to the overgrown pond. She couldn't risk one of the FBI agents forcing her to leave, not before she knew whether Tiffany was in the water.

"Haley."

It was Mac. He took the damp blanket from around her shoulders and draped a jacket in its place.

Haley started to sob.

"Shhh," Mac whispered, enveloping her in his strong arms. She breathed in his familiar soapy scent and suddenly felt much safer. "It's okay. It'll all be okay."

"Here are two more!" a diver on the far side of the pond yelled.

Haley reluctantly turned back to the pond. Mrs. Perron's howls pierced the air again, and her husband grabbed her by the shoulders. Then he and a deputy led her away as she kicked and screamed.

About ten minutes later, while Mac held her close, Haley watched as they pulled the second and third bodies from the water. She felt nauseated.

A few minutes later, they sliced open the first bag. "It's in really bad shape," she heard the coroner say. "This appears to be the body of an older woman, from what's left of it."

"Lord Almighty," the sheriff said, making the sign of the cross.

"Any other women go missing around here in the last several years?" Guitreaux asked.

The sheriff shook his head. "Not that have been reported." He knelt down, so that he was closer. "Well, lookie here. A backpack."

A backpack had been weighing down the body. The sheriff muttered something about initials embroidered on the backpack's front flap. He read them aloud.

Suddenly, Erica screamed, and her notebook tumbled to the ground. Her voice trembled as she shouted: "What? What did you just say?"

"Erica?" Haley said, reaching out to her friend. "Erica, what's wrong? What's going on?"

Erica glanced at her, her eyes wide, but she said nothing. The girl shuffled stiffly past Haley, toward the pond. She kicked off her flip-flops, bent, and turned the left one over. Then she straightened and walked closer to the water's edge.

She started weeping.

"What the hell?" Mac muttered.

Startled, Haley watched her friend bend over again and plant her palms against her knees. Haley hurried over to her.

"Miss, you can't be out here right now," Special Agent Jones said, finally noticing Erica. Tears rolling down her cheeks, Erica ignored her.

Jones touched her shoulder. "C'mon with me, Miss Duvall."

Erica screamed and pulled away.

Suddenly, Erica's father was at her side. He brushed the agent away and pulled his daughter into his arms. "It's okay, hon. At least we know now. It's all going to be just fine. We'll get through this."

Erica kicked and screamed, resisting her father.

Haley's mind raced: Austin, the pond, the remains at its edge, Mac appearing to be his old self once again, Erica reacting so oddly. Everything was just too much and became a blur to her. This wasn't reality. It couldn't be.

A diver shouted: "Found another one!"

Then she heard the sheriff. "What the hell is going on here?"

EPILOGUE

RACHEL WALKED FROM room to room, her footsteps echoing through the empty house. She still couldn't wrap her head around everything that had happened. She dug in her pocket for another tissue and blotted her cheeks and eyes. Then she headed downstairs.

Although the house was empty, it looked so much smaller than it had just six weeks ago. Smaller and entirely different. Like they'd never lived there at all.

She walked to the kitchen and ran her finger along the wall by the back door where, for years, she'd measured her children's heights. It felt like only yesterday when Kelsey had been small enough to hold in her arms, when Tom still fawned over her.

She thought of the young man who had taken so much from her family, from the town. Of his sickness and the strange fascination he seemed to have had with her.

Why me? she wondered for the millionth time.

He'd confessed it all in the letter, part of a package addressed to her that the authorities had found in the Seacrests' mailbox the night of his suicide. It contained her gold bracelet, strands of hair, and a note confessing that he had been inside her house, had borrowed her belongings, and was sorry. He said that he wasn't well and had finally come to the conclusion that he never would be.

It had made total sense to him. Protect her and her honor by killing her cheating husband. He'd been sick all right. Just thinking about him sent chills up her spine.

The kids, especially little Tommy, still struggled to come to terms with Tom's death. His father had been his world. Unfortunately, Tom's death had caused a newfound hatred for Rachel in Tommy's heart.

She didn't understand it. It hadn't been her fault. Besides, she'd lost someone, too, someone who had once meant everything to her.

But Tommy was a child. One day he'd understand that none of it had been her fault—at least, she hoped he would.

That morning, Rachel had said good-bye to Erica. The two promised to keep in touch. Somehow Rachel knew that they would. A bond had formed that stormy night that felt strangely like one between a mother and a daughter, like the one she and Kelsey were rebuilding. A bond that could possibly last a lifetime.

Grabbing her purse from the kitchen counter, Rachel walked to the mouth of the foyer and took one last look back. She wiped her nose, turned, and walked forward and out the front door.

———

Erica set down her pen and leaned back on the bed. Since the night at the pond, she'd completely immersed herself in finishing her novel in order to not break down completely.

Saying good-bye to her mother as she had been laid to rest in the cemetery on Harper's Road was the toughest thing she had ever had to do. Yet although she was hurting worse than ever, she also felt a little relieved. Something inside of her had always told her that her mother hadn't made it to New York. She'd ignored that little voice out of necessity.

She also said good-bye to Rachel that morning. Her teacher had taken care of family affairs in town and was now off to Phoenix to start a new life with her children. She'd miss her. The woman genuinely cared about her, *believed* in her. That warmth and belief were the only things that made life manageable these days.

Before that summer, Erica felt she had no one, just a burning desire to reconnect with her mother. Now she had Haley and Rachel and strangely enough even—

There was a knock on the door.

She wiped her eyes with the heel of her hand. "Yeah?"

Pamela's voice. "May I come in, *cher*?"

She watched the door slowly inch open. Pamela came in and sat on the bed. "You okay today?"

"Um, what do you think?" Erica murmured.

Pamela patted her knee. "Well, then, I think you should go."

Erica's brow furrowed. "Go?" *Is she trying to kick me out of my father's house?*

"To New York."

Erica was confused. "I don't understand."

"Well, hasn't that been your plan all along?"

Erica eyed the woman. "How did you know?"

Pamela got up and tapped the Heineken bottle that Erica had been using as a bank. The masking tape Erica had stuck to the neck read "New York City" in black marker.

Pamela winked. "I told you I was observant, didn't I? I've got a keen sense for these things. I'll never be a worldly one, but God did give me that."

Tears rolled down Erica's cheeks, tears she vowed no one would ever get to see.

Show them your weakness . . .

But she didn't care anymore. "I just don't understand. She never did anything bad to *anyone*."

Pamela sat back down and patted her on the shoulder. "Maybe she got too close to something, *cher*. That's what your father seems to think anyway."

Erica blinked through her tears. "How would *he* know?"

"He knew she was writing a mystery book about this town and that she was talkin' to some people, including that Dariah Thibodeaux. See, your mama, she had a keen sense for things, too. And, like you, she loved them woods. Your daddy thinks that the book had something to do with what Dariah was doing to all the men she was laying up with. Too bad we'll never know for sure. Her manuscript was in that backpack."

Erica was shocked. "How would he know about the book? They never even talked!"

Pamela thought about this for a moment. "Memories from childhood aren't always accurate, baby girl. I'm sure your parents had some good times. I'm sure they talked more than you think."

Yeah, maybe.

Pamela reached into her back pocket and handed an envelope to Erica.

"What's this?" Erica sniffed.

"Something to help you out while you're gettin' on your feet in New York." She pointed to the Heineken bottle. "That money of yours isn't goin' to carry you too far, I'm afraid."

Erica opened it reluctantly and saw a sticky note with a name and number on it and a bunch of hundred-dollar bills. "Where'd you get all this money?"

"Just somethin' I had tucked away. My needs are cheap. Always have been. And I was waitin' to put this to good use. Can't think of a better one than helping you git a fresh start. Call that number there, and ask for Mitchell. He's a good friend of mine. He'll give you a job and a temporary place to stay in the city."

"But she's not *in* New York. Don't you understand that? That's the whole reason I was going."

Pamela shook her head. "That's not true, *cher*. You see, she *is*. She's much more in New York than she was in that old pond. Or in the ground out there on Harper's Road. You know that. That was just her shell. New York . . . that's where her heart is. Her dreams, her passion. That's exactly where yours are, too. Now you take that book of yours to New York, and you start fresh. Find a new job, meet people who are more like you, and make a happy life for yourself. And if you find that you don't like it out there, feel at peace that you always have a home here."

Erica shook her head. "No, I have to find out what happened to my mom."

"There are plenty of folks doing that, as we speak. Doin' much more than you'll be able to do. I'll keep my ear to the ground and make sure to ring you up any time there's new information."

Pamela was right . . . about it all.

It was scary.

Erica glanced at the money again. "Are you sure about this?"

"Never been surer of anything else. Well, except for your daddy, of course." She grinned. "And speakin' of him, one day you'll find out that there's more to him than what you see now. I know he didn't always treat your mama decent and maybe he hasn't been the best father, but you have to give people the benefit of the doubt that they can change. And I know in my heart that he has. He loves you more than anything, although I know he's terrible at showin' it."

The next thing Erica did surprised both of them. She reached out and hugged Pamela tightly. "Thank you . . . and this is just a loan. I'm going to pay you back."

Pamela's laugh was warm, genuine. "You're more than welcome, Sugar. My fingers are crossed that you get that book of yours published. Never seen anyone work so hard on somethin' my whole life."

For the first time that summer, Erica smiled at her.

———

Austin's memory haunted Haley, and she imagined it always would. His broken head in Seacrest's lap as she screamed for him, blood pooling around her bare thighs. The way Haley had trusted him.

Many of the same opportunists who had appeared at Charles's funeral showed up for Austin's. But they merely came and went. In their eyes, he wasn't worth paying the respect.

Allie Seacrest hadn't shown. She'd disappeared just minutes after the shooting, and no one had seen her since. There was an alert out on her, and nearly every man from Grand Trespass to Carencro had searched for her those first few days after Austin's suicide.

There were several questions left that they were hoping she could answer.

Haley now understood that Austin was Tiffany's mysterious crush. Why hadn't she put two and two together before? Austin was handsome and, as far as she was concerned, unavailable—the way Tiffany liked them.

The two even worked together, for God's sake.

But Austin had been cunning. He'd shown up on time at Luke's for every shift; he had been a model employee and well-liked. No one knew who he really was or just how sick he had been.

Until it had been too late.

As far as anyone knew, Austin's girlfriend, Beth, didn't exist. She'd only been a figment of his imagination. Part of his facade.

Haley shivered, thinking about being in his truck so many times. She'd also had countless intimate dreams about him.

He'd been Tiffany's murderer—and not just Tiffany's.

After the Seacrests' pond had been drained, the remains of about thirteen other bodies had been found. According to the sheriff and the press, most of the murders had taken place a decade earlier: three out-of-state truck drivers that had been reported missing; a former Winn-Dixie cashier; five yet-to-be identified men; Austin's mother, Dariah Thibodeaux; Erica's mother, Norah Duvall; Sarah Greene; and Chris Guidry. Rachel Anderson also had identified the body that Guitreaux and Erica had discovered in the woods as that of her husband, Tom.

The FBI was investigating the multiple homicides and there was still yellow crime-scene tape up at the Seacrest property. There would be for a long time.

Haley pulled her last suitcase out the front door and let the screen door snap in place behind her. The morning was crisp and clean, comforting, a fresh start. Haley let go of the suitcase and pulled her cardigan tighter across her body.

"You all packed and ready, baby?" her mother asked. She was sitting in a rocking chair, sipping coffee.

"Yeah," Haley said, and sat next to her.

Haley was heading to Lafayette to check into her new dorm room. She was finally starting school, getting out of Grand Trespass.

Her mother's fingers stroked Haley's cheek. "Remember how strong you are. Stronger than any of us. You'll always come out on top. You just remember that."

Haley nodded. She thought of Erica wrapped in that wet blanket, shivering, blinking the cold rain from her eyes. It seemed as though she'd instantly known that they'd found her mother. The initials embroidered across the front of the backpack was just a confirmation. Her mother hadn't left her in the middle of the night for

New York City ten years ago after all. For some reason, she'd been murdered and discarded in the Seacrests' pond.

Aside from her mother's funeral, Erica had refused to see anyone, even Haley, the first four weeks after that night. "Sorry, she don't want to see anybody just yet," Pamela would tell her at the front door. "Not even you, I'm afraid. But soon. Hopefully, soon."

When Haley was finally able to see her, it was as though she was looking at a different girl. Erica's mannerisms were softer. She seemed less angry, somehow more at peace. Haley would have thought the opposite to be true after all that had happened. But that year she'd seen it all and didn't think she could be shocked again by anything.

She looked at her mother, someone who was also making a fresh start. She and Becky finally had their mom back. She was alive again, not off and on, but all the time. She was almost the same as she had been before the accident—but not quite.

She smoked now, and her personality was still a little off, but Haley was convinced that she'd be okay—at least, as okay as any of them would ever be.

"I'm so glad to have you back, Mama."

Her mother patted her hand.

A truck pulled into the drive, and Haley glanced at her watch. Ten o'clock on the dot. Dependable as always.

"Good luck. Not that you'll need it," her mother said.

"Thanks, Mama," Haley said, kissing her mother on the cheek.

The screen door creaked, and Becky stepped out, her eyes heavy with sleep. "You going now?"

Haley nodded.

"But you'll be back on the weekends, right?"

"Yep, each and every one."

Haley said her good-byes, then rolled her suitcases up the drive to meet Mac. She was relieved that Mac was just Mac—and that he always had been. He hadn't been a stranger after all.

The boy with the great smile, the one she'd fawned over and decided she could trust . . . he'd been the stranger. She just was thankful that she and her family were okay.

Finally, she could separate herself from the town and begin working on the person she was meant to become. She'd needed that for so long.

She opened the passenger door and hopped in. A ray of sunlight shone across her face, but she didn't shield herself from it. She just closed her eyes and let it warm her forehead.

ACKNOWLEDGMENTS

There are many people to thank for making this novel finally happen.

My husband, Brian, who believed in me from day one. His encouragement, support, creativity, and insight have meant the world to me. I'm very lucky—in so many ways—to have met you. Reida and Terry O'Brien, who have always been incredibly supportive of everything I do—and who have always been there during the tough times.

Ken Atchity and Chi-Li Wong at AEI for offering to represent me. Todd (*Jefe*) Grover, the best boss ever. Thank you for reading several drafts of this book and offering such valuable advice. The late and very talented Diane Domingo, Vanessa McDaniel, Ayla Dyer, Chris O'Brien, Brian Cartee, Andy Corso, and Augie Corso.

My good friend, Mark Klein, who for over a decade and across many projects has read my work, offered honest critiques, and boosted my confidence. Your friendship and support have been priceless. You deserve many more glamorous roles in upcoming movies.

I'm also extremely grateful to my amazing and spirited twin sons, Christopher and Ryan—who helped me learn what's truly important in life and whose existence taught me to push past fear in order to achieve my dreams and pursue work that fulfills me.

NEXT IN THE
STRANGER SERIES

Read on for a sneak peak of *Ugly Young Thing* by Jennifer Jaynes, the follow-up to *Never Smile at Strangers*.

PROLOGUE

URINE SKIDDED DOWN her leg, warming her bare skin. She was more terrified than she'd ever been, and in her short fifteen years, there had been plenty of reasons to be afraid.

A heavy downpour pummeled the small house, battering the living room window next to her. But Allie wasn't aware of the storm outside.

Only the storm inside the house mattered.

Her older brother was facing her, his eyes unfocused. In one hand he held a gun. In the other was the smooth stone he kept on his nightstand while he slept. The gun was pointed at her and he was rolling the stone around in the palm of his hand.

Hatred flashed in his eyes—and she could see just how much he'd come to loathe her.

"Please," she pleaded, tears flooding her eyes, making it difficult to see. "Please don't do this. I'll change. I will. I promise."

Please don't hurt me.

Thunder boomed outside, overpowering her words, so she wasn't sure if he even heard her. He just continued to stare, his eyes glassy. He swayed a little, and she wondered if he was on something, even though it wasn't like him to medicate with anything stronger than a beer or two.

The thunder died down and she tried again. "Just wait. You'll be so surprised at how nice I can be. How *normal.*"

"No," he said, his words slurring. "You'll *never* be normal."

"I will. I cross my heart. I . . . I love you."

His handsome face twisted. "Don't say that to me!"

"I'm serious. You're all . . . you're all I've got," she cried, holding her palms out to him, showing him how vulnerable she was, just in case he didn't already know. "You're all I've *ever* had. Mama was sick. I knew that. I hated her for what she did to you. For what she did to everyone, but *especially* you."

At that, he cocked his head. He seemed to weigh her words, trying to decide if, for once, she was telling the truth.

"I guess I just didn't know any other way to act," she added.

He stared at her for a long moment, then his face filled with rage. He shouted an expletive and sounded so angry Allie's face burned with shame.

But it was true. She *didn't* know how to act. At least not like others did. She didn't fit in like most others did. She was always the outsider.

Her brother had been her only friend, so when he started avoiding her, she lashed back. She said nasty things to him and told him he was a loser, although she didn't really think he was . . . and the more he ignored her, the nastier she became.

She was also frightened because he had grown sick, just like their mother had, and that summer he'd killed two teenage girls. The sheer fact that he'd done it really freaked her out. But what scared her even more was she feared he'd eventually get caught and be taken away from her.

Then what would she do?

How could she possibly live without him?

She didn't want him to be sent away. She loved him more than anything, but she was also deathly afraid of rejection. So, instead of saying "please love me again" or "I need you more than anything," she did and said hateful things. She wasn't really sure why she did what she did; all she knew was that she didn't know how not to.

Her brother's countenance shifted. The hatred and loathing in his eyes was now replaced with something different. Something that looked like pain. His face went fish-belly white, his expression blank.

Allie realized that the moment had come. She slowly backed away from him.

Please, no! Give me another chance, she wanted to yell, but her mouth wouldn't move.

The stone tumbled onto the living room carpet. The light draining from his eyes, he pressed the old army-issue .45 to his temple—and stared at her.

"Quit causing people pain," he said. "Just stop it. It's wrong." He blinked a few times. "And don't think this is about you, because it isn't. It's me. It always has been." With that, he inhaled sharply and his eyes flickered to the wall behind her. "God, please forgive me," he whispered.

And he pulled the trigger.

———

Allie clamped her hands against her mouth. "No!" she wailed. But, of course, it was too late.

"No, please. My God, no!"

Don't die! Don't leave me!

Her ears ringing, she went to him. Her older brother, the only person who had ever meant *anything* to her, was about to be gone forever. Just minutes before she was sure he was going to kill her, but in the end he had decided to kill himself.

He made a gurgling sound, his eyes now frozen on the popcorn finish of the ceiling, a flood of red spreading out beneath his head. His eyes fluttered once, then stayed at half-mast.

He went very still.

"No! NO! NO!" She fell to the carpet. Trembling, she lifted his shoulders and scooted her legs beneath his back so that his head lay on her lap. Ignoring the warm blood soaking her legs, she held on to his arm and sobbed.

Yes, he had murdered people. But he'd never hurt her. In fact, he'd taken excellent care of her over the years: protecting her from their psychotic mother, buying groceries, making sure she had most of the things she needed.

She studied his face, trying to burn a mental image of it into her mind so she would never forget what he looked like—and she noticed something different about him. The edges of his mouth were slightly upturned, as though he had been trying to smile. Like maybe, just maybe, he had finally found peace.

"I'm not as mean as I pretended to be," she whispered through her tears. "I've always loved you so much. I just wanted you to love me back and you . . . you wouldn't." She placed her brother's hands in hers and squeezed them tight.

Eyes clouded with tears, she realized she had to leave, and quick. Either go or risk becoming a ward of the state, and she couldn't let that happen. No one had ever controlled her or told her what to do—and she sure as hell wouldn't let anyone do it now, especially the government that her brother had hated so much. After all, if he hated it, *she* hated it.

Scooting away from his body, she ran to pack a bag. Three minutes later, just as she heard the first of the police sirens, she threw open the screen door at the back of the house and disappeared into the woods.

Thirty minutes after that, she was sitting, bloodstained and paralyzed with fear, in the passenger seat of an eighteen-wheeler.

She was headed west on Highway I-10, toward Texas.

CHAPTER 1

Nine Months Later . . .

HE STOOD OUTSIDE Sherwood Foods, a small supermarket in Truro, Louisiana, clutching a paper grocery bag as though he was waiting for someone.

And he was.

Just not in the sense that people might think.

The day was overcast and uncomfortably humid, but he persisted. Since he'd arrived thirty minutes before, there had been heavy foot traffic. Couples and families in and out. Hundreds of screaming, red-faced children.

Most people didn't seem to notice him. And the ones who did probably forgot about him two seconds after making eye contact. He wasn't especially memorable, which, of course, worked in his favor.

So far he hadn't bothered to smile at anyone.

No one had been worth a smile.

He'd managed to stop hunting for years, but like all addicts, it was always on his mind, somewhere, well concealed behind several layers of thoughts. Or, sometimes just barely cloaked, behind one or two. But the desire was always there. Fortunately, he'd managed to keep it in check.

Until now.

He thought about the headlines he'd read of the kid who had killed people in an adjacent town a year earlier and wondered if he and the kid had shared any of the same thoughts. He wondered if the kid felt vindication or remorse after the attacks or if he just went numb. In fact, he thought a lot about the kid. About how alike they might or might not have been. About how awful it was that he ended his life just as it was getting started. It disheartened him just thinking about it.

The newspapers reported the kid had always been a loner. That he'd had weight issues when he was younger. That maybe his desire to kill had been fueled by being bullied at a fragile age . . . which, of course, described *him* to a T. But who really knew exactly what drove people to the type of madness that made them kill? Was it nature or nurture? Or a combination of the two? Over the years he'd studied the topic relentlessly, but the more he studied, the more confused he became, so he'd decided to stop.

The itch was back. He barely slept, and the rare times he managed to, he woke up in a pool of sweat. And, as always, when he had the itch, the rage flooded in, sickening every cell of his body. The problem was that he only knew of one short-term cure for his itch: hunting. He first discovered this, almost by accident, at the age of sixteen.

When he hunted he abided by three rules: the prey had to be a woman, she had to be a certain type . . . and she had to smile at him. He had learned the hard way that men didn't satisfy his needs. Nor did just any woman. And the smile did two things: It gave the woman some control over her fate. It also provided more of a challenge, because most people didn't like to smile at strangers, which meant he often had to work for it.

The new life he was leading had him on edge. He'd been waiting around for months for something big that might not ever happen, something he wasn't sure about, and it made him tense. He needed the release.

His thoughts snapped back to the foot traffic. Just as long as SHE didn't find out, he'd be okay. So with HER, he'd been very careful. Out of self-preservation he'd learned how to lie very well to HER over the years. Still, something had changed. SHE was guarded now . . . not nearly as warm. They even argued—something they never did before. He sensed it was because SHE was still suspicious, and that disturbed him . . . and only made the itch worse.

He stared deep into the parking lot, his eyes narrowing as he watched a young, blonde woman step out of her white Honda Civic.

She was cute, but plain.

Not his type.

Plus, she didn't have that certain *attitude* he usually went for. That cool, confident, even arrogant one that usually meant trouble but also deeply attracted him. The type other women would call bitchy. The type who made his life miserable when he was a boy. He knew that this woman didn't fit that profile, so he dismissed her.

He shifted his attention to the next row of cars and he spotted a curvier, more fashionably dressed young woman who had just eased herself out of a Pathfinder. She was a brunette, and he could gauge her attitude in her presentation and movements alone.

His pulse quickened.

The woman's dark hair was sprayed stiff and she was wearing a sassy little shorts set, tall wedges, and oversized designer sunglasses. Her chin was tilted toward the sky, her spine straight as she fussed with her linen shorts, yanking them lower around her thighs.

Bingo.

But then the Pathfinder's back passenger door flew open and a young boy jumped out.

He frowned. No, too messy.

Loosening his grip on the grocery bag, he halfheartedly turned his attention back to the plain-Jane blonde as she approached the supermarket's automatic doors.

On closer inspection, he realized she was much prettier than he'd first thought. In that natural, girl-next-door sort of way. She appeared to be in her early twenties and had a thin, athletic build. Her blonde hair was long and pulled into a high ponytail.

As she drew closer, it was also more obvious that she was very self-conscious.

She would be so easy.

If only she were right.

It surprised him when, a few seconds later, his heart gave a little tug. He sensed something about her. Something special. He wasn't sure what it was, but now that she was closer, he could feel it.

Suddenly he was excited.

But . . . was she going to smile?

Please, let her smile, he thought, strangling his grocery bag. For the true test was always the smile. It was an important rule he kept because it gave them a little control. Made what he did to them a little more fair.

Made him feel a little more human.

If they smiled, they were meant for him. If they didn't, well, maybe they'd live long, happy lives. Maybe they'd become grandmothers. Great-grandmothers even. Happy ones.

If anyone's even capable of being happy anymore.

When he and she were not ten feet apart, she stumbled in her sandals.

"Whoa there," he said, his tone playful. He smiled at her.

She caught his eye and grinned sheepishly back, her face blooming into something truly beautiful. A light scar blemished her face, running the length of her forehead to her cheek, but it only added to her intrigue. "Guess I'm a little clumsy," she laughed.

His smile widened.

No . . . no, you're perfect.

ABOUT THE AUTHOR

Since graduating from Old Dominion University with a BS in health sciences and a minor in management, Jennifer Jaynes has made her living as a content manager, webmaster, news publisher, editor, and copywriter.

Her first novel, *Never Smile at Strangers*, quickly found an audience and, in 2014, became a *USA Today* bestseller. Her second novel, *Ugly Young Thing*, will be published in 2015.

She lives in the Dallas area with her husband and twin sons. When she's not spending time with her family or writing, she loves reading, cooking, studying nutrition, doing CrossFit, and playing poker.